PRIEST

TRIDENT AGENCY
BOOK TWO

KIKI CLARK
E.M. LINDSEY

There's a fine line between lust and love...

Feeding on the pleasure of other creatures might sound like the perfect life, but Priest knows the truth. The bottomless hunger and the never-ending need for more will eventually drive him to the brink of madness.

It's the fate of all Incubi.

But until then, he's determined to spend as much time as possible checking on the human bookstore owner who turns Priest into a tongue-tied mess. Oliver doesn't seem to mind, treating him with a kindness he's never experienced from anyone outside his Trident Agency family.

Fumbling flirtations is all it can ever be though. The risk of draining Oliver is too great, and Priest refuses to put him at risk.

But then the bookstore goes up in flames, and Priest learns he'll do just about anything to keep Oliver safe.

Protecting the reckless human he has been obsessed with for months may be the only truly good thing he does with his life. But the longer they're together, the more difficult it is to resist his demon's cravings, and the more secrets they uncover. About Oliver... and supernaturals like Priest and his friends.

As the Alpha Team investigates and attacks keep coming—forming a terrifyingly familiar picture—Priest and Oliver have to learn to trust each other... and themselves.

Priest is the second book in the swoon-worthy Trident Agency series by co-writing duo, E.M. Lindsey and Kiki Clark. It features an endearingly awkward Incubus, a bookworm ready for his gorgeous stalker to make a move, a trash panda of a fallen angel who doesn't really do *friendship*, one wonderfully dexterous forked tongue, truckloads of possessiveness, and touch him and get unalived vibes for days.

PRIEST

The door slammed shut behind Priest, but he barely heard it. He was caught up in the vicious cycle of his never-ending hunger. It was something he'd learned to live with. The insatiable cravings that came with who—and what—he was. He wasn't like Knight. He'd never known what it was like to exist as a human.

He wasn't even good at playing pretend the way Jeremiah could when he needed to blend in.

Of course, his nature—being an Incubus Demon, which made him a pariah in the supernatural world—was the first thing that had bonded him and Jeremiah. It was the reason the rest of the team trusted him with their lives. He understood what it meant to exist outside of the polite, pandering social norms. To live with a strength that also made him a complete outsider.

But gods, he was so tired of being *hungry*.

And he was so tired of never being satisfied every time he attempted to take his fill.

He appreciated Azriel's club, of course. A den of iniquity, as the Angel liked to call it, and the perfect feeding grounds for lonely Incubi who needed a quick fix. Not that Priest knew many like him. They were one of the rarest beings walking the planet, and it was one of the reasons he wasn't killed on the spot when he and Jeremiah had been picked up as children.

He was valuable. Powerful in ways even he didn't fully understand and susceptible to coercion when he was too young to know better.

He'd lucked out growing up with Jeremiah instead of being captured and molded by some foreign power that would use him for their own gain.

And really, *luck* was the only word for it. He should have been like the others: sold into the service of some royal family, brainwashed into thinking he was serving his own best interests as he destroyed the people he was meant to be protecting.

Instead, he became one of the founding members and the second-in-command of the Trident Agency, working his ass off for a lot of money and a fraction of begrudging respect from the people they served.

It wasn't the worst life, but it wasn't the best.

And life felt a little odd and a little lonely now that he was witnessing Jeremiah slowly but surely tumble into love with a Siren prince. He was happy for his best friend, but a small piece of him was terrified that the moment Jeremiah and the prince realized how good they were for each other, he'd abandon everything he and the other agents had built.

After all, the world the Tridents inhabited had no place for a royal prince groomed to rule a kingdom, even if he was abdicating his throne. So what would Jeremiah's options be except to leave the agency behind?

Priest was steadfastly keeping that to himself, of course. He wasn't about to cause an upset in the office dynamic before shit actually hit the fan. He told himself that maybe Jeremiah and the prince needed to scratch an itch, and it would all fizzle out once they took care of the threat against the royal family, and things could go back to normal.

But he also saw the way Remi made Jeremiah smile. The way he made the stoic, loveless Hellhound soften in ways no one ever had before.

Jeremiah's heart was doomed, and all Priest could do was hope that didn't mean the end of who and what they were to each other.

Taking a breath before stepping into the main club, Priest felt the last vestiges of his feed settle under his skin. If he didn't know better, he'd say the effects weren't lasting as long as they once had, and it was starting to scare him. Priest grew up with horror stories about Incubi like him, who could never find a steady partner. The unsatiated hunger drove them to irreversible insanity, and if that happened... his friends would have to take him out. There was no cure for that kind of madness in Demons like him.

There were no other options, and while he knew he had a while longer to spare, the walls felt like they were closing in on him.

Death was an inevitability, but he hoped he had a couple of centuries to live before it came to being put down like a rabid animal.

Shoving his hands into his pockets, Priest nudged the swinging door open with his shoulder to avoid whatever sticky, glittery shit was always all over the furniture and made his way past the stage, where a couple of Siren go-go dancers were entertaining a group in the front seats. Other dancers—he spotted another Siren, two Felidae shifters, and a redheaded Dragon with an impressive bulge in his thong that Priest had fed off a few times—were perched in laps, grinding against whatever patron had the biggest wad of cash that evening.

There were a handful of demons and a Hellhound monitoring the main room and watching the feeds from the "private" spaces.

Azriel might be a giant asshole most days, but he made

sure his dancers were well protected, even if he wasn't there himself. Few things could get past an Angel, fallen or not.

Priest could smell sex, and it settled under his skin, tantalizing and almost cruel because he couldn't have it the way he wanted it. He'd learned when he was young that to truly satisfy his hunger, he'd have to drain a partner dry, killing them in the process. He fed on arousal and lust, but when he took from someone, it wasn't just their pheromones he ingested. If left unchecked, he could turn their organs into dust, saturating himself with the very essence that made a person who they were.

He'd almost done it as a teen, when he'd had so little control over his Demon he could barely be trusted to go a store without supervision. Knight had pulled him from the brink when that happened, and he knew he couldn't go there again. And yet... he kept torturing himself by hanging out at the Pearly Gates whenever he was in town. Meals were easy for him to get. It wasn't like he *needed* to go to a strip club to feed.

He had no idea why he kept doing this to himself.

Well, okay. That was a lie, but it wasn't one he wanted to admit aloud just yet. If he let himself think about the shop next door and the human who was almost always behind the front desk, he would start to spiral. And when he started to spiral, he got hungry.

And when he got hungry...

He got reckless.

"Well, well, well. Look what the... hmm, *who* dragged you in here today? Was it an awkwardly adorable human who runs a shop across the street?"

The voice accompanied a cloud of smoke that was most definitely not tobacco. It was something foreign and spicy, like it came from one of the Dragon kingdoms. Azriel leaned over the bar and smiled at Priest. He looked the way he always did: pale and muscular, like he was cut from ancient marble. His messy, blond hair hung over his forehead, just a little too long, though it gave him an innocent boyish look, which was immediately ruined by the blunt clenched between his teeth.

He was shirtless, like always, wearing impossibly tight jeans and ice-blue glittery eyeshadow that made him look doe-eyed and naïve. Not that anyone who spent more than five minutes with Azriel would believe that, but it was one of the reasons people had believed Angels were kind and loving for so many generations after they began to fall and live amongst earthbound society.

"I need a drink," Priest said, ignoring his friend's words. He did not need to be given shit tonight about the human. Even if Azriel was mostly right.

Azriel rolled his eyes, but he reached under the bar and came up with a moderately clean highball glass and used his hands to throw in a few cubes of ice. Priest stared him dead in the face as Azriel lifted the whiskey bottle and filled the cup halfway.

"Want to start a tab?" the Angel asked.

Priest scoffed. "I'm not paying for your shitty liquor." He snatched the glass and took a long sip. It tasted like piss, but he choked it down for the sake of it. He had no ability to get drunk, but Gargoyle liquor did dull his senses, and today, he needed it.

"How's the whole"—Azriel wiggled ring-covered fingers at him—"hero thing going?"

His shoulders tensed, and Priest knew what was coming. The Angel leapt, and though his wings weren't visible at the moment, the rush of wind battered Priest as they helped to lift Azriel into the air so he could land on top of the bar with his legs neatly crossed.

Priest focused on Azriel's knee, which was showing through a rip in his jeans. There was a dark curl of ink on his skin, and even over the scent of arousal and sweat, he could catch hints that the tattoo was fresh, which meant a touch of something so alluring his mouth watered: Angel blood.

He fought the urge to press his finger against the tattoo to see if it would hurt his friend.

"Same as it was last week," he finally answered. "Jeremiah's barely able to tear his focus from the prince, Knight's quietly having a panic attack that something bigger's going on, Slate's still off on his *super-secret* assignment, and Storm's grumpy because he had to visit his brother's Hoard."

And Priest was left in the city, trying to hold all the pieces together.

Azriel hummed softly as he stretched his legs out and let his knees press on either side of Priest's biceps. The Angel leaned back on his elbows, tipping his head toward the ceiling. There were two bodies suspended above them, but Priest wasn't going to look. By the waves of lust he was getting, he didn't need to in order to know what was going on.

The horndog that he was, Azriel licked his lips, his pupils dilating and dick hardening twelve inches from Priest's face. He refused to move back, knowing the Angel wasn't really coming on to him. He just got bored and liked to push to see if he could get Priest to crack sometimes.

There was a surge of Angelic power, and a high-pitched, feminine voice cried out, practically showering Priest in pheromones as she orgasmed for a long minute, a masculine grunting growing louder and getting faster.

Priest couldn't even imagine how much the couple had paid to get played with like this by the dirty fallen Angel who ran the place.

As if nothing had happened, Azriel focused his softly glowing eyes on Priest and tilted his head to the side. "Whose side are you on?"

"Knight's," Priest answered without thinking.

Fucking Angels, always loosening his tongue. They were

the only Supes who had the ability to enthrall him, and his only saving grace was that Azriel was one of his best friends and never did it to hurt him.

"He's paranoid after all the shit he went through, but I think he's onto something." He glared right at his gorgeous face. "Also fucking stop that."

Azriel blinked, and his soft grip on Priest's brain released. He shot him a wide, unapologetic smile as he snatched his drink out of his hand and swallowed down half.

Setting the glass on the bar, he scooted closer to the edge and touched the underside of Priest's jaw with one finger. "You're still hungry."

"I'm always hungry," Priest muttered. And he meant it. Right now, it was just a quiet itch. His sessions here at the club kept him functional but never satisfied. No one who frequented the club was strong enough to keep him properly fed for more than a few meals at most.

"You could always book me." Azriel gave him a shit-eating grin, running his straight white teeth over his bottom lip.

Except maybe the Angel, but that was a *bad* idea.

"I'd probably kill us both. And half the city."

"Yeah, but what a ride, right?" Azriel shivered and winked—like the idea of their mutually assured destruction was something he found positively delicious—then swung a foot up and pressed his bare toes with black polish into the center of Priest's chest. "Time to go, my little sex Demon."

Priest blinked at him. "Excuse you?"

"You're sitting here wasting time when we both know you want to be next door flirting with your adorable bespectacled human. Your woe-is-me attitude is bringing the whole place down."

Priest fought back a sigh at his friend's mercurial temperament. It wasn't really Azriel's fault. He was an unmoored, unbonded Angel with no interest in finding his fated mate, so he couldn't always control the swings in his mood or how his attention would hop around. It was what made him and his club so popular though.

Priest stared up at him, trying to picture him the way the myths of Angels existed in human society. White robes. Feathered wings. A glowing halo. The lie of kindness in their eyes.

He bit back a snort.

Azriel took a long drag of his spice blunt and blew the smoke into Priest's face, making his head spin for a second. Fuck, whatever was in that thing was strong as shit. "Seriously. Your pining is getting on my nerves."

Priest tossed back the last of his drink and stood without really thinking. He wanted to blame Azriel's thrall for that, but deep down, he knew the truth. He'd met the human from next door—Oliver—several months ago when he'd stumbled into Azriel's bar looking frazzled and panicked.

For a moment, Priest had thought the human was going to be torn to shreds. Historically, humans weren't welcome in places like Azriel's. It was meant to be a safe space for Supes, and humans had a long history of being anything but safe.

Only, it hadn't happened that way.

Azriel's face had gone uncharacteristically soft. He'd hopped over the bar and taken Oliver by the shoulders, pulling him into a dark corner and talking to him in a tone so soft not even Priest had been able to make out the words. Priest had watched as all the tension drained from Oliver's face.

It wasn't long before Oliver was sitting two stools away from Priest, sipping an odd-looking drink—honest-to-gods glitter swirling around blue liquid. He smiled shyly at Priest, and while he wanted desperately to deny it, he couldn't hide the fact that something deep inside him felt like it was waking up. It was a slow, cautious burning—like the lust he fed on, only... different.

It terrified him and created an obsession that he couldn't run from.

And there was no trying to pretend like he didn't come up with the most clumsy and ridiculous excuses to see Oliver every time he came in to feed. It was easier if Oliver was in the club having a drink, but those moments were actually rare, so instead, Priest invented reasons to be in a little human shop to torment himself.

Azriel had been merciless in his teasing since he realized how Priest felt, but he also didn't understand why Priest wouldn't actually pursue him, and Priest couldn't make an Angel understand why he'd never cross that line. Azriel had far more control over his powers than Priest did, and his powers weren't meant to consume and destroy.

Priest wouldn't be able to live with himself if he let himself get close and Oliver suffered. Some Incubi loved feeding on humans. They loved the rush of being able to drain them. Humans were so responsive, after all. They were bound by their emotions with so little control, and it was a heady rush. But Priest had only sampled that once in his life, long before he dedicated himself to protecting others, and he vowed never again.

It was far too addictive. Far too dangerous.

"Stop looking at me like that," Priest muttered.

Azriel rolled his eyes and kicked his leg, sending Priest flying. Luckily, he'd been expecting it, so he landed on his feet, only slightly rumpled. He stood, straightening his shirt as he glowered at the smirking Angel and walked back up to the bar.

"This is for your own good," Azriel said with a shrug, swinging his legs like nothing had happened. He reached behind him again and came up with a stack of mail, slapping it against Priest's chest. "Here. I got some mail delivered here for him. Now you have an actual reason to go in there besides stalking him."

"I'm not stalking him. And unless you want to pay me, I'm not your goddamn errand boy," Priest growled.

Azriel laughed and flicked the end of his nose, and Priest flinched away. "Keep telling yourself that, gorgeous."

"I'm going home."

Azriel stared at the pieces of mail Priest was still holding close to his chest. "Sure you are, bud. Whatever helps you sleep at night—though there's a pretty little thing next door who could probably do wonders for your insomnia." He motioned at his mouth with a closed fist, his tongue poking at his cheek.

Priest let his eyes flare black for a second, showing his Demon. "Don't talk about him like that. I will end you."

Azriel just winked, then turned his attention to the Siren who'd wandered up to sit at the bar and stare, mouth gaping at the couple still caught in their Angel-induced haze of ecstasy. "Hey, gorgeous. First time at the Pearly Gates?"

Priest knew a dismissal when he saw one.

Squaring his shoulders, he turned, ignoring several stares from the dancers as he made his way toward the exit. The night air was a little too cool on his skin, in spite of the fact that the Siren kingdom was one of the warmer, more humid climates. He shivered and did his best not to glance to the left as he waited for a lull in traffic.

He stared down at the mail in his hands. Most of it looked like pointless junk. He could probably throw it all away, and Oliver wouldn't miss it.

"Just go," he muttered to himself. "Slip it through the mail slot and walk away."

His feet were already moving, his hand reaching for the door handle, and his resolve shattered.

Looking around the empty shop, Priest thought maybe he was going to be unlucky. Then the back door swung open, and his heart gave a single, heavy thud. But it wasn't the man he was there to see. It was Oliver's best friend and business partner.

Poe was also good-looking, but he was rugged and sharp where Oliver was delicate and soft. He was just as kind, though, and just as protective of supernaturals as Oliver seemed to be, so Priest had no choice but to like him a little.

"I'm just here to—"

"I'll let Oliver know you're here. He's in the back digging around some antique boxes," Poe interrupted.

"I just—" Priest tried again, but Poe was gone.

His shoulders sagged, and he hurried toward the counter, determined to just leave the mail and go this time, but before he could turn away, the door opened once more, and Oliver was there. Priest's heart stuttered in his chest, his throat going tight. He had never and would never understand his reaction to this single human. There was no sense behind it.

Oliver was short and lithe—the body of a kid who had probably once been malnourished. He was gorgeous, with light brown hair that was prone to waves and hazel eyes behind black-rimmed glasses full of happiness and mischief. He was everything Priest wasn't. He was kind. He was gentle. He wore sweater vests, and his hair was always mussed like he'd just rolled out of bed.

Priest was helplessly and hopelessly charmed by him, and he didn't understand why or how.

The only thing he knew was that he never wanted to stop being in his presence. Even if it was slowly killing him.

"Your... uh... mail," he said, gesturing weakly.

Oliver glanced down, and then his mouth spread in a wide grin. He adjusted his glasses, then walked over and picked up the envelopes. His perfect, delicate fingers flicked through all of it, and then—as Priest predicted he would—he tossed it all into the trash.

"Did Azriel send you?"

Priest rolled his eyes. "How'd you guess?"

Oliver laughed, the sound of it almost melodic, and Priest's heart sped up a bit when he leaned his forearms on the counter, his eyes soft and crinkled in the corners. "He's such a lazy asshole. You should start charging him for running his errands."

"That's what *I* told him," Priest said. He leaned against the counter and stared down. They were inches apart, and the world seemed to narrow down until only the two of them existed. "He just laughed in my face and started flirting with a Siren at the bar."

Oliver's smile softened, and he shook his head. "I keep telling you to skip that hole and come hang out with me. Everything in here has ten layers of dust, but I promise the liquor is better. And I won't charge you. Plus, you know my company's better."

Priest grinned. "Can't argue there. I have way more fun over here."

"Minus the lack of go-go dancers," Oliver mused. "I mean, I guess I could wear booty shorts and high boots, but I'm trying to attract customers, not drive them off."

Priest sucked in a breath. By the gods, was Oliver trying to kill him? He'd never be able to get that mental image out of his head—not that he really wanted to.

"Oh, sweetheart," he murmured. "Trust me, you'd have a line around the block."

Oliver's eyes darkened, and he shook his head. "You don't have to flatter me, Priest. I already like you." His hand splayed flat on the glass counter, and he moved it closer—like he was begging to be touched, and gods, Priest wanted to know how warm he was.

Priest's exhale trembled. He shifted closer, and then their

hands were touching. Sparks flared to life under his skin, and the scent of lust was thick between them—both Oliver's and his own. He stared into the human's eyes, watching as his pupils dilated. Priest wanted to pull him close—not to feed but to taste.

He licked his lips, and Oliver mirrored him.

Everything in him felt coiled, poised to strike like a goddamn cobra. "Oliver," he whispered.

Oliver leaned in close. "Yeah?"

They were less than an inch apart now. Priest could smell everything on him—his cologne, the soap he'd used in the shower, the cotton from his bedding, the faint traces of come after stroking himself off. He shivered, and Oliver swayed closer, prepared to take what he was all but begging for.

Bang!

Priest jumped, head twisting and fangs descending on instinct at the loud sound from the back room. Poe's muffled "Sorry!" brought him back down to reality, and he took a stumbling step back, panic rising in his gut.

Oliver's head dropped, groaning slightly. "I hate him. I'm going to *kill* him."

Had they almost just…

He looked at Oliver—at the flush in his cheeks and how his eyes were a little red-rimmed. He knew that look, those signs. He was far too close to being under Priest's thrall, and he could never live with himself if that happened.

"I have to go, sorry."

Oliver started to reach for him, but Priest carefully stepped away from his grasp. "No. It was my fault. I—"

"It wasn't," Priest interrupted in a hurry. "It's not you. I have a massive case going on right now, and I've already been away too long."

That wasn't a lie. The Siren royal family was waiting, and Jeremiah would most definitely kill him dead if his fucking hunger got Remi hurt.

"I'll see you soon, yeah?"

He ignored the shattered look on Oliver's face and told himself it meant nothing as he rushed out the door without a real goodbye. Oliver was forbidden fruit. He was the temptation Priest could never give in to.

It had to be that way. For both their sakes.

2

OLIVER

*O*liver was a polite person. He understood social niceties. It was one of the things that helped him survive when he was younger, and it was one of the things Poe was trying to cook out of him now. Well, mostly. Poe wanted him to stop being such a people-pleaser, and rightfully so.

And right then, he was the closest he'd ever been to cracking and giving someone a real piece of his mind. Priest, to be exact.

The Demon. The Liar.

I'll see you soon, yeah?

Those had been Priest's last words to him before doing the exact opposite. Oliver hadn't seen him in weeks, and if it wasn't for the news talking about the Trident Agency's involvement with the Siren royal family, he would have assumed Priest was lying to get out of having the conversation Oliver was so desperate to have.

The truth was, Oliver wanted him. He understood the risks that came with falling for an Incubus Demon, but he didn't care. Priest had been nothing but kind to him. He was what he was, but he was also an adorably awkward nerd who acted like he'd never learned how to flirt.

And Oliver was no fool. He knew there was danger lurking behind Priest's gorgeous eyes. He knew what he went to Azriel's club for, and the only thing Oliver wanted to do was offer himself. Not that he would, of course. Not without some kind of commitment.

Oliver had already grilled Azriel on whether or not it was safe to be with someone like Priest.

"Could he kill me?" Oliver had asked a few weeks after meeting the Demon.

Azriel rolled his eyes and muttered several words in a language Oliver didn't understand before flashing teeth in a grimace trying to be a smile. "Yes, he could kill you. But he wouldn't. That's not his nature."

"That's not an Incubus's nature?" Oliver asked, his entire body humming with skepticism.

Azriel laughed. "Oh, darling. *No*. An Incubus would definitely consume you until you were dead. But Priest wouldn't. It's not in *his* nature. He's a bodyguard. A *protector*. His entire life is keeping little lost lambs like you safe."

Oliver flipped him off and ignored it when Azriel laid an apologetic kiss on his cheek. "I don't even know why I'm asking," Oliver had said when Azriel pulled back. "It's not like he'd want someone like me."

Azriel looked at him, sighed, and shook his head. "Oh, honey," he said in that devastating tone that cut right to the quick.

It was the last time Oliver had brought up the Demon with his Angel friend. Now, Poe had to suffer Oliver's pining, which he complained loudly about but still sat through all of Oliver's poetic ranting. Poe gave him shit but also told him to be patient.

"He's probably not used to wanting a human for more than a midnight snack," Poe had told him.

And he was probably right. Oliver knew that should scare him off, but instead, it just added to the intrigue. How would it work? How would it feel to let Priest feed off him? He groaned and opened his eyes to find a mug hovering over his face.

He jolted, then realized the mug was attached to the arm of his best friend. He sat up, carefully dodging Poe's hand, and rubbed his face. "What are you doing?"

"Making you tea," Poe said, waving the mug back and forth. "Here comes the train," he singsonged. "Open up. Choo-choo!"

"I will hire the biggest Gargoyle I can find to sit on you," Oliver growled.

Poe grinned over the rim of the mug. "Don't promise me a good time. Now, drink your tea like a good boy. That or go jerk off, but I literally can't take the pining or the pheromones, and since you won't go ask Azriel where your stalker is..."

"He's not my stalker," Oliver said, standing up and brushing past his friend, heading into the kitchen. He opened up the fridge and got a bottle of Siren Water out. The damn stuff wasn't great for humans, but by the gods, it was addictive.

Behind him, Poe snorted and set the tea down. "Yeah, he's totally not a stalker. Never mind him randomly showing up at a grocery store where you happened to be shopping. Or the kebab place. Or the—"

Oliver cleared his throat, cutting Poe off. "Correlation is not causation."

"Oh, my love, that's not what that phrase means." Poe slung an arm around Oliver, jolting him hard enough that he choked on his swallow of water. "And denial is not really a cute look on you. I'm sorry he totally ditched you though."

Oliver flinched, the words cutting deeper than Poe meant them to. He let out a bone-deep sigh and sank into one of their kitchen chairs, staring out the window. The apartment

17

was above the shop, and it had an amazing view of the city. There was a little peekaboo strip of ocean on the horizon, and usually, Oliver could sit out on their tiny, one-chair terrace and feel at peace.

But not today.

"I just don't get it, you know?" Oliver said as Poe hopped up on the counter and tapped a little pattern against the cabinet with his bare heels. "He flirts with me for weeks."

"Months. Almost a damn year," Poe pointed out.

Oliver rolled his eyes, but he couldn't exactly argue with that. He just hadn't noticed until both Poe and Azriel pointed it out. For far too long, Oliver thought he was just quietly pining and that Priest was just... nice. That was probably why he was a pathetic, single loner who hadn't had a hookup, much less a boyfriend, in years.

"I know what you're thinking, and stop," Poe said. "You're a catch, and he's a Demon. If there's anything defunct about this whole thing, it's him."

"That's not very kind," Oliver said quietly.

Poe shrugged, not looking sorry. "You're sitting here alone on your one day off, sad because he strung you along and then ghosted you without a word."

"He was working," Oliver defended weakly. Working hadn't stopped Priest before when he wanted to come to Azriel's to feed, and he'd never failed to stop in at the shop. At least, not until now. But Azriel swore up and down he hadn't heard from Priest since the last time he'd been in and then come over to the shop and nearly kissed Oliver, and he knew the Angel wouldn't lie to him. Not about this.

Poe bit his lip, his expression torn, and then his shoulders sagged. "I just hate seeing you waste your time. You're my brother, and I want you to be happy."

"I'm not unhappy," Oliver told him gently, and that was true. He wanted to be in love. Meeting someone and having a life together had always been a goal of his. But it wasn't something he needed to survive.

More than anyone, Oliver knew what unhappiness felt like. He'd grown up unloved, trapped in a family with a vendetta against every supernatural community. He'd spent his formative years surrounded by hateful bigotry and rhetoric, and none of it had ever made sense. Their views terrified him to the point that at sixteen, when he realized he would never be like them, he ran.

It was his only escape. If he'd stayed—if they'd found out about him—he wasn't sure he'd ever see the light of day again. He'd heard rumors of other people in their little community, young like him with minds of their own, who went missing and never returned.

Oliver wasn't going to let that happen to him.

Shortly after he'd run, he understood what being cold was like. And what hunger truly was. He learned how to pick-pocket and shoplift to make it from one day to the next, hating himself a little more each day. There was little sanctuary for humans outside of his own borders, but just before his seventeenth birthday, Poe found him.

Oliver was huddled against the tide wall near the touristy beach in Midlona, trying to blend in. He'd bathed in the sea and was hoping he could just get a little peace—a little rest. Then Poe had stumbled into him, literally, and for whatever reason, he hadn't left Oliver's side again.

He dragged Oliver back to his house, where he had his first real meal and a shower in months. Poe's mom put on a strong face, but he could see the anger in her eyes, and he thought maybe he was all wrong here too. But when he offered to leave, she just put her arms around him and told him he'd always have a place to land if he ever fell.

Then she asked him not to go.

Oliver hadn't realized what it was like to be loved—truly loved—until that moment. He watched Poe's family dynamic, and he realized he fit. There was no hatred or bigotry at the dinner table. Poe's parents were both activists working in Midlona and the surrounding kingdoms, frustrated at their lack of progress but never losing hope.

And Oliver knew he was home.

He and Poe had settled into their life, running the book-shop and sharing their tiny apartment. He could never, ever call this miserable, even if his heart was aching now. Even if he still believed he was the one who was all wrong somehow.

"Seriously, drink some tea," Poe said, dragging Oliver out of his thoughts.

Oliver blinked, then shook his head. "I don't want tea. I want to get laid."

"You literally have a Guardian Angel who owns a strip club and has fucked half of Midlona," Poe told him dryly. "If you want to get laid, I can help you with that. Or hell, you can go next door and pick up one of the Angel's patrons."

Oliver flushed, but he didn't bother telling Poe that he didn't want to be fucked by just anyone. He wanted to be ravaged by an awkward Incubus, and that was apparently not going to happen anytime soon.

Or ever.

"Am I hideous?" he asked.

"You know you're not. If it didn't feel like weird incest, I'd totally be into you," Poe told him.

Oliver shuddered at the thought. "Thanks, I think?"

Poe tapped his chin. "I bet Azriel would be really good in bed. I mean, I've thought about it once or twice. He probably has moves that are illegal in half the kingdoms on the continent."

And then he shivered and bit his lip.

Oliver gaped at him. "Stop talking for at least one hour. I've had enough of your mouth for now."

Poe laughed and hopped off the counter. "I'm gonna go

shower and jerk off. Go visit your friend unless you want to listen in."

That was enough to get Oliver up off his ass and out the door. He loved sharing a place with his best friend, but sometimes, he also really hated it.

Sitting in the club, Oliver felt a little pathetic. The Pearly Gates was usually always busy no matter what time of day, but today, there was a noticeable lull in business now that the sun had set. There were a couple of dancers on the side stages, but the main stage was dark, the curtain drawn, and Oliver was the only one sitting at the bar.

"Does it seem weirdly dead in here today?"

"There's nothing weird about it," Azriel said. His voice sounded harsh and cold, which was completely unlike him. He never talked to Oliver like that. "You haven't seen the news?"

Something ran up Oliver's spine. He'd been feeling odd all day long, and he just figured it was melancholy over Priest. But maybe it wasn't. Oliver had always had an almost sixth sense when something was about to go wrong or when someone he loved was hurt. Some of the time, he was right, but sometimes, he was also just being paranoid out of fear of losing the only people who cared about him.

He'd learned to ignore it unless the feeling was pressing, and today had been nothing more than a dull hum.

Azriel snapped his fingers, and a TV Oliver had never noticed on the wall above the rows of bottles turned on. There was a reporter talking about the arrest of a human senator, and then he started paying attention. The sound was off, but the slow-moving captions told the story of what really went on.

The Trident Agency had just uncovered a plot against the

Siren royal family. The crown prince and the young prince and princess had been taken by an unnamed anti-Supe organization, and several members of the notorious Alpha Team were instrumental in bringing them home.

Now, fingers were being pointed at one of the human governments, though the news didn't name who had done it or why.

Oliver felt bile rising in his throat. He did his best not to think about where he'd come from, but that wasn't easy when he knew far too many people who would applaud something like this. The feeling along his spine got worse.

And then it exploded when the camera panned over, and he got his first glimpse of Priest in weeks. His heart felt like it was trying to climb out of his throat.

"I hate this."

Azriel stared at him for a long time, an expression on his face Oliver couldn't read. "Something wrong?"

"No," Oliver lied.

Azriel leaned forward and captured his gaze. Oliver had seen this move before. Usually, the person cracked open like a damn walnut and spilled their guts, but Azriel rarely used his power on Oliver for that. "Talk to me."

"I really don't want to."

The strange look on Azriel's face deepened, and then he sighed and leaned back. "Is this about Priest?"

"Is there, like, a group chat with all of you who want to talk about my pathetic crush?" Oliver groaned.

Azriel laughed. "Let me guess... Poe?"

"He thinks I'm pining."

Azriel's smile widened. "Oh, honey. You *are* pining. It's really quite disgusting and it totally throws off the vibe in here. The only reason I don't mind is because everyone's at home shaking in their panties, and there's no one left to entertain me."

Oliver frowned at him. "You're not going to take all of that seriously? You know they'd come after you too. Angels aren't exempt."

"I've never taken anything seriously in my whole existence, and I'm not about to start now," Azriel said with a wink. He grabbed one of his spice cigarettes from his silver case, blew on the tip, and Oliver sucked in a breath when it lit. Azriel drew in a deep lungful, then let it out with a happy sigh. "Anyway, this whole thing with Priest is not one-sided, okay? So quit worrying."

"I'm not. And yes it is. The last time I saw him, I swear he was going to kiss me. I was laying it on as thick as I could, but he panicked and ran."

"Yeah, that's a *him* problem, not a *you* problem. Trust me," Azriel said, patting Oliver's hand.

Oliver licked his lips, then repeated his question to Poe earlier. "Am I hideous?"

"You're gorgeous. I'd put you up on that main stage if I could, babe. But dancing isn't the life for you."

Oliver flushed. It hadn't exactly been a fantasy of his to get dressed up, throw on some glitter and lipstick, and dance for a crowd. But it wasn't *not* a fantasy for doing that privately for one man. Or Demon, as it were. But he'd made a go-go dance joke the night Priest panicked and left, so maybe that wouldn't be appreciated.

Letting out a small sigh, Oliver turned his attention back to Azriel, but suddenly, he got a chill up his spine too intense to ignore. He'd felt things like this before, usually before some disaster struck. Half the time, it was some angry customer, and the other half, it was Poe picking drunk fights with people.

But this was something else. Something new. Poe was in trouble. No, it was more than that. A vision of Poe's bloody, lifeless body filled his head, and his chest felt like it was cracking in half.

He jumped off his stool. "Something's wrong." His voice

was trembling, and he realized he couldn't just stand there. He didn't know why or how, but he knew his best friend was in trouble, and he would be damned if he didn't save him.

"Oliver!" Azriel called, but Oliver was running for the door.

He burst out into the street, then started for the shop. There was a van nearby looking odd, though he didn't know why, but when he locked gazes with the driver, the feeling in his gut only got worse. Poe *was* in danger. Something was very wrong.

He was steps from the side of their building when he first heard the rumble, and then—between one breath and the next —there was heat.

And then there was pain.

He was falling through the air. His skin was burning, and he knew he was seconds from hitting the ground, and when he did, it would all be over.

And finally, just before his body shattered apart, there was blessed darkness.

3

PRIEST

*H*e woke up with a gasp, bile in his throat, his heart racing so hard for a moment he thought maybe he was dying. Rolling onto his side, he groped for the little trash can he kept near his bed and unleashed a torrent of bitterness. His stomach ached, and his heart began to stabilize, but he couldn't shake the feeling something was wrong.

And not just a little wrong.

Priest was a Demon. An Incubus. He sure as the nine hells was not clairvoyant, and he'd never had a premonition in his life. But somehow, he knew that shit had just hit the fan. Swinging his legs over the side of the bed, he scrubbed at his face and made his way into the living room. He could hear a low murmur, and he immediately recognized Knight, who appeared a second later, his brow furrowed.

"Mm. Okay. And he's—yeah. You and I both know he's going to lose his fucking shit."

"Who is that?" Priest demanded.

Knight waved him off, turning his back. "Yeah, well, it's not like I have a choice, do I? He's going to find out on the goddamn news if—"

Priest didn't usually move faster than human speed, but

this time, he was at Knight's throat in the blink of an eye, grabbing him by the collar, careful to avoid actually touching him. He ripped the phone out of Knight's hand and pressed it to his ear. "Who the fuck is this, and what the fuck happened?"

"Well, hello to you too, my darling." Azriel.

Priest's heart sank to his feet. He knew. Fuck—he didn't know how, but he knew. "Is it Oliver?"

Azriel sighed. "Before you panic and do something we both know you'll regret, know that he's alive."

Priest felt relief knock into him like a damn freight train, and it was only his grip on Knight's shirt that kept him upright. "Okay, so what happened?" It became very clear in Azriel's beat of silence that he had said Oliver was alive, not that he was fine.

That was a big distinction.

"Azriel! What fucking happened?"

"There was an attack." Azriel sounded pissed, but not at him. "The cops are here, but they're so absolutely useless. I got a call from the head of your adorable backups—I mean, *Bravo* Team—who told me to let you know they were standing by when you got here. I'm assuming this is because your fearless leader is unreachable while his dick is stuck in his cute little prince's ass—"

"Enough," Priest said tiredly. He was in no mood for Azriel's bullshit. "How alive is he? I mean... how hurt? How—"

"He's breathing, and he's not going to die. I was right behind him, so I was able to shield him from a lot of the blast, but his bookshop is gone, and so is a good chunk of their neighbor's living room wall."

Priest let out a sound of grief he didn't know he was capable of making. Oliver loved that place. They could rebuild, but fuck, it wouldn't be the same. Taking a breath, he listened to the sound of Azriel on the line, and he realized there was more. There was something worse than the shop. "What aren't you telling me."

He loosened his grip on Knight, who took a very grateful step back and wrapped his arms around his middle. Their gazes connected. Knight knew.

"They haven't found a body," Azriel said very slowly, "but they're pretty sure that Poe didn't make it."

Priest's ears began to ring. He knew Poe. He *liked* Poe. He was a lot like Az but less obnoxious, and from the bits and pieces he'd overheard about their lives, Poe had saved Oliver after he'd run from his heinous, bigoted family. He'd picked Oliver up off the streets, and they'd been inseparable ever since.

If Poe was gone—if he was actually gone—Oliver would never recover.

Priest didn't fight when Knight took the phone back. He backed up, sinking down on the end of his bed as Knight finished the call. Oliver was hurt. The shop was destroyed. Poe was likely dead. And someone had done this deliberately because there was no way the shop had blown up by accident. This wasn't some gas leak or wrath of the gods.

Someone had targeted them.

But why?

"We have a flight," Knight said as he walked back into the room. His hands were trembling a little, and Priest knew that was his fault. He'd gotten too close.

Knight was okay with touching them sometimes, but it had to be on his terms.

"I'm sorry," Priest whispered.

Knight shook his head and sat, a larger-than-normal space left between them. His dark brown hair was starting to look a little too long on top, nearly falling in his eyes, and his five-o'clock shadow was beginning to become more of a beard than just stubble. Protecting the Siren royals had taken a lot out of all of them.

"How did you know?"

"I didn't," Priest told him, not even pretending not to know what he was talking about. He pressed his hands to his face and let out a trembling breath. "I woke up, and I felt… something. Like I could sense something was very wrong. I don't know how to explain it. It's never happened to me before."

When he dropped his hands, he saw Knight's brow was furrowed.

"You're starving."

"I'm not starving," he started to argue, but Knight held up a hand.

"You're weaker, and you're sleeping too much. You never nap, but you've been out cold in here for nearly two hours." Knight ran his fingers over his pursed lips. "You just fed a couple of days ago. Something's going on with you."

He hadn't, actually. He hadn't fed in far too long. But the very idea of feeding on someone who wasn't a bespectacled bookworm had begun to repulse him so much he hadn't been able to go through with any of his attempts.

Priest knew what was happening—the first signs of lacking a feeding partner who could satisfy him were starting to take a toll on him. Luckily for him, it could last years and years before he got to the point he wasn't able to function. And a few years after that before he went mad and began to kill.

"Seriously, I'm fine. My hunger has nothing to do with Oliver."

Knight's mouth twitched. "I didn't say it did."

"Can you just…" Priest groaned. "Do you know what the fuck is going on? Who would bother targeting a human book-shop? This can't be related to the thing with the Sirens, can it?"

"No one's sure right now. I've been on the phone since this whole thing went down. Storm got an unsubstantiated threat report a couple of days ago, but we thought it was just people still stirred up and venting about McCornal and his kid. People say all kinds of shit online, and there wasn't a specific target or upcoming incident mentioned, so it went in the pile."

Priest bared his teeth in a furious grimace. "Sunshine is going to kick both your asses for not sharing that, you know."

"Maybe." Knight's lip curled back in distaste, his canines pointed and deadly even while his friend was completely in control of his Vampire. "But we've been getting dozens of reports like that from the analysts since news broke about the princes and princess getting rescued, and most of them haven't turned into anything we can actually investigate or even hand off to local law enforcement. Just whispers of anger and larger-than-normal piles of bullshit being spewed in hate groups."

"Except there's obviously more going on. Something like this? It doesn't come out of nowhere."

Knight's eyes went red. "No. There have been a few instances in the last few weeks of people going missing." His gaze turned distant. "Humans. Not enough in a single place to draw most people's attention, but…"

Priest sat up. "But our analysts aren't most people. They caught it, and you think this is connected."

"It wouldn't surprise me if—whatever the fuck this is—it's an escalation. I think McCornal and his piece-of-shit son were just the beginning of a new, bigger problem. Something unlike anything we've ever seen."

There was a note of a lie in his voice, and Priest played the words back in his head before realizing what it was. People going missing. Anti-Supe hatred.

"The labs," Priest murmured, staring at his friend's profile. Mentioning the worst thing to ever happen to Knight wasn't something he did very often—and Knight *never* talked about it willingly—but the dots were connecting and leading him to one place.

Knight stiffened and swallowed heavily, pushing to his feet and keeping his back to Priest. The scent of his anguish stung his nose, riling his Demon, who was just as protective of the Vampire as Priest was. "We shouldn't assume. Not yet. But I'll fill Sunshine in on the plane and, if you're in agreement, have him order the other two teams to be on standby. Since most of Bravo Team is already there, we'll have them create a perimeter around Azriel's, but the Alphas will be in charge."

Priest felt an almost violent wave of relief. He needed to see Oliver. To touch him. To breathe in his scent. He needed to be there when he opened his eyes so he could be sure that he was as okay as he could be. And he needed to find who'd hurt him and make them hurt a hundred times worse.

And considering the potential magnitude of what Knight was hinting at, they were looking at a possible war on their hands. Were they ready for that?

He almost broke a rib trying to hold in his laugh. They'd be completely and utterly fucked.

"When do we leave?" They had returned to HQ about a week ago, the high-security building sitting right on the border between the Siren's kingdom, Midlona, and the Gargoyle's, Averna. There were few others in the area, most clustering around the castles their royals lived in, but Jeremiah and his new princely mate were in a cozy—and private—little house nearby.

The bookshop was on the edge of the Midlona city in a slightly seedier area than Priest would have liked—or it had been.

"As soon as your go bag is packed," Knight said.

Luckily, Priest was nothing if not prepared.

The rooms he stayed in at HQ weren't really home to him, and he always kept his bag ready. Snagging his duffel from the closet, he pulled out his phone. He didn't give a shit that he was in running pants and a tattered T-shirt. The only thing that mattered was getting to Oliver as quickly as he could.

As they headed out to the elevator, Knight texting their new pilot to let him know they were on their way, Priest called the only person who could help him get through the next few days.

When his best friend answered, he didn't give him a chance to speak. "I need you. Something happened."

The flight was short, but it felt eternal, and Knight threatened to pin him and drain him if he didn't stop pacing. Priest flopped on his back over two seats in their new jet—a thank-you gift from the king and queen of Midlona—and started counting divots in the plane ceiling. Loudly.

Jeremiah was on his phone in the last row, Remi curled up against his side. The waves of worry mixed with lust coming off the prince were driving Priest's Demon to distraction, which added to his inability to settle.

Knight gave him a flat look, then slipped noise-canceling headphones over his ears—the good ones he'd bought after he and Priest had experienced a *particularly* hellish stakeout together a year or so ago—and Priest flipped him off before turning his face toward the windows, not really seeing anything beyond the glass.

He couldn't stop shaking on the descent, and by the time they landed, he was all but crawling out of his skin.

Jeremiah squeezed his shoulder on his way past, telling him and Knight he'd call when he knew something, and then jumped in a vehicle with Remi and the head of the Bravo Team.

Knight didn't put up any kind of fight when Priest snagged the keys to their waiting SUV and quickly climbed in after him. Priest drove the way to Azriel's on pure muscle memory, pulling around the back of the club, and he was unsurprised to find the Angel sitting outside waiting for them.

Az looked the same as he always did—shirtless, artfully torn jeans, his hair still hanging in his face. But there were dark circles under his eyes Priest was unused to seeing, which he knew wasn't from lack of sleep but from a power drain. It meant he'd gone above and beyond to heal Oliver... which meant his injuries had probably been worse than he'd admitted over the phone.

The scent of smoke and charred wood filled the air, and he could see the blackened outline of what used to be a corner of the bookstore. The sight nearly brought him to his knees, making the whole thing so much more real. Turning his fear and anger on the only outlet he had was a terrible idea, but he couldn't stop himself.

He slammed the SUV door shut and rushed Azriel, ripping his spiced cigarette from his mouth and flinging it away. "How bad was it? How could he have survived that? There are char marks on your fucking club!"

Azriel followed the trajectory of his blunt, a small frown on his inhumanly pretty face. "Your little pet will be fine."

Priest's hands curled into fists. "Call him that one more time. See what happens."

Smiling, Azriel shook his head, clapping his hand against the side of Priest's neck and pulling him close so their foreheads touched. There was an instinctive twitch under his skin, his Demon repelled on a cellular level by an Angel touching him, but he shook it off and allowed the soothing scent and heat of his friend to ease his anxiety.

"He's alive. He hasn't woken up yet, and I'm not sure when he will, but he's not dying."

When he will, yes, or *if* he will, but Priest refused to acknowledge those unspoken words.

"How bad are his injuries? Are they permanent?" Priest whispered hoarsely.

At that, Azriel pulled back and glanced away. "I don't know yet. I've given him everything I've got. And before you make a complete fucking ass of yourself, you might want to feed. I can smell your hunger, babes."

Priest shoved Azriel away from him and marched for the door. "He's upstairs, right?"

The Angel lived on the third floor, above the rooms where people usually went for the more... *indiscreet* services the club offered. It wasn't often anyone was invited all the way to the top floor, but Priest knew that Azriel wasn't going to stop him.

He didn't wait for an answer, and he took the stairs three at a time before pressing his hand to the lock and willing it open. What should have been little more than a parlor trick left him staggering against the door for a moment. The drain on his power was worse than it had ever been before. His legs felt heavy, and he knew Azriel was probably right. He should feed. But the very idea of taking anything from anyone in that club who wasn't Oliver felt...

There weren't really words, but betrayal was the only thing that came close.

He took a breath, scenting his human behind Azriel's apartment door, and he was relieved when the knob turned, worried his surge of power hadn't actually been enough to get the job done. Just as he pushed inside, he felt a hand on his shoulder, and then Azriel and Knight were at his side.

"You need to calm down. You're going to cause an orgy downstairs," Azriel murmured. "And I don't have the staff on hand to deal with that—no matter how good of a time it would be."

Priest looked down and caught the outline of Azriel's rather impressively large cock pressing against his jeans, and he flushed with embarrassment. He hadn't lost control of himself like that since he was young and untethered to his best friends. He took a breath as Azriel brushed a hand against the small of his back and ushered him inside.

"Are you sure you don't want to feed?"

Priest shook his head. "I'd love a drink though. And to see Oliver."

"Let him rest," Knight rumbled as he breezed past them both, his phone in his hand. "Sunshine's calling. He's probably got an update."

Priest was struggling to give a shit about the rest of the world. Knight stepped out onto the balcony, closing the glass door behind him but keeping his attention on Priest.

He ignored his friend, gaze tracking Az where he was rummaging around his small kitchen. The Angel let out a quiet *"aha"* when he pulled a bottle of vodka out of the freezer.

The bottle was frosty by design, which meant it was something Angel made. And that meant it was going to be very good and very strong. Exactly what he needed. Azriel, being as extra as he was, pulled out two massive spheres of ice and settled them in short glasses, letting the vodka rain over them.

He took out a little dish of lime slices from his nearly empty fridge, and he squeezed one over the top, then ran it over the rim before finally handing it over. Priest took down half the glass without even tasting it, ignoring the pointed look Azriel was giving him.

"Tell me everything," he finally said as his throat ached in the best way, a wonderful numbness settling over his extremities.

Azriel picked up his own glass, then hopped up on his kitchen counter and crossed his legs. He tapped his bare foot against the edge of the sink as he let his head fall back to rest against the fridge. "I should have felt it. Things were weird, but shit was getting weird everywhere. The bar was really dead."

That was bizarre. The Pearly Gates was the house of scandal in more ways than one. Royal families and politicians alike bought VIP rooms and engaged in all manner of speakable and unspeakable things. And, so long as they paid and all parties consented, Azriel and his entire crew kept their mouths shut. Because of that, no matter what the economy was like, the place was always booming.

"Oliver pointed it out. He came by to vent. Poe was giving him shit about you."

Priest felt a strange, unfamiliar emotion in his chest. Was it grief? Or humiliation because he was the one leading Oliver on only to pull back.

"What next?" he demanded. He needed to focus. He wouldn't let what had almost happened between them happen again. He couldn't. But he needed to know everything, and he needed to make sure Oliver was safe. That he could fully heal, even if he'd never get over the loss of his best friend.

Azriel scrunched up his face. "He just kind of... lost it. He ran out of the club like a Dragon hatchling out of the nest. That's when I felt something was wrong. I don't know how to explain it. I've never experienced anything so intense. It was this feeling that went deeper in my gut. Like I just knew something was about to happen, you know?"

Priest did know. He didn't get the feeling often—and *nothing* like what had awoken him earlier—but when he was close to danger, there was a sort of buzzing under his skin. It was most likely different for Angels, but Demons were the other side of the same coin, so it was probably at least similar, if not from the same source.

"I was too far behind him," Azriel said, his voice a little choked. "The blast caught him before I could. I was able to shield him from the worst of it, but..." He closed his eyes and drained half his glass. "Some fucking Guardian Angel I turned out to be, hm?"

"That wasn't your job." *It was mine.* "You did what you could. You saved his life."

"I should have been faster, but I was distracted," Azriel spat, setting aside his glass and scrubbing at his face. "He's such a stubborn little shit though. He wouldn't listen. He started running before I'd even picked up on the danger, and he was so far ahead of me when the blast went off."

Priest couldn't help his smile, even though it hurt. He tipped back the rest of his drink, then set it on the table. "And then you brought him here, yeah?"

Azriel nodded. "Seemed the safest place for him. No one can break in if I don't want them to."

"And you didn't see anything suspicious in the street?"

"Not really, no." He could tell Azriel was holding something back, but there would be time to grill him later. "I didn't really have time to investigate. I brought him up here as quickly as I could. He was going to die if I didn't act fast, and I wasn't sure how much I could heal. Like I said, I gave him everything I had. He's probably going to be in a world of pain if he wakes up."

His heart constricted. *If.* He'd finally said the quiet part out loud.

"*When*," Priest whispered.

Azriel met his gaze, his eyes glowing heavenly blue. "He's only human."

Only. As if Oliver was *only* anything.

"He's mine," he snarled, then snapped his jaws shut. He shouldn't have said that because it couldn't be true, but he wasn't going to take the words back. "Where is he?"

Azriel hesitated for only a second before jerking his chin toward the closed door on the other side of the open-plan apartment. "Don't do anything you'll regret," he warned.

There wasn't anything Priest could do. He wasn't a healer.

His nature was to take—to feed, to bend others and objects to his will. All he could do was stand there and hope like some kind of useless fool.

But he'd be damned if he didn't do at least that.

It was dark inside the room, the shades drawn, but Priest could smell blood, soot, and charred skin. And he could smell fear. And pain. His chest ached as he approached the bed and fell to his knees. Oliver was lying beneath a thin sheet, and his face was mottled with bruising, his lip fat, his right eye still blackened.

There were no burn marks, but they were likely the first things Azriel had managed to heal, and that was at least something.

But hells' bells, if this was how he looked after draining an Angel, Priest could only imagine what he'd looked like before. It was a miracle he hadn't died. Literally. He felt an aching sense of regret crawling up the back of his throat like bitter bile.

The last time he'd seen Oliver, he'd tried to kiss him. And by the gods, what Priest wouldn't give to go back to that moment. He should have let him. He should have said fuck it and given in because he was terrified now he might not get the chance.

He knew there was more to focus on than a single injured human, but Priest had no idea how to explain to anyone why it felt like Oliver's pain seemed like the end of the world.

The human let out a groan, and Priest's heart began to hammer in his chest. "Come on," he whispered. "Come back to me."

He felt something in his chest—like tendrils of a thread—reaching for Oliver. It was strange, but he couldn't focus on that now. He was probably just losing it a bit more to his hunger.

Maybe the others were right to be worried about him.

His hand crept across the sheets, taking Oliver's battered one into his light grasp. "Come on, sweetheart. Please."

Oliver's fingers twitched against his palm.

"Wake up," Priest begged, tightening his grip. His whole chest seemed to be reaching for the human's soft, warm, glowing soul. *"Wake up."*

It felt like the world stopped turning.

And then Oliver opened his eyes.

4

OLIVER

*W*arm. God, he was so *warm*, and everything around him was so soft. Except... no. It was hot. Everything was hot, and he was *burning*, and...

Oliver's eyes opened, his breath stuttering in his chest as he tried to gasp for air. Everything around him was unfamiliar, and the first thing he became aware of was the pain. He couldn't pinpoint where it was coming from because it felt like every single muscle was on fire.

"Mrrfpfh." He wasn't sure what he'd tried to say, but that was the odd noise that escaped his lips. But a second later, a hand touched his, and some of the agony began to ease.

Azriel? He was the only creature Oliver knew who could heal, and... wait. Wasn't he with Azriel? Shit, where was he? How did he get there, and what in the name of all the gods had happened?

"Hey. You're okay. I'm right here."

Ten minutes ago—or was it maybe ten hours or ten years —Oliver would have given his right arm to hear that voice. He managed to turn his head, and he found Priest on his knees beside the bed he was lying on in an unfamiliar room. Oliver tried to lick his lips, but his tongue felt like sandpaper.

"What…" He got the single word out before he started choking.

Priest was on his feet, screaming at the top of his lungs for water before Oliver had time to react.

He forced himself to sit partway up. "No. I'm—"

"Lay down," Priest shouted, then slapped his hand over his mouth while using the other one to forcibly shove Oliver back to the sheets. Oliver stared at him with wide eyes as Priest snatched his hand back and stared at it like the thing was possessed. "I'm so sorry. I'm so sorry. But don't move. Please? Because you're hurt, and… *where the hell is that water*!"

Oliver managed to lift his arm and pressed his hand over his eyes. His head was pounding. "Can you," he rasped, "maybe… not scream right now?"

He heard the sound of Priest slapping his mouth again and then muffled words against his palm. Gods, why was he so head over heels for this disaster Demon?

Another beat later, Oliver heard the door creak open, and he dropped his hand, breathing out a sigh of relief when he saw Azriel leaning in the doorway holding a frosty glass bottle of Siren Water. "Good morning, Sleeping Beauty."

Oliver managed a scowl, and as he tried to push himself up, Priest was instantly at his side, offering his very warm, very strong arms. Oliver did his best not to melt, considering the situation seemed pretty damned dire.

"Here," Azriel said, sitting on the edge of the bed.

He twisted off the aluminum cap and helped Oliver take a few sips. The water was the perfect temperature, and the healing properties began to ease some of the internal aches. When he tried to move again though, pain shot through him, and he collapsed back against Priest.

"Easy," Azriel said, setting the bottle on the table. "You basically just died, so no marathons."

Oliver sucked in a breath and fought off a coughing fit. "I'm sorry. I *what*?"

Azriel and Priest exchanged a look, and Priest's arms tightened around him, giving Oliver comfort he hadn't realized he'd needed.

The Angel took a breath, then asked, "What do you remember?"

Oliver's brow furrowed. Everything was so... foggy and off, like he'd been sleeping for too long. What had he been doing? "I was at the shop. I came to see you," he recounted. There was something else he was missing. "The club was pretty dead."

Azriel sighed. "Mhm. Remember why?"

Oliver started to shake his head, wincing at the pain, but a memory slammed into him. "Something... something was wrong. I felt it." He lifted a weak, trembling hand and pressed it to his sternum. "I ran out. I... I don't...I think my shop is gone."

"Yeah," Priest whispered, and Oliver felt a sudden, crushing grief. "I'm so sorry."

Closing his eyes, Oliver leaned back into Priest's arms and took a few trembling breaths. "Poe must be so pissed." It was the silence that was so telling—the tension in the air. Oliver opened his eyes and looked between them. "Tell me he's woken up."

Azriel couldn't meet his gaze, and Oliver felt like his soul was trying to escape his body. There was no way. No way in any level of hell that Poe was—

"We haven't been allowed in the shop yet to look for his body, but..."

"No," Oliver said. No. Absolutely not. That wasn't right. Not just because he refused to lose Poe but because he could feel it. He'd know if Poe was gone, and that just wasn't the case. "You're wrong."

Azriel looked like he wanted to cry. It was an expression that might have broken Oliver's heart if he hadn't known deep in his soul that Poe was still alive. "There's no chance he survived that, Oliver. I'm so sorry."

Oliver shook his head and tried to wriggle out of Priest's arms, but the Demon was refusing to let him go. "You didn't even look for him. He could be hurt! He's not dead, but he might be bleeding out, and—"

"He's gone," came a voice from the doorway.

All of them looked over, and Oliver's eyes rested on Easton, the Dragon he'd met once or twice when he'd come around with Priest. He was very tall and gorgeous, with massive shoulders, short dark curls, and brown skin that shone with barely-there scales whenever he turned just right in the late afternoon sun. His eyes were narrowed and serious, his mouth tipped down.

"What do you mean?" Priest asked, running a hand down Oliver's bare arm. The gesture might have been soothing if Oliver hadn't been reeling from the news that his entire life had just been blown to bits.

Easton sighed. "Just that. Knight and I got access to the building after Sunshine made some calls. There's no body. But the blast destroyed pretty much everything. I don't know what kind of weapon they used—"

"One that could have done significant damage even to an Angel," Azriel said, sounding furious.

"Thank you, Storm," Priest said quietly. He bowed his head, his nose resting very close to Oliver's ear. "I'm so sorry."

Oliver shook his head. "I don't know why you're sorry. There's no body."

"There's a damn good chance the explosion..." the Dragon didn't finish his sentence.

Oliver felt like he was going to throw up all over his lap. He understood that the others were making sense, and maybe he was just being stubborn because there wasn't a chance in hell he wanted to live life without Poe in the world, but he couldn't shake the feeling that they were wrong. Poe was alive. He might be hurt, and he was definitely missing.

But he wasn't dead.

He tried to move his legs, but he realized he could barely feel them, and panic raced up his spine. "I can't move."

Azriel nodded. "I know. You're healing. I gave you literally everything I could, but your body's going to need to do the rest."

"Am I… will I walk again?" Oliver asked, his voice barely above a whisper.

Azriel gave him a pat on the hand. "Yes, darling. Even dancing eventually, but right now, you need to rest. I'm going to make a couple calls and get you some potions that work on humans, okay?"

Oliver let out a shaking sigh, then nodded. What he wanted was to jump out of the bed and follow the odd sensation in his chest. It was tugging at him like someone had attached a string to his soul, and he knew it would lead him to Poe.

But he physically couldn't, and right then, he couldn't stop his eyes from getting hot.

"Do you want me to leave you alone?" Priest asked after Azriel and Easton left the room. He'd finally moved away from Oliver, but the empty space felt all wrong.

Oliver realized that was the last thing in the world he wanted. "Will you stay? I, uh…" Oliver's gaze cut to the window. The shades were mostly drawn, but he realized right then he could see flashing lights from the fire trucks and the police.

Gods, it all felt so real suddenly.

His eyes got hot, and he looked away, mortified, as tears began to spill down his cheeks. There was a crushing grief for everything he'd lost and a sudden fear because while he knew Poe wasn't dead, if he wasn't in the shop rubble, where was he?

"Hey," Priest said, dropping to his knees beside the bed. "What can I do?"

Oliver shook his head. He couldn't speak, or he'd fall apart.

"Would you like touch? Comfort? I mean, I don't think I'm super great at—oh," Priest gasped when Oliver blindly reached for him and yanked him close.

Considering the way Priest had reacted to him before, he wasn't sure he'd be allowed to have this again, so he was going to be greedy. He didn't think a Demon would mind if he indulged in that—especially an Incubus. He closed his eyes as Priest wrapped his impossibly warm body around him and held him tight.

Sobs lodged in his chest, but eventually, the edge of hysteria faded, and he could breathe again. "Sorry," he managed.

"Shut up," Priest replied, then stiffened. "Sorry. Gods, I don't know what's wrong with me. I just... I mean... please don't apologize for needing—um—this."

You, Oliver finished for him. And maybe that's what Priest had been about to say. He buried his face in the Demon's shirt and breathed in his scent. It was heady and rich and spicy. If he hadn't been in so much pain, both emotionally and physically, he might have even responded to it.

"I hate feeling weak and useless," Oliver said, finally giving voice to his raging emotions. "I should be out there looking for Poe."

"Ol—"

"No," Oliver interrupted at the sound of Priest's pacifying tone. He pulled back and looked him in the eye. "I know it sounds nuts, but he *is* alive."

"How do you know?" Priest asked. He didn't sound like he was mocking Oliver, which was the only reason he felt safe to answer.

"I don't understand it. It's just this... feeling." He touched his aching sternum. "It's right here. It's like this little pulse trying to tell me that he's still here. And I should be out there looking for him because something is definitely wrong, and he needs help."

Priest's brow furrowed. "Well, something *is* wrong, that's for damned sure."

It was obvious he didn't agree with Oliver that Poe was alive, but he didn't immediately dismiss him either, which was something, at least. Oliver closed his eyes and sagged against Priest again. "Promise me when I'm better, we can go get him. Wherever he is."

Oliver felt Priest dragging fingers through his hair. The gesture was kind and soft and soothing enough that Oliver felt himself slipping toward unconsciousness again. The edges of his vision were going black, and his limbs were heavy.

Just before he slipped away, he swore he heard Priest say, "We can do whatever you want. I'd do anything for you."

But maybe that was part of a dream.

When Oliver woke next, his heart sank when he realized his pain wasn't much better, and he still couldn't really move his legs. He got a few wiggles out of his toes, but his body felt shattered. Which, he realized, it probably was. Azriel was an Angel, so he'd been able to stop Oliver from actually dying, but Angelic miracles had limits.

With a small sigh, Oliver turned toward the nightstand and saw a small vial sitting beside the little digital clock. He'd seen something like it before. Poe liked to keep a nice stock of magical treatments along with human ones. Magic was always iffy on their kind—sometimes, it worked too well; other times, it made them sick. But he trusted Azriel to know what he could and couldn't take.

Mostly.

But he didn't have much to lose at this point.

Oliver grabbed the potion, uncorked it, and grimaced at the smell. It wasn't particularly bad—it was just chock-full of so much lavender it smelled like his adoptive mom's fancy soap in her guest bathroom. Saying a small prayer to whatever god might be listening, Oliver pinched his nose and tipped it all down his throat.

"You're a literal child," came a voice from the doorway.

Oliver set the vial down and looked over at Azriel, who seemed not quite himself. Almost rattled, which wasn't something Oliver ever expected to see.

"It's disgusting," he said with a sniff.

Azriel attempted a smile, but it fell short, and a beat later, he was across the room and dropping down to Oliver's side. Barely able to get a breath in, Oliver found himself crushed against the Angel's chest, the powerful hands holding him like he might fall to pieces.

"Hey," Oliver said after a beat. "Is everything okay?"

Azriel sniffed and pulled back. "Don't you ever, ever fucking do that to me again, okay? I'm not actually a Guardian Angel. I'm just some piece of shit who owns a strip club. I'm not good at the whole"—he waved his hand—"being good thing."

Oliver's chest warmed a little. "Didn't know you cared. And for what it's worth, you're better at it than you think."

Azriel punched him in the arm hard enough to hurt, laughing when Oliver scowled. "Shut up. I don't care about a lot of people. You and Poe are different. Special. He's..." His voice cracked, and Oliver quickly grabbed Azriel's hand.

"He's not dead."

"You didn't see the blast," Azriel argued. "There was no way he survived it. Honey, I am so sorry, but—"

"No," Oliver interrupted again. "Look, I don't know how to explain it, but he's not dead."

Azriel closed his eyes in a long, slow blink. "Death is hard to accept. Trust me, I get that more than most, and I don't wish this kind of pain on anyone. But at some point, you need to face the reality of this situation."

Oliver flopped back down, covering his face with both hands. "If I could walk right now, I'd get out of this fucking bed and lead all of you to him."

Azriel was very quiet for a moment, then cleared his throat. "You know where he is?"

Oliver groaned and peered at the Angel through his fingers. "Well, no, but I can feel him. Don't ask me how. I just... can. It's like having a second heartbeat or something. He's alive, but he's in danger, and I hate that we're sitting around on our asses when he needs our help."

"That's the grief, babes," Azriel said.

Oliver was too tired to argue, and he realized that the potion was kicking in because his limbs were as heavy as stones. "What did you give me?" His tongue struggled to form words.

"The good shit. Gargoyle shit," Azriel said. "It won't heal you, but it'll let your body rest so it can heal itself."

"Being human sucks," Oliver mumbled.

Azriel let out a hum that sounded off. Like there was something Azriel wasn't saying. But his head was far too foggy to follow that trail.

"Where's Priest?"

Azriel laughed and gave him a tiny shake. "Even drugged up and injured, you're still a little horndog."

Oliver would have blushed, but the potion was making it impossible to care about shame or propriety. "He held me. Was nice."

"Oh, I bet. But I sent him out for some supplies. I thought he was fucking awful when he was just hungry. Now, he's hungry and stressed," Azriel said with a small sigh.

Oliver forced his eyes open. "Hungry?"

"You know how he feeds, babes. Right?"

Oliver managed to roll his eyes before they slipped shut again. "M'not stupid."

"Of course not. Well, he's been a little reluctant to take someone upstairs for a while now, and I think I know why." Azriel gave him a little pat again, and in spite of the potion doing an amazing job, Oliver still got what he was saying.

He blindly swatted at the Angel. "Lies. Wouldn't even kiss me."

"That's probably because he's afraid to drain you, darling. Priest doesn't feed on humans. Too fragile."

"M'strong," Oliver mumbled. He was drifting now. Azriel was there, but so was Priest. He was naked and gorgeous, and his eyes looked like he was starving for Oliver. A warmth pooled in his chest—something tugging at him a little like his feelings about Poe, except entirely different. When Priest got close, it felt like he was the other half to Oliver's whole, and they fit together like they were fated to be.

Which was impossible. Humans didn't have mates, and Incubi rarely even fed on them, let alone allowed a true bond to form.

So it was nothing more than a lovely dream.

"Rest well," Azriel said off in the distance.

Oliver tried to answer him, but he was too busy reaching for dream-Priest, who was there and willing, unafraid, and most definitely not going to run.

5

PRIEST

"So," Azriel said, folding his hands under his chin.

"Eat shit and die," Priest muttered without feeling.

"That is so not nice to say to the Angel that saved your precious human." Azriel leaned back on the barstool, kicking his feet up on another one. The club was closed, which was a bizarre feeling being in there without the pulse of booze and sex floating around him. It was a terrible way for Priest to realize how hungry he was.

And that was the reason why he hadn't gone back upstairs.

He pinched the bridge of his nose and tried to chase off his irritation, but it was next to impossible with his hunger clawing at his insides. He was not far from begging Azriel to bring in one of the dancers so he could feed enough that he could stand Oliver's smell without jumping him. He shouldn't have let it get this bad. If he couldn't handle feeding in person, he should have slipped into a dream of one of his regulars and siphoned off enough to hold him over.

But it hadn't felt *right*. And now, he was fucked.

"Have a drink," Azriel said after a beat. When Priest

didn't move, he sighed and stood, propping his ass on the bar and spinning around. He dropped to the floor, and Priest couldn't help but watch him.

He was literal grace, the way he moved. His feet were light, like his wings were carrying him, though Priest knew that wasn't the case. Not for this Angel. Still, he was ethereal, and being around him sometimes made Priest feel every bit the Demon humans thought he was.

Well, most humans.

Never Oliver.

His chest burned with the need to run upstairs and cradle Oliver close to his body. He was still healing though, and Priest's presence wasn't going to do him any favors. Whatever Azriel had done to save Oliver's life made it impossible for Priest to use his Demonic abilities to try and heal him further. He was basically shrouded in Angelic magic for the time being, and that didn't mix with his own. So he was starving, feeling useless, but unable to leave the premises while Oliver was unconscious and helpless upstairs.

He startled in his seat when a glass appeared in front of him, and he stared down at it. It was pale, opaque, and kind of glittery.

"The hell is this?"

"Just drink it. You'll thank me later," Azriel said.

Priest did trust his friend, so he tipped back a long swallow, and while he was expecting to taste something like pine or almonds—his least two favorite things; they were equally terrible—instead, it tasted a little floral and barely sweet.

And suddenly, his hunger abated.

"It won't help long term," Azriel said before Priest could get any ideas. "But it'll take the edge off for a while. There's just a small caveat."

Priest sighed. "It's going to make me ravenous when it wears off, isn't it?"

Azriel grimaced. "There's always a price when it comes to the Fae."

"Oh, fuck you, man. I don't want Fae shit in my body." He spat, but it was no use. He was already craving more. The Fae rarely interacted with anyone at all in their world, almost all of them having crossed over through their portals eons ago, but their influence still trickled in from time to time.

"The detox isn't hellish. You'll just need to increase your feed and probably sleep for a good few hours," Azriel said.

"Like I have time for sleep," Priest grumbled. He jolted when Azriel's warm fingers closed over his own, but he refused to look up.

"Claude."

"Don't," he growled, tensing all over, "call me that."

The name always felt like mockery—posh and distinguished. Everything he would never be. His name now, the one he embraced, had come because he'd been found in a human church, aching all over, curled into himself under a long stretch of empty pews.

When he was younger, he found it hilarious. Now, he just ached for that small child who'd wanted nothing more than to be protected.

"I think your name is beautiful," Azriel said softly, refusing to let him go.

Priest hated how comforting the touch of an Angel could be—and he hated that he couldn't bring himself to pull away. "You think everything's beautiful."

Azriel laughed. "Yes, I do. That's why I'm here running this club. That's why I left…"

Heaven. None of them knew exactly what had driven Azriel out of the Angelic Kingdom, but Priest had gotten enough hints and clues over the years to be pretty sure it hadn't been a flippant choice. Or one that had been accepted by the rest of the Host.

It might not have been a *choice* at all.

Priest understood more than most. He knew what the other Incubi thought of him—fighting his hunger day in and day out, choosing to live as his own man—but like Azriel, he couldn't bring himself to give a shit. He'd die in the throes of madness before he gave himself to the control of corrupt leaders that did little more than whisper pretty lies.

"I need you to tell me he's going to be okay," Priest said after finishing the last of his drink.

Azriel drew his touch away, and Priest took a few deep breaths, weak with relief when the Fae magic began to work immediately, edging down his ravenous hunger to a tolerable background noise.

"He's going to be okay for now, but I'm worried that won't last."

"And you should be," came a growly voice from the doorway.

His chest pulsed with happiness as Jeremiah strode into the room, the scent of smoke and anger thick in the air around him. Priest was on his feet, flinging himself at his best friend before he could think twice. He'd been with Knight for far too long and was starved for physical affection and reassurance. Not having the Hellhound there next to him as he'd seen Oliver's bruised and battered body had made everything harder. No one leveled him out like Jeremiah.

"Yeah, yeah," Jeremiah said, gently petting his hair before shoving him off. "Such a demonic octopus."

Priest grinned good-naturedly, then grimaced, his Demon rippling under his skin. "Oh dear gods, you smell like Siren come."

Jeremiah flushed. Hard. "Watch it. I'll burn you to a crisp."

"You'd miss me too much," Priest declared. He was halfway over to the bar before he really processed what Jeremiah had said before. "Hold the fuck up. What do you mean *we should be*?"

Jeremiah sighed as he sat, rubbing a hand down his face. Being mated suited him, but he'd also been on edge since their rescue of Remi and his siblings, worried something else would pop up to try and take Remi away from him. Priest was pretty sure the terror of almost losing his fated mate had taken a few decades off the Hellhound's life.

"Knight filled me in on the reported threats and disappearances, and I assigned Charlie Team to dig into them. But after tonight…" He exchanged a glance with Azriel that Priest didn't like one bit. "We now know what to look for in the threats. Certain phrases and words. Particular targets."

Priest had assumed the bookstore was related, but hearing Jeremiah agree rose the hairs on the back of his neck. Oliver and Poe had been targeted because of their proximity to *him*. Because Priest hadn't been able to stop himself from fixating on the sexy human.

How could Oliver ever forgive him?

"Why are they taking humans?" Priest asked absently, eyes turning upward, even though he couldn't see Oliver's slumbering body. "McCornal's kid targeted Supes. Royals at that."

"Half Supes," Azriel corrected, pouring himself a large glass of liquor. "And half human."

Jeremiah shook his head. "Considering how half-cocked most of those attempts were, I doubt daddy dearest was looped in on everything Thad was doing. He just took his cues from the hatred McCornal spewed and focused them on the one person he knew and could get to."

"And used his dad's name and resources to recruit others to help."

Azriel threw back half his drink. "Lovely people all around."

Jeremiah side-eyed the Angel before focusing on Priest. "There's clearly a connection between what happened today and McCornal's bullshit. Not to mention…"

Priest understood what he wasn't saying. What Knight had endured was likely part of it. That was something they'd always kept at the back of their minds. The few details Knight had shared—or maybe he couldn't remember most of what happened—always made them believe there was something bigger behind it. Definitely bigger than infecting one random person with Vampirism and then seemingly letting him go.

Knight had survived, but none of them had believed it was over.

"What do we do?" Priest asked.

Jeremiah looked torn. "For now, I think you need to take Oliver somewhere safe. He's clearly a target, and being here isn't going to help. Azriel's drained for now, and I don't have the resources to create stronger wards."

Priest barked a laugh. "Where the fuck do you suggest I take him? Headquarters? Everyone will be looking for him there, and he can't be left alone in a safe hou—"

Jeremiah lifted both brows.

"No," Priest said. "No. Fuck no, even. A great big, grand, shining, sparkly hell no—"

"Why not?" Jeremiah said, cutting him off.

Priest threw up his hands. "Because I... He's... I'm... If he's there, and my things... and his scent, and..."

"He's in love," Azriel said loudly from behind his glass.

Priest narrowed his eyes at him. "Shut the fuck up."

"Please. Everyone knows. You're not exactly Captain Subtle."

Jeremiah looked thoughtful. "Give me one good reason why."

Priest felt himself crack and then shatter. "I can't control it. I'll feed on him and drain him, and I'd rather fucking die, okay? I'm starving, and it's getting harder to stay satisfied."

The words hung in the air around them for a long moment, Jeremiah studying him, but Priest couldn't meet his eyes. Laying his shame and failure out for the man he respected more than any other to see was slowly killing him.

"Priest…"

He flinched at the growly understanding in his voice. He didn't want his best friend's fucking pity. They just needed to understand why Priest couldn't be alone with Oliver in his house.

Jeremiah looked at Azriel, his expression helpless in a way that sliced through Priest's chest, and the Angel sighed and reached behind the bar, producing a small frosted glass bottle adorned in a way Priest had rarely ever seen.

"You can't use it forever, but you can use it long enough for Oliver to heal. Then you will *have* to feed. And I mean far more than what you've been taking," Azriel warned, his voice a low rumble.

Priest wanted to say no, and all the gods save him, he wanted to say yes because he wasn't sure he'd ever get the chance like this again. He was smitten with the human, and he doubted he'd ever feel this way about another creature ever again. If he was capable of being lucky enough to have a fated mate, Oliver would be his.

He had no idea how he knew that—he just did.

His hand crept across the bar, and very carefully, very slowly, he curled his fingers around the neck. It was cool to the touch, and his body hummed for more of what he'd just consumed. "How long will it take me to detox?"

"If you feed sufficiently," Azriel said, "a matter of hours."

And if he didn't, well…

"Get him a sedative for the drive," Priest said. "And safe transport."

"I've got Slate on it," Jeremiah said. "And I've got two of the guys from Bravo working on your townhouse now."

Priest turned his gaze up to the ceiling and wished he could see through the walls. But somehow, he knew Oliver was still sleeping, still healing. And he could only hope the drink was enough to get him through until Oliver was well enough to protect himself.

Then, Priest would deal with the consequences of his choices alone.

As he was always meant to do.

Oliver was half-sedated when he agreed to the trip, and luckily, Priest had a town house not too far from the border, so the drive was less than an hour. Priest lived in a gated community that had official royal protection, but he wasn't there often since it was more convenient during certain cases and missions to stay at HQ. He and Storm both tended to stay there, but Jeremiah had always preferred his own space—and now, his cozy little house he shared with the prince—and Knight started getting fangy if he didn't get enough alone time to decompress.

Plus, it'd be hard for him to take care of his damn moths if he was staying in a skyscraper.

Slate had... *family* obligations that made it more convenient for him to stay in Averna most of the time.

He pulled his bulletproof SUV into his garage, watching until the door was fully closed behind him before getting out and retrieving Oliver from the back seat.

The place was dark and a little musty from the infrequent cleaning service, but Slate had arranged for a delivery of supplies for Oliver—mainly food and a few medicines that would be safe for a human to consume.

Priest managed to get Oliver up the stairs and into the master bedroom, which, arguably, had the most comfortable bed, and he was snoring quietly as Priest took his second dose of the Fae wine. He noticed almost immediately the effects weren't as strong, but he also noticed that while the bottle didn't replenish itself completely, it replenished itself some.

Which was probably what made it more dangerous.

Living like this, he could see himself offering his name—or several years of his life—in order to take the edge off his hunger. In fact, the absence of it was almost heady. It wasn't something he'd known since he was very young, and by the gods, he wished it could be like that always.

He was terrified of what was coming, but he'd make do. Oliver needed rest, and Priest would give that little human literally anything in order to keep him safe.

He showered just after midnight before picking the closest guest room to sleep in. He woke twice for a drink, but Oliver hadn't stirred. It wasn't until morning that Priest could hear him rustling around, so he forced his heavy limbs to carry him to the kitchen.

Oliver was in no condition to walk anywhere, so he took his time putting together an appropriate breakfast for a human—at least, he was pretty sure. He wasn't actually sure what humans preferred for each meal or how much of it, so he went with what he liked.

He stared at the tray with an entire pot of tea—and one of coffee, just in case—six oranges, two apples, half a loaf of toasted bread with raspberry jam the royals had sent him away with—the twins had told their parents Priest loved it, so they'd basically given him a lifetime supply, the little shits laughing their heads off as he'd been forced to take it with a smile as he planned his retaliation in his head—and a rasher of bacon.

Was it enough? Oliver needed to heal, and his body would need fuel for that... He decided he could always get more if Oliver was still hungry after he finished.

Priest carefully balanced the tray in his hands and made his way into the master bedroom. Light was filtering in through a gap in the curtains, and Oliver was sitting halfway up, looking put out.

"I'm about to literally piss in your bed, and I can still barely feel my legs."

Priest rushed to set the tray down on the edge of the mattress, then scooped Oliver into his arms and marched toward the bathroom.

"Uh, the fuck?" Oliver demanded.

Priest smirked down at him. "I don't know how to work the laundry in this place, and we can't have cleaners coming in here, so you get to piss in the toilet like a big boy."

"I'm going to cut your head off," Oliver snarled.

Priest threw his head back and laughed as he kicked the door open and plopped Oliver down on the toilet. He took a step back and folded his arms as Oliver glowered up at him. "Well?"

Oliver's eyes widened in fake innocence. "Do you use the toilet? I mean, you must."

"Yes," Priest said slowly.

"Do you do it with your fucking pants on?" Oliver hissed.

Priest flushed. "Right. Let me just…"

"Hands off," Oliver said, batting him away. "Just leave the door cracked open. And if you hear a crash, give me thirty seconds to preserve my dignity before you come in."

Priest swallowed and nodded, then let himself out and rested the back of his head against the wall with a soft thud.

"And for the sake of all the gods, don't listen," Oliver shouted, exasperation bleeding through the door.

Priest threw himself away from the bathroom and paced in front of the bed until he heard Oliver call his name. He took tentative steps toward the doorway, then peered around the jamb.

"I didn't make a mess," Oliver said dryly.

Priest smiled. "You're pretty grumpy in the morning."

He was only slightly disappointed to see that Oliver had

managed to get out and then back into his sweats. But Oliver did deserve dignity, and Priest was a little more careful when lifting him and walking him back into the bedroom. He gingerly placed him against the pillows, then tried to fluff them until Oliver sighed heavily.

"I'm usually not," he said, pulling the covers over his legs and smoothing his hands over his thighs a few times. "Poe always..." He swallowed. "He says it's annoying how cheerful I am, but now he's missing and I can't *move* and it's... it's just all a lot."

"Oliver..." He shook his head, deciding against addressing his insistence about Poe still being alive. Instead, he lowered his gaze to Oliver's legs. "They'll get better. Azriel said it'll take some time. That's why we're here."

"At your place," Oliver said slowly, glancing around with a frown.

Priest knew his bedroom was a bit sterile and lacking in personality, but it was hard to give a shit about the place he rarely had the chance to do more than pass out in. His job came with some fantastic perks, but they didn't feel like luxury when being inside the town house, only made the loneliness more profound.

He was better off staying at HQ and entertaining himself by pestering his teammates when he wasn't working.

"It's the only place right now with wards strong enough to fend off whoever's after you," Priest said. He walked around to the edge of the bed and carefully nudged the tray closer. When Oliver didn't react, he nudged it closer still. Then closer, until it hit his hip.

Oliver startled and looked down. "Uh. Are you eating some of this?"

"No, no. I'll eat later. I made this for you. You need to refuel your body to help you heal."

Oliver stared at the tray and then glanced up at him, lips pressed together but the corners twitching in a way that made

Priest think he was trying not to laugh at him. "But you made enough for, like, twelve people."

Priest offered a sheepish smile, his face heating. "Oh, uh, I didn't know how much you ate. I thought you needed it for, you know, healing."

Oliver opened his mouth, then closed it again. Then he took a breath. "Thank you, Priest. It'll help."

Priest preened a little, puffing out his chest. He felt like a godsdamned peacock, but he couldn't help it. Something about Oliver's careful praise went straight to his core and made him all... hot. It was a very new feeling. His gaze fell on Oliver again as he dug his fingers into an orange and ripped it in half without peeling it.

Fuck.

Why was that so...

"Do you know why they're after me?" Oliver asked, the fear in his voice eclipsing whatever Priest had been feeling.

He flopped his arms at his sides. "Not exactly. We're pretty sure it's related to what happened to the crown prince and his siblings and the vague threats we've been receiving since, but we don't have any solid leads yet. The best thing we can do is keep you safe while we continue to investigate."

Oliver narrowed his eyes on him. "What does that mean? Not exactly."

"Um." Stomach twisting, Priest glanced away. "It's *possible* you were targeted because of me."

The silence in the room was suffocating, and he couldn't help but look back at Oliver to try and gauge his reaction. He was sitting frozen, his scent a strange mix of shock, anger, and sorrow. When he pinned Priest with a hard stare, he flinched away.

"Because of you how?"

"Whoever did this, they might have been watching me, us. They would have seen the way I... well. They may have thought you were connected to the team from how often I stop by." Priest cleared his throat, reaching over and grabbing a cup from the tray and pouring himself some coffee.

Oliver watched his restless movements. "And you think these people who did this, that they're connected to what happened to Prince Remington?"

Priest nodded slowly, taking a careful sip. "Seems likely. I can't share everything at this point, but yeah. It's too big of a coincidence."

He stared at the orange in his hands for a long, excruciating moment, Priest's heart racing in his chest, and then Oliver shook his head. "This isn't your fault."

"Oliver—"

His sharp eyes landed on Priest, silencing him. "No. You haven't been around in weeks, and even before that, it was sporadic and short visits. If these assholes were watching you, me and my shop aren't the way to hit back at you and your team."

"But—"

"Start again," Oliver insisted, taking a large bite out of one of the halves of orange. "Don't make assumptions because you know me. You need to look at all the pieces before you put the picture together."

Priest sucked in a sharp breath. Gods, the way Oliver's mind worked had always fascinated him, but the fact he could still see clearly through his grief and anger and call Priest out on it? His whole body began to heat with hunger and desire.

"I will. You're right," Priest said softly, running his teeth over his lower lip as he watched Oliver carefully devour his fruit. "While we do that, you need to stay here though. If your shop wasn't a message to us and you were targeted specifically, that's even more reason to keep you tucked away here where you're safe."

"At least until I'm healed up and can walk again," Oliver said as he finished half of the orange, then moved on to some of the toast. "Then you can use me as bait while I look for Poe."

Priest almost choked on his tongue. "I'm sorry. Repeat that, but do it in a way where you aren't talking like the blast knocked all the sense out of you."

Oliver's eyes narrowed. "I'm not going to just sit here on my ass when someone has my best friend."

"Oliver," Priest said very softly.

His eyes narrowed. "No. Nothing you can say will convince me that he's not alive. I feel it. I don't know why or how, but that doesn't fucking matter." He rubbed at his sternum, and then he met Priest's gaze. "Tell me you're going to try to stop me. I dare you."

Priest wanted to rise to that challenge, but before he could, Oliver grimaced, and the bed began to tremble with his leg spasms. He cried out softly, and Priest was immediately kneeling next to him, moving the tray and rubbing his hands firmly over Oliver's shaking thighs and calves.

"Hey," he whispered softly. "Hey. It's okay. I'm here."

Oliver groaned, flopping back. "It hurts."

"I know," Priest murmured. "But it'll be okay. This is a good sign."

Oliver swallowed heavily, and when Priest started to stand, he caught his wrist. "Don't go."

"I was just going to get you something for the pain," Priest said, putting his hand over Oliver's.

"No. I'm tired of feeling like my head's in a cloud. Just... can you sit with me? Can you..." He hesitated, biting his lip.

"Anything," Priest said, kneeling once more. In spite of himself, in spite of all manner of self-preservation he should have been using, he lifted Oliver's hand from his and kissed his knuckles. "Just ask. You can have anything."

Oliver breathed out. "Hold me for a little while. It feels better when you do."

Priest's hunger flared up, like a beast rising from the abyss to swallow the world whole, but he shoved it down with every ounce of his power and carefully slid beside Oliver. Once Oliver was asleep again, he could take more of the Fae potion; he just needed to hold on until then. A small, fragile human body curled into his own, and Priest wrapped his arms around him. He'd never brought comfort to another being before—not... not really. Not like this. He and Jeremiah used to huddle for warmth when they were on the streets, and Priest often hugged and snuggled against his teammates when *he* needed the tactile reassurance.

But that was almost always for him, not the others. His Demon always wanted more touch, more food, more warmth, and Priest needed the peace and safety he felt when near the only people he trusted in the world.

This was very different from that.

He buried his nose in Oliver's hair and breathed him in. "I'm here," he whispered. "Get some rest. You'll be walking soon enough."

Oliver nodded, murmuring something into Priest's shirt, and not too long after, he was boneless and heavy against him. He settled Oliver more firmly against his chest, then offered a quiet thanks to the gods who allowed him to have this moment.

It wouldn't last. It couldn't.

But for a moment in his long, lonely life, he let himself be selfish.

6

OLIVER

It had taken exactly six days of choking down whatever the hell Azriel had sent Priest home with for him, but Oliver was finally able to stand on his own. Not that he exactly minded the last week of being doted on. Priest was exactly the way Oliver had expected him to be—a complete disaster of overattentiveness that often led to him literally tripping over himself to help.

It only made Oliver's feelings worse, and it was the one thing that kept him from hyperfixating on the fact that Poe was out there somewhere, probably injured and definitely in trouble—because it wasn't like his best friend had gotten lost. He'd been taken, and that was haunting Oliver to the point he was driving himself insane with his inability to do anything about it.

Even now that he could walk himself to the bathroom and take a piss without Priest carrying him, he still wasn't strong enough to leave. He would be, but the gods only knew when that would happen. His healing was a slow climb, and he was profoundly aware that he'd almost died.

Or, to hear Azriel tell it, he had basically died, and the Angel had brought him back from the edge of the veil.

Luckily, he didn't remember any of it, so he didn't have to deal with the trauma of knowing what was on the other side. It was like he'd taken a very long, very powerful nap, and he'd woken up in the arms of the one person he'd wanted for far too long.

Gods, he wished Poe was there to relentlessly mock him over Priest feeding him soup and combing his hair.

His chest hurt from missing and worrying endlessly about his friend.

He washed his face with trembling hands and grimaced at the state of himself. Priest had helped him get in and out of the shower, but washing was a huge chore, and he'd only managed to scrub the sweat from his hair twice in the last week. He wanted a long, hot soak in a tub, but more than that, he wanted to get away from the bed.

His legs felt barely strong enough to support his weight, but he managed to make his way down the stairs and followed his nose to the scent of toasting bread. He couldn't get over how big Priest's place was. It was obviously a very cushy job working for royal families and the like. Oliver wasn't exactly jealous, but he'd grown up in a cult that found any semblance of wealth akin to the worst sin a human could commit.

Well, almost the worst.

They would have considered his *biggest* sin to be lusting after a Demon. It almost made him smile to think about what his parents might have said. Their idea of love was cruelty and hate, and he was more than grateful every day that he'd escaped them.

Even now, hurt and very lonely, there was nothing to miss except Poe.

"I need to tell his parents," Oliver whispered to himself as he turned a corner and found himself in a large kitchen full of black cabinets, marble counters, and stainless steel appliances. His heart gave a little staccato beat against his ribs when he found Priest leaning over the sink, his head bowed, hand curled around a wineglass full of something very shiny and very white.

Oliver had never seen anything like it before, and it made his skin itch.

"What is that?"

Priest jolted and spun, giving Oliver an almost hysterical and very guilty laugh. "This? Oh, it's... well. It's a... it's nothing."

Oliver peered around him to find a bottle he did recognize, only because he dealt in things like that—rare books and magics. And Fae magic was the rarest. He blinked at Priest as his tired brain connected the dots.

"Tell me you're not drinking that."

"I'm not drinking that," Priest said, like he was incapable of disobeying Oliver. Then, he tipped the glass back and drained it in one go.

Oliver spluttered, and surprising himself with his own speed, he was at Priest's side and reaching for the bottle. Priest's eyes had gone black from the magic, and they widened at him, though he seemed too stunned to do anything but watch as Oliver grabbed the bottle and heaved it into the sink. The glass shattered, but the white liquid hit the metal and sizzled, turning to smoke and drifting into the air. Oliver waved his hand, helping it to disperse so they didn't breathe in too much.

"Shit," Priest whispered, sounding brokenhearted. "What did you do?"

"Saved you from yourself, you moron," Oliver snapped. "Do you have any idea how dangerous drinking that is?"

"Do you have any idea how dangerous *I* can be?" Priest's eyes seemed even blacker somehow, hypnotic if Oliver wasn't so furious at his recklessness. "Do you even know what it was?"

Oliver scoffed, then stumbled. His legs went weak, and in

spite of Priest's very real anger, he caught him and lifted him like he weighed nothing. "It's poison," he said, lifting his chin despite being held like a child. "It could kill you."

Priest bared his teeth, and they were... sharper as he set him on a barstool. "It might not have been the best thing for me, but it was protecting you."

Oliver couldn't help but laugh at that. "Protecting me? From what?"

"From me. My hunger is..." He swallowed thickly, glancing away as the blackness seeped away from his eyes. "I had to let you heal before I could go out and feed. It was the only thing that took the edge off."

Oliver felt his heart sink. He knew what hunger could do to an Incubus. He knew that eventually, it would drive him mad because someday, he wouldn't be satisfied without taking a life. And Priest would never do that. It would be the end of him. He'd allow himself to starve to death.

Or he'd order the agents of Trident to kill him. Either way was too painful to think about. Oliver wanted to weep. But he also knew that would be decades from now, if not centuries.

"I have to call Azriel," Priest said, sounding exhausted.

"You're not bringing more of that shit into this house," Oliver said. "Fae wine will ruin you."

"He doesn't have more," Priest replied, pulling out his phone. "But now that he's juiced back up from healing you, he can sit with you while I feed."

Oliver opened his mouth, not sure what he was going to say, but Priest kept talking, trying to reassure him, even though he was so wrong about what was upsetting him.

"Don't worry, I won't bring someone in the house," Priest said, making a face. "And I'll stay close by, but while I'm feeding, I'm unaware of what's happening around me, and I won't be able to sense if it if you're in danger. With Azriel here, you won't be defenseless."

Something in Oliver snapped. He didn't know how or

why. He just knew that six days of having Priest beside him—close but not touching the way he wanted, loving but not loved the way he needed—it was too much. He felt a rush of possession and fury at the thought of Priest touching anyone else, even if just through their dreams.

He slapped the phone out of Priest's hand.

The Demon stared at him, eyes wide. "Oliver… I need to feed. When this wears off—"

"Then you'll have me," Oliver said.

Priest closed his eyes very slowly. "You know I can't do that."

Oliver scoffed, leaning against the counter because he was dizzy. It took him a minute to realize it wasn't from his injuries. It was from his proximity to a hungry Incubus. *This* hungry Incubus. One that he wanted with an almost soul-crushing need. "I don't know that, actually. Why don't you explain it to me."

When Priest opened his eyes, they were black. Not like his usual color—a sort of gorgeous onyx that covered the entire surface—whites, irises, and pupils. Now, the abyss consumed them. He parted his lips, and though his teeth weren't sharp like a Vampire's, his canines had lengthened to short points.

Oliver shuddered. Maybe Priest was trying to scare him, but it wasn't working.

"Oliver." His voice was a low, strange rumble that sent sparks over Oliver's skin. "Go back upstairs and go to sleep."

Oliver stared at him, then rolled his eyes. "No. I just woke up. You're out of your mind if you think I'm going back to bed in the middle of our conversation."

Priest's eyes faded back to their usual appearance, and he blinked rapidly before clearing his throat. He was softer—the sweet sort of awkward potato he'd been since Oliver got there. "Um. Please go back to sleep?"

Oliver sighed. "Cute, but no. I'm going to waste away if I

sleep any longer. And since you won't let me go look for my best friend, I say we do the second-best thing."

Priest swallowed heavily. "Which is…"

Oliver drummed his fingers on the counter. He felt oddly brave in a way he hadn't been for the months he'd known and pined after Priest. Maybe it was the whole near death experience. Or maybe it was the trauma of losing everything in his life. Or maybe he was just tired of waiting around.

Whatever the case, he was done letting Priest shove him off when he knew damn well the Demon not only wanted him but was holding himself back by a tinsel-weak thread.

"I'll go back to bed… if you go with me."

Priest choked. "I need to leave."

He started away, but Oliver caught him by the wrist. He tugged, his strength obviously replenished from all the napping he'd been doing because Priest stumbled toward him and landed right up against Oliver's front, bracing himself against the counter with his free hand.

A beat passed, and Oliver swore he could feel Priest's heart beating beneath his own skin.

"I'll hurt you."

"Something tells me you won't," Oliver murmured. He reached up, boldly drawing a touch over Priest's jawline. "You'd stop yourself before we got anywhere near that point."

"You have no idea how dangerous this is." Priest's voice went rough again, his eyes darkening. "I've wanted you for so long. I'd die if anything happened to you. If I *let* anything happen to you."

"So don't let anything happen to me," Oliver said. "I'm stronger than you think. And I want you too. I want you to take what you need from me. I can't stand the thought of you suffering or feeding on someone other than me."

Priest closed his eyes and tipped his head forward. For a moment, Oliver thought he was going to be kissed, but Priest pressed their foreheads together and breathed deep, like he was taking his scent into his body. "This temptation is going to send me straight to hell."

"As a Demon, I figured you'd be at home there," Oliver quipped.

Priest pulled back, eyes wide, and then he burst into low chuckles seconds before he grabbed Oliver by the waist and lifted him, settling him on the counter. His laughter died, and then he licked his lips, and not only were his little fangs back, but Priest's tongue had thinned and lengthened, the end split and forked like a snake.

Oliver's dick pulsed in his loose pants.

Priest sucked in another deep breath and let it out on a groan. "Gods, I want you. Your lust is so fucking sweet."

"So have me. Be delicate, but take what you need. I know what it'll cost, and I'm giving it to you," Oliver said. An idea struck him. He stuck his thumbs under the waistband of his pajamas and did his best to shimmy them off while sitting on the counter and having Priest between his knees.

Taking the hint, Priest stepped back and grabbed handfuls of the fabric, his nails sharper and almost clawlike, and between one blink and the next, Oliver was naked from the waist down. For a moment, he couldn't seem to make a sound. Tendrils of pleasure were curling over his skin as Priest groaned, and he felt like he was going to lose his mind from ecstasy before Priest even touched him.

"Please," he whispered.

Priest looked up at him, eyes fully black now. He smiled. "Oh, sweet thing. I'm not going to make you beg. Not today."

Oliver's head cleared after a second, like he was waking from a dream. He curled his hand around his hard dick, then used his other one to grip Priest by the chin. The Demon seemed startled and unsure, but Oliver wasn't toying with him. He traced the head of his cock over Priest's lips.

"I don't know if it'll be enough to take the edge off, but..."

"It'll be enough," Priest growled. His eyes closed again, and when he ran his tongue over his lower lip, Oliver sucked in a sharp breath. It was thin. And forked. Priest met his gaze, and his tongue licked out farther, the ends curling around the head of Oliver's dick.

He let out a sharp moan, sagging backward and being held up by Priest's hands alone. "Yes," he hissed.

Priest shoved his face against Oliver and breathed in a last time before his lips parted, and he took his dick in a single, perfect swallow. Oliver's hands twisted into Priest's hair. He felt wild with desire in ways he never had before. He'd heard a thousand rumors about what it was like to fuck an Incubus, but he felt far from weak or like he was being drained.

Instead, it felt like all the cracked pieces of him that were still healing were suddenly solid again. And then Priest slipped the thin ends of his tongue into his slit, and his balls tightened, threatening to spill into his mouth.

"Want it," Priest said, as though he sensed Oliver holding back. "Need it. Need you. So delicious," he said, his voice like a hiss between long pulls of his lips.

Oliver was nearly blind from how good it all felt. He let Priest's hair go, only to grab the countertop and thrust forward. Priest moaned sharply, encouraging, and Oliver fucked his hips against Priest's face.

His impending orgasm began to light up under his skin like fireworks, and he realized there was no stopping it. His head lolled back as his thrusts turned sloppy, his elbows weak. Priest curled that glorious tongue, wrapping it around him and tightening in pulses of eye-rolling pleasures.

Oliver let go.

He came with a sharp cry, spilling hot ropes down Priest's throat, feeling every single swallow as the Demon drank him down. He waited for the drain, for the weakness, for the years of his life he'd sacrificed, but all he felt was strong.

His hands were steady when Priest pulled off him, and he

used a firm grip to yank Priest to his feet. His eyes were hot, almost like they were blazing with fire, and he grabbed Priest by the hair once more and kissed him.

The taste was euphoric. Salty from his own release and something else—the essence of the Demon. *His* Demon. He felt a strange, possessive sensation unfurling in his chest, and for a moment, he wanted to burn the world down just so no one could ever get close to Priest again.

And then, with each breath, the feeling faded. Something was lodged in his chest he couldn't explain, but the fatigue of it all hit him. All the strength in his muscles released, and he started to sag off the counter, Priest catching him and sweeping him up like he'd done when Oliver couldn't walk.

"I told you, I shouldn't have—"

"Shut up," Oliver murmured. "I got blown up a week ago. Sue me if my first orgasm since then makes me a little tired."

Priest sighed quietly as he carried Oliver back to the bedroom. "We shouldn't have done that."

Oliver winced, unable to stop from being a little hurt at his quick dismissal of what they'd just shared. "Did it help?"

Priest didn't answer until he'd laid Oliver back down. "It helped."

He started to pull back, but Oliver caught his arm again. "I don't think so, you obnoxious little martyr. You don't get to suck my brain out through my dick and then leave."

Priest choked on his tongue—which looked back to normal. A shame. But he put one knee on the bed. "I really should let you rest."

"You should lie here with me for a while," Oliver countered.

Priest hesitated before finally doing as Oliver asked, and for a moment, it felt like his heart was singing. Literally. Priest hummed a tuneless sound as he curled up around Oliver, then laid his head next to his on the pillow. "I can't risk you."

"I don't think you have to," Oliver told him. He assessed himself, and he was tired, but it was no more tired than he had been since he was hurt. Maybe Priest was all wrong about his effect on humans. Or maybe it was something else. Either way, he felt good. He traced a touch over Priest's jaw. "I feel... good."

Priest stared at him, then cupped his cheek, running his thumb beside his eye. "You're not lying, are you?"

Oliver shook his head. "I'm still a little tender from everything, but you made me feel..." He had no real words for it.

Priest carefully stroked a hand through his hair, gently petting him and lulling him to sleep. Just as he started to drop off, he swore he heard Priest mutter, "What are you? Because after that... there's no way you're fully human."

7

OLIVER

*H*is Demon was avoiding him.

And Oliver was tired of it.

He'd been in a bad mood all day after waking up alone. He was still sleeping more than normal, but he was surprised at how good he'd felt—especially considering all of the horror stories he'd heard about humans being fed on by Incubi and being left for dead.

Deciding to forgive being left alone in bed, he'd gone to search for Priest... and come up empty. He'd eaten breakfast by himself. And then lunch. It was nearly dinnertime before he found where Priest had been hiding all day.

"What is this place?" He was more than a little pleased at the way the Demon jumped and whirled around at his question.

"Oh. Uh. Hi." Shoulders hunched a bit, Priest glanced around the strange and amazing room before carefully setting a pot holding a spiky plant with bulbous purple flowers on the waist-high table he was standing behind. "This is my library. And workshop."

Oliver ran his eyes over the floor-to-ceiling shelves full of books and glass bottles with mysterious liquids and puzzle boxes—one of which was emitting a soft pink smoke. "Workshop, huh?"

Priest shrugged. "Not, like, officially. I just enjoy tinkering with things."

Tinkering with things.

None of Oliver's books had ever talked about a Demon like Priest. He would have been annoyed normally—he hated not knowing what to expect or feeling out of his element—but since the Incubus seemed to be just as off-balance, Oliver found he didn't actually mind.

But he was still unhappy with being ignored all day.

"Why are you hiding in here?"

A week ago, he wouldn't have had the nerve to flat out ask Priest something like that. If he had, they wouldn't have been tiptoeing around each other for months. But nearly dying and having your life's work destroyed had a way of convincing a person to just say *fuck it*. Sleep with the sex Demon. Ask the hard questions. Eat all the donuts.

Priest's face made a series of complicated expressions. "I'm not. I've just been busy."

Oliver clenched his teeth. "Don't do that."

"Do what?"

"That!" He waved a hand at Priest, a ball of hurt sitting uncomfortably in his stomach. "Don't lie to me, and don't act like you aren't still scared."

For the first time since he'd entered the room, Priest's gaze met his own, and blackness swallowed his eyes, turning them into the dark abyss of his Demon. "Oliver, it's better if we—"

"And don't fucking make decisions for me!"

His chest heaved with his panting breaths, and he was more than a little surprised to find himself only a foot away from Priest. He didn't remember crossing the room, his anger blotting it out.

The blackness seeped away, and Priest cocked his head,

studying Oliver in a way he wasn't completely comfortable with. "That was... peculiar."

"What—*shit*." He reached out blindly for the worktable, a wave of dizziness washing over him and nearly taking him out at the knees. Warm, strong hands gripped his arms, steadying him until he could refocus his eyesight. Priest's worried face was only inches from his own. "I'm okay. I guess I'm not quite as recovered as I thought."

Even as he said the words, he knew in his gut that wasn't what was wrong. He tried to pull away, but Priest tightened his hold and tugged him closer. "Do you know what you just did, *little human*?"

Oliver licked his dry lips, a shiver rolling down his body at the emphasis the Demon put on those last two words. "I didn't do anything."

Priest hummed and cupped the side of Oliver's face, tipping his head back and leaning closer. "Very peculiar."

"Priest..." He breathed out the word, his lids lowering and lips parting without his permission.

"Yes, darling?"

"I'm still mad at you." He definitely was. Even though goose bumps were rippling across his skin at the sinful sensation of that damn forked tongue tasting just inside his mouth. His anger was just somewhere else now.

"I'll make it up to you." The words were said directly against his lips, tearing free a moan from deep in his chest, but before Priest could do more than press their mouths together, someone cleared their throat behind Oliver.

Loudly.

"If you two wouldn't mind," Azriel said, voice more serious than usual, as Oliver jerked backward, only somewhat relieved when Priest let him that time. "I need to talk to Oliver. Alone."

He whirled around to face the Angel, surprised to find

him leaning against a bookshelf a good ten feet from the door. "How did you get here so fast?"

Azriel rolled his eyes and pushed himself upright, striding across the room with the same loose-hipped strut that always made Oliver a little uncomfortable no matter how long he knew him. "Used my wings, of course."

"But..." He hadn't felt a breeze like he usually did when Azriel used the invisible limbs to get around a little faster.

"Come along," Azriel said, not pausing as he exited the room.

"Um." Oliver bit his lip and turned to face Priest once again. "To be continued?"

His skittish Demon had retreated a few steps and was back to looking more awkward and less straight-up lustful.

Pity.

"Sure, if you want," Priest said, a strained casualness in his tone. "Knight and Jeremiah will be here soon to give us an update."

A surge of hope crashed through him. Would they bother coming to give an update if they didn't have something important to share? Maybe they'd found a clue about where Poe was and finally believed him.

"Okay. If I'm still with Azriel when they get here, come and get me." He retreated toward the door but turned back at the last minute, biting his lip and then giving Priest a soft smile. "Please?"

Priest's throat bobbed, and the room sizzled around them. "I—"

"Knock it off, you sex fiends!"

If Oliver didn't like the Angel so much—and wasn't more than a little scared of his powers—he'd kill him for his rotten timing.

Groaning, he spun away and marched out. His gut told him where to find Azriel, though he probably could have guessed. The den at the back of Priest's house had an extensive wet bar. Sure enough, the Angel was lounging on the couch with a glass of brown liquid in hand. He was wearing his signature torn-to-hell jeans and a white T-shirt so thin and ratty there were holes near the collar and seams, and Oliver could see his nipples through the fabric.

It was not a look that should have worked, but combined with Azriel's supernatural beauty, it really, really did.

"There you are." He set the drink aside and patted the spot next to him on the couch.

Sighing, Oliver perched on the edge. "What's going on?"

"I have a theory about what you are." The Angel turned to face him more fully, brushing his bare knee against Oliver's arm in the process.

He gasped and jerked away at the sharp, electric pain the brief contact had caused. "What the hell?"

"I think you mean what the heaven."

"Azriel!" Oliver scrambled away from him, putting a solid two feet between them. "Why would you use your powers on me like that?"

Instead of even pretending to be sorry, the Angel smirked and sank his elbow into the back of the couch, resting his head on his fist. "I didn't. I just didn't protect you from them like I usually do. If you were one hundred percent human, it would have fried your brain inside your skull."

Oliver jumped to his feet, fury building inside him. "You tried to *kill* me? What the hell is the matter with you!"

"Settle down, babe," Azriel drawled, grabbing his glass and taking a noisy slurp. "There's no need to get all dramatic about it. I was pretty sure you wouldn't die, and you didn't. Everything's fine."

"Everything is not fine!"

Bright, glowing white eyes were suddenly right in front of his face, the air buffeting him from every side. The scent of magic and feathers was thick in the air, cooling his rage with a dose of bone-chilling fear. This was the side of Azriel that had always scared him but he'd rarely seen, and never directed at him. He became very aware of how weak and fragile he was compared to the fallen Angel.

But a small, ignored part of him woke up at the threat.

And it was pissed.

Heat began to build inside his veins, and his fingers and shoulder blades tingled with a phantom desire to do... *something*. Anger that wasn't his own and yet *was* at the same time flooded his chest, cracking him open to make room for something big and powerful.

"What's... happening..." Oliver clutched at his sternum, his breathing becoming labored as the force pressed against his lungs and heart and up into his throat. "Azriel..."

"Shhh. Don't fight it." Warm, gentle hands cupped his face as the wind in the room eased back down to nothing. "It's time to wake up, little brother."

"I don't—"

Azriel lifted two glowing fingers and tapped his forehead.

Darkness swallowed him whole.

"There you are. How are you feeling?"

Oliver rubbed at his face and squinted at the bright room around him. His head ached like he and Poe had drunk too many shots playing Never Have I Ever again. Gods, why did he let that little asshole talk him into doing dumb shit like that?

Wait.

That wasn't right.

Poe was...

He sat up, nearly smoking Azriel in the face with his head, and glanced around. The den looked exactly the same, and so did he. Carefully, he touched his chest, but he couldn't feel the swelling power anymore. He just felt like... him.

"What happened?"

"Apart from confirming my theory was correct—as I usually am—you were unconscious for a little while."

Something about his arrogant tone triggered a memory. Azriel fucking with him—using powers on him. Something heavy in his chest trying to claw its way out. He glanced at the Angel's smirk and remembered something else. "I'm still pissed at you too."

Azriel's head tipped back with his chuckle. "I'm sure you are, little brother."

Little brother… It's time to wake up…

"I'm not going to ask again. What happened?"

"You woke up." Azriel leaned back against the couch, one knee crooked up, his arm resting over it. "I've suspected for a while that you weren't fully human, but I thought it might just be us rubbing off on you. So to speak."

"Don't," Oliver warned, in no mood for his crude sex jokes.

Azriel held up his hands in surrender, and his tone shifted into something far less playful. "I'm being serious. I've been drawn to you since I met you. I thought it was because you were an ally—and trust me when I say I treasure my human allies. But the longer you were here, the more I started to wonder. Today proved it."

"That I'm not human?" Oliver couldn't help his bitter laugh. "Do you know who my family is, Az? There's not a chance in hell."

"The most bigoted families have the deepest secrets, Oliver." Azriel dropped his legs to the floor and stood up, pacing in front of him. "I've seen it a thousand times, and usually it doesn't matter, but that's because I haven't seen a descendant from an Angel in a long, long time."

Oliver's ears began to ring. An Angel? There was no chance in hell.

"Trust me, it makes sense. You were drawn to me, weren't

you? You're not the kind of man who frequents clubs like mine. Not for fun. You'd come over to drink a fizzy water and sort your taxes, darling."

Oliver's cheeks went hot. Azriel wasn't wrong, and Oliver couldn't really explain it. The club felt like home. Except… maybe it wasn't the club. Maybe it was because Azriel was there. Fuck, no, he could not be entertaining this.

"I'm human."

"Not entirely." Azriel dropped beside him and brushed a lock of hair off his forehead. "Those feelings you get in your gut? Humans don't have those. Or, if they do, they're called paranoia and treated with medication. Yours are real. You know they are. Your little premonitions always come true."

Oliver tried to swallow, but his throat was too dry. "I'm… how…"

"My guess is that a grandparent or a great-grandparent had a little tryst. I'm not the only Angel around who likes to—"

"Slum it?"

Azriel looked angry and offended. "The people who came up with that term were trying to make it sound like we thought humans were dirty. We don't."

"I'm sorry," Oliver whispered. All these years away from his family, and sometimes shit like that popped out of his mouth. "I didn't mean it."

Azriel relaxed and took Oliver's hand, holding it gently. "I know you didn't. And I know this is a lot. Take time to process, okay?"

Oliver nodded, then sucked in a breath and looked frantically into Azriel's eyes. "Don't tell Priest. I… I can't deal with this right now, okay? Poe's missing, and he's being a weird, overprotective dick who's also avoiding me, which—make that make sense."

"It's because he's a Demon, and he's afraid to hurt you. He's always been afraid to hurt you," Azriel said.

"You can feel that?"

Azriel snorted and rolled his eyes. "No. That little shit gets drunk and dumps his unrequited love all over me every time he sets foot in my club."

Oliver's ears burned. "Oh."

With a soft smile, Azriel tilted Oliver's chin up. "It's going to be okay."

"Is it? Because I don't know what this means for me. Do I have powers? Will I get wings? What do people with Angel blood like mine even do?"

Azriel studied him for a long moment, then sighed. "To tell you the truth, I don't know. And I'm not sure you'd want me as your teacher even if I did. But I can put you in touch with someone if you want to learn more."

"If? Is that a serious question? Why wouldn't I?"

Azriel's smile was soft and a little sad. "Because accepting what you are will change things. The more you know, the more your Angel side will emerge, and once it does, there's no going back."

Oliver swallowed heavily. "And if I stop here, I stay human."

"You're definitely not human, Oliver. Not fully. You never have been. But you can pretend it's not there and go about in society as you were. Mostly undetected."

Oliver understood what he was saying. "That feels like denying a big part of who I am."

"I can't help you there. I've never been in that position," Azriel told him. He squeezed his hand tighter, then slowly let go. "Take your time. Like you said, there's a million things going on right now, and this is the least important one of them."

The Angel was right. Poe had to come first and then whatever strange dance he was doing with Priest. The world was also on fire, and the gods only knew when things would go back to normal again. If they ever could.

Whoever he was—whatever he was—could probably wait. "I think I—"

"Priest is here," Azriel interrupted.

A second later, the Demon himself appeared in the doorway. He looked just as awkward as before, but maybe a little more tired, and definitely apologetic. "I'm sure you two aren't done, but I wanted to let you know that Jeremiah and Knight are here. And they have news."

"About Poe?" Oliver asked, jumping to his feet.

Priest bowed his head and took a breath before looking up. His irises had thick black rings around them. "Yes, Oliver. About Poe."

8

PRIEST

*P*riest hadn't given in to his urge to listen to Azriel and Oliver when they were speaking, as much as it killed him to not know what was so important. But he knew whatever Azriel had to say, it was for Oliver. He couldn't be selfish. Not after everything.

So he paced, and he drank a little, and he paced some more. He did his best not to relive the moment when he finally got to taste Oliver. And of course, he failed at that because shutting that out only led him to the moment of tension between them before the Angel showed up.

The bastard.

He'd been beating himself up over being so weak, but he had been on the verge of giving in when the winged dickhead showed up. Priest could only hope that one day, karma would come and bite him on the ass. He'd like to see Azriel knocked down a peg or two from love. Actual love. The kind that made Demons weep.

He started pacing again when his phone buzzed, and he didn't bother looking at it when he picked up. "What?"

"Excuse me," Jeremiah said, voice low.

"I'm in a shit mood. Don't start with me."

There was a heavy silence full of warning, letting Priest know Jeremiah had even less patience than normal. "We're pulling up now, and we need to see you and Oliver both."

Priest's spine went stiff. "Tell me you found something."

"We found something. We found a few somethings. Including evidence that Oliver might be right about his friend."

Priest sat down hard enough to make his jaw click. Oliver was right? He'd already been on the verge of believing him, but if Oliver really was having premonitions, it confirmed what he was so damn sure of: he wasn't human. Not entirely. He was mostly mortal, but there was something inside him—in his *essence*—that Priest had only experienced feeding off some of the dancers at Azriel's club.

It was more delicate though. And it was strong. There were only a few creatures with that kind of strength—the kind that grew when it was diluted instead of weakening.

"Priest," Jeremiah barked.

"Yeah. Right. Um. Let yourselves in. I'll go get Oliver."

"Where is he?" Jeremiah demanded. In the background, a car door slammed. "You're supposed to be watching him."

"Step one, grab stick. Step two, remove from ass," Priest told him. "He's here. He's just with Azriel right now."

Jeremiah groaned. "I do not have the patience for that fucking Angel today."

"Don't worry, I don't think he's interested in staying. I've invited him to lend a hand on cases a couple of times, and he claims that helping others gives him hives."

"Of course it does. We're at the door now."

Priest hung up, then slowly made his way back to Oliver and Azriel, freezing in the doorway when he saw how close they were. But there was no lust in the air. He parted his lips and inhaled deeply to be sure, but all he could taste was shock and wariness. And maybe a little fear.

It showed all over Oliver's face. Priest hated it. He wanted to grab Oliver away from Azriel and wrap him tightly so nothing bad could ever touch him again. He felt an irrational hatred toward the Angel for disrupting what little peace Oliver had managed to find during his recovery.

And yes, he supposed there was a little jealousy too. Azriel and Oliver had always been close, and although it wasn't in Priest's nature to feel like this, he couldn't help it. It was new. It was different. Alien to the very core of his being, and he didn't like it at all.

"I'm sure you two aren't done, but I wanted to let you know that Jeremiah and Knight are here. And they have news." He hoped everything he was feeling wasn't obvious in his tone.

Oliver leapt away from Azriel, and Priest breathed a little easier. "About Poe?"

He didn't know what answer to give, because yes, it was about the missing human, but he wasn't sure it was good news. He answered him anyway. "Yes, Oliver. About Poe."

Azriel stretched his arms above his head and climbed to his feet slowly. He moved like a cat, something Priest had always liked until this moment. He closed the distance between them, and his cool palm touched Priest's cheek. "Relax. He's all yours," he murmured so softly Priest doubted Oliver could hear it. The Angel pulled back, then winked at him before turning a smile on Oliver. "This is my cue to leave. But you know where to find me, little brother."

Little brother? What—

Azriel rarely used his abilities to teleport, but one second, he was there, and the next, he was gone. Exactly like Oliver had done. There was a loaded moment before Oliver touched his arm, and all of the tension fled Priest's body.

"Come on," he said, pulling away, "they're waiting for us in the living room."

Priest could feel Oliver's confusion and his worry when he followed him down the hall and into the brightly lit room, but it was laced with concern. Priest didn't blame him. Jeremiah was sitting on the sofa with his ankle hooked over his knee, and Knight was at the window, eyes closed as he basked in the light streaming in through the filtering glass. Like all Vampires, his skin was highly sensitive to sunlight, turning most into night dwellers. With their jobs, Knight didn't always have a choice in going out during the day and often suffered the consequences.

The mood in the room was somber, and Priest's heart began to kick up because the last thing he wanted to hear was bad news.

"Sorry to interrupt. Where's Azriel?" Jeremiah asked.

Oliver took a seat on the larger sofa, and Priest followed, drawn to him like a magnet. He kept a cushion of space between them, but all he could think about was having a moment to pull the man into his arms.

"He's gone," Priest said.

Jeremiah scoffed, shaking his head. "One day, he'll have to get off the damn sidelines."

"Having an Angel on the team wouldn't be the worst idea," Knight murmured. He turned his back to the window but kept far from the group. He'd been tense lately—like he was in the early days when his trauma was overwhelming him. "Their tracking abilities put all our technology to shame. It would make things easier."

Priest swallowed heavily and stared at Oliver. He was tense—more than he had been a moment ago. There was something different about him. Like his body was operating at a higher vibration. The longer they sat there, the more pieces of the puzzle started to fall into place.

Oliver was different than most humans. He was more clever and quicker on his feet. He was still a fumbling, anxious mess, but when he stood in front of danger, he didn't crumble. And then there was the incident in Priest's workroom.

No human could do what he did.

There was not a chance in hell Oliver didn't possess some kind of supernatural blood, and there was only one logical conclusion. After all, what would Azriel need to speak to him privately about? Why would he call him little brother?

Gods.

An Angel?

Priest couldn't deal with this right now.

"... around the shop, and we picked up on a scent." Jeremiah was staring at him—his face a mask of irritation, which apparently meant getting good dick on the regular wasn't going to change who he was at his core. The thought was oddly comforting. "Are you with us, Claude?"

Priest's eyes narrowed, and he felt them go hot and black. His vision changed, all the heat in the room more visible. "If you think I won't tear your throat out—"

"Claude?"

Priest's Demon immediately fell back, and he turned his face to Oliver. "Please don't ask."

Oliver's lip twitched. "I won't. Clau—"

"Don't."

Oliver held up his hands in surrender. "Okay. I'm sorry."

This was no time to be biting Oliver's head off. Priest took a breath and turned his attention to Jeremiah. "I'm here. I'm listening. But multiple piles of shit are hitting multiple fans, okay? I'm trying to process."

Jeremiah stared, then gave a stiff nod. His gaze flickered to Oliver, his brow raised, but when Priest gave a single, sharp shake of his head, he backed off. "We picked up a scent," he repeated, and it took a second, but eventually, Oliver sucked in a breath.

"Poe's?"

Knight walked closer to them, resting his hands on the back of a tall chair. "Yes. It was faint, but it was there. The police finally let us inside the shop, and there was no sign of

89

his body. I was able to pick up a little blood, but not enough to indicate a human had died."

Oliver swallowed roughly. "I knew it."

"We followed the scent down the alley, and there was a shoe—a black-and-white sneaker. The smell of blood was strong enough for me to tell it belonged to the same human in the shop. But again, no indication the human had died there. The scent simply... vanished." There was a tightness in his voice that Priest recognized.

This was killing Knight inside. They couldn't let this go on for much longer.

"Okay, so where do we start?" Oliver asked, jumping to his feet. "There's probably no point in me going back to the bookstore. But we can start with the scent, right? I mean, we need to contact Poe's family first—see if they've gotten some kind of ransom call? And you have other teams, don't you? Bravo Team, Charlie Team..."

"Pump the brakes," Jeremiah said, putting up a hand. Oliver backed away from him, but he didn't stop pacing. "You're getting ahead of yourself."

"How?" Oliver's eyes blazed. "Poe's been out there alive, just like I said, for how long now? While we're just sitting on our asses! The gods only know what they're doing to him. It could be torture. It could be—"

"Control your human," Knight said, his voice a low rumble, fangs dropping.

Priest was on his feet, pulling Oliver close. "Oliver, I need you to stop."

He had no idea if Oliver's not-quite-human side made him aware that the situation was on the verge of getting dangerous or if he just had good natural instincts, but his jaw snapped shut. His gaze flickered from Priest to Knight to Jeremiah before he stepped out of Priest's hold.

"I'm not going to sit here while my friend is in danger."

"Yes, you are," Priest said.

Oliver's mouth dropped open. "You can't be fucking serious."

"I'm fucking a lot of things. I'm an Incubus," Priest quipped.

"I'm not joking!"

"Neither am I," Priest said, though he was lying. Since Oliver, he hadn't fucked anyone else. But it was the only thing he could think of to try and diffuse the situation because it was getting out of hand. "This is what we do, darling. This is our job. And we are the best at it. We don't know Poe is alive—"

"Are you still on that?" Oliver looked like he wanted to tear his hair out. "He's alive, and the fact that you don't believe me goes to show exactly what you think of me. And since I'm not a prisoner here, I'm out. I'm going to find him myself."

"Alone?" Priest asked, raising a mocking brow.

Oliver spun and met his gaze. "No. I have the Angel you all said would be helpful on my side. He'll help me. He'll give me anything I ask."

He turned and started away, and that was when Priest snapped.

It was jealousy. It was possession. It was fear because whatever Oliver was, he was still mostly human. He was strong, but he was fragile. He was mortal. He could die too easily, and Priest had seen what could happen to supernaturals with the right spells and the right power. The very idea of Oliver suffering made him want to rip his human face off and raze the city with his claws.

He didn't do that, of course. Instead, he used his speed and strength to stop Oliver from taking another step. His hands dug into Oliver's shoulders, and Oliver met his gaze.

His eyes flashed bright blue. Something was emanating off him, coming at Priest in waves. Dangerous. Tantalizing. It made him feel like he'd been starved for a thousand years, and Oliver was his first taste of food.

Priest's eyes went black again. He was done fighting. He was done with Oliver resisting. He almost never used his thrall, but he called on it now for the first time in years. His voice rumbled sweetly in the back of his throat. Tendrils of his power reached out and caressed Oliver's skin.

"Enough of this," he murmured. Oliver swallowed thickly. "Relax. Let it go. Head to my bedroom and wait for me."

There was a long pause... and then Oliver opened his mouth and laughed in his face. "Are you out of your fucking mind?"

And then Jeremiah sneezed loudly—a full-on dad sneeze that rocked the room.

The tension immediately evaporated. Oliver sagged like he was exhausted, and Priest caught him before his knees buckled.

"Sorry," Jeremiah said, sniffing and wiping his nose. "Angels always make me sneeze. I thought you said Azriel was gone."

Priest locked eyes with Oliver. "He is."

Oliver looked guilty, swallowing heavily. "Priest..."

"Go up to my room. We're going to talk about this once the guys and I figure out our next steps."

"But—"

"No," Priest growled, and he was hit with a sudden wave of lust from Oliver. It took everything in him to control it. "Upstairs. Now. I'm done with this argument."

Oliver looked like he wanted to keep going, but after a beat, he nodded and stepped back. "Fine. But this doesn't mean I'm backing down. Poe saved me. He is my family. I am not going to sit by while you all try to decide whether or not he's worth going after."

"That's not what's happening. But we've been through this before," Knight said, his voice carefully measured.

"Firsthand. So please, trust us. Whatever choices we make, they'll be in everyone's best interest."

Oliver stood fast for another moment, then finally turned and left the room. Priest followed his aura as long as he was able, and when he was sure Oliver wasn't planning an escape attempt, he turned back to his brothers.

"I need to handle this."

"Clearly," Jeremiah said flatly. "And when you're done, you're going to tell us what the fuck you're hiding."

Priest felt his face heat, but he didn't give in. "It's not important right now."

Knight barked a laugh. "You tried to put him in your thrall, and he laughed in your face. You're telling us that's not important?"

Jeremiah was staring at him curiously. "Do you love him?"

"Oh, fuck off," Priest started, but Jeremiah moved faster than he was ready for, and suddenly, he was backed into the wall.

"Do you love him?"

"I don't know."

Grabbing his face, Jeremiah pulled at his cheeks until his lower eyelids sagged. He stared into his eyes for so long Priest wanted to throw him out the window. And then he let go. "We're going to talk about this later. Right now, you need to take care of your hunger."

Priest realized he was right. His claws were still out, and his eyes were black. He was starving for the man upstairs. "You should probably put some distance between yourselves and this house for a little while."

"We have shit to do anyway." Jeremiah gave his cheek a soft pat, then jerked his head at Knight. Priest felt their gazes linger on him as they left, and it was only when they were no longer under his roof that he turned and headed for Oliver.

And he wasn't going to stop until he had him.

9

PRIEST

*T*he moment he was in the bedroom, he kicked the door shut so hard it rattled on the frame. Oliver, who was perched on the end of the bed, didn't move. He didn't startle. He just stared with his wide eyes and lips parted, lust still rolling off him in waves.

Priest took a moment to drink it in, to feed on the tendrils of what he would be having like an appetizer. Then, he reached for the buttons on his shirt as he stalked forward. Oliver's breath hitched when Priest's chest was exposed. He dropped his shirt on the floor next to the bed, then pressed his hand to the center of Oliver's chest.

His heart was beating rabbit fast—like prey.

Fuck.

"Do you know?"

Oliver licked his lips slowly. "Do I know what?"

"What you are?"

Oliver nodded.

"Did you know before Azriel told you?" Priest's head ducked, and he nuzzled against Oliver's throat, breathing him in. Oliver tilted his head to the side, giving him better access, and Priest licked at his thrumming pulse. "Have you been hiding it all this time?"

"I had no idea," Oliver said in a broken whisper. He grabbed at Priest's waist, clawing at the button on his trousers. "You figured it out. How?"

Priest pulled back, gripping Oliver's chin tightly. "It was obvious, little human."

Oliver's swallow bobbed thickly in his throat. "Little Angel?"

Priest smiled. His teeth felt sharp in his mouth. He pushed Oliver, who moved back like he had no control over his limbs, and Priest followed, crawling along the mattress until Oliver was pinned to the headboard. "Little Angel." He lifted a claw and traced the sharp point over Oliver's shirt, then curled them in the hem and tugged until his chest was bare. "You teleported."

"I did?"

"In my workshop." Priest bent his elbows until he was eye level with Oliver's nipples, and his tongue—thin now, slightly forked—flicked out and licked at him. Oliver let out a heavy, soul-deep groan, and Priest felt his lust like the strongest drink in Azriel's bar. His gaze lifted. "You resisted my thrall."

Oliver's jaw ticked with irritation. "Not something I appreciated."

Priest felt a small wave of guilt, which paled in comparison to the desire that was coursing through him, but it was enough to knock a little sense into him for that single moment. "I know. I'm sorry. I panicked at the thought of losing you."

Oliver softened, lifting a hand and pressing it to the side of Priest's throat. It was like a test, seeing how willing he would be to bare his vulnerable spots to this man. Priest tipped his head to the side, and Oliver dragged two fingers over his pulsing artery. "You won't lose me, Priest. It's been you and only you for a long, long time now."

Priest groaned, then surged in and pressed their lips together. Oliver's mouth was hot, perfect for the wet, messy kiss Priest was taking. His claws managed to get Oliver's pants undone and shoved down toward his ankles, and he couldn't help a smile in spite of the raging passion between them as Oliver kicked them away.

"I'm scared," Oliver said as Priest broke the kiss so he could remove his own trousers.

His hands froze, and he looked up. "Of me?"

"Of what I am. Of what it means," Oliver whispered.

Priest's eyes closed in a slow blink as he continued to undress. He needed to feel Oliver's skin against his own. He shuffled forward, bracketing Oliver's hips with his knees, and he thrust his hips, his thick, needy cock rubbing against Oliver's stomach.

"It changes nothing." He pinched Oliver's chin, careful not to prick his delicate skin. He might be part Angel, but he was still so human. He was so warm. So perfect. He dipped his head and knocked their foreheads together. "You're still the man I fell for."

Oliver's breath trembled in his chest. "I want you. I can feel your hunger. I want to feed you."

Priest shuddered. "Oliver—"

"Let me. I'm strong. You know I'm strong." His hands dug into Priest's sides, urging him to fuck his hips forward. Oliver was rock hard, leaking at the tip, and Priest was desperate for a taste. "I can take it."

Priest looked into his eyes and believed him. Fuck, he believed him. He stole a single, furious kiss before pulling away, and as Oliver made a noise of protest, Priest opened his mouth, grabbed Oliver's cock, and took him down in a single swallow.

There was a beat of silence so thick Priest thought maybe

he'd gone deaf. And then Oliver let out a noise so inhuman it could have shattered glass if he'd been any louder. His Angel voice. Melodic, powerful, and, in this moment, wanton.

Priest sucked hard as he pulled up, dragging Oliver's essence from the core of him. He tasted like summer, like wind, like rain. It rushed through his limbs, chasing away the edges of madness, sating hunger in ways he'd never been sated before.

Behind his closed lids, he saw something—two glowing threads, reaching for each other, not quite there, but somehow, he knew if they could touch, everything would be right.

It terrified him to his core.

He pulled away with a gasp, his eyes hot as he stared into Oliver's, which were still bright but rimmed with dark black like his own. Then he blinked, and it was gone.

He and Oliver were both breathing heavily, and his heart was going a million miles a minute.

"Priest," Oliver said, his voice thready.

He wanted to ask what the hell that was—and if Oliver had seen it too—but he was too far gone to his hunger. He pinned Oliver back with a hand to his throat, and then he gripped their cocks in his palm and began to stroke them.

He kept his gaze locked on Oliver as he fed on him. It flowed through him in every groan, every pant that Oliver gave. *Beloved*, he thought as he leaned in. *My beloved*. His forked tongue darted out, licking the sweat from Oliver's skin, and then he tilted his head back and took his mouth.

Come for me, little human. Little Angel. Come for me.

Oliver's body began to shake as his orgasm raced through him. Priest could see nothing, feel nothing except the waves of pleasure that were giving him the strength he needed. He could see Oliver's soul, bright and wild and different to anyone Priest had ever fed on. It was warm. It enveloped him, cradled him. It nourished him in ways nothing ever had.

For the first time in his life, he didn't feel like he was

taking something from someone. No. He was being given this gift. This power. This strength.

He was only peripherally aware of his own climax—of hot ropes of come spilling on their dicks as he stroked them. And it was only when Oliver moaned in genuine pain that Priest let go with a gasp. His hands trembled as his vision returned.

Oliver was pale.

"Sweetheart—"

"No," Oliver said. His voice was still strong. He opened his eyes, and they were bright Angel blue. "I'm okay. I'm here."

Priest collapsed against him, rolling them to the side and wrapping around him like he was afraid to let go. "Promise me you won't leave me."

"I'm not going anywhere."

Priest buried his face in the back of Oliver's neck. "Can we stay like this for a little while?"

He heard Oliver's smile in his happy hum, and he grinned when Oliver nuzzled back against him. "For as long as you want."

For as long as he wanted was a lie, but it wasn't Oliver's fault. His beloved was still dead to the world when Priest woke, and it took him a second to realize it was his phone. He attempted to ignore it, but when it buzzed a dozen more times, he finally grabbed it off the nightstand and extracted himself from the only place he wanted to be.

Still naked, he shuffled out of the bedroom and down to the kitchen as he answered. "This better be fucking good."

He started the coffee machine with the push of a button, then stared at the glowing numbers on his stove.

It was ass o'clock in the morning. Of course.

"There's been another attack." Jeremiah sounded more tired than angry. "Just like Oliver's shop."

With those words, Priest didn't need coffee. "Where?"

"Dawson and Zimmerson. It's a—"

"Law firm." Priest gripped the counter. "Fuck. They were in the news recently, weren't they?"

"One of the partners—Zimmerson—he made a statement about McCornal and his shit-for-brains son, calling what happened to Remi and his siblings horrifying and a product of McCornal's crusade of hatred," Jeremiah said with a heavy sigh. "The firm has a lot of very important clients—some human and some supernatural—and most of them have been quietly distancing themselves from the senator since."

That… was a lot of information to have on hand for such a fluid situation.

"Have we been monitoring the firm?" he asked, rubbing at his throbbing temples.

Jeremiah didn't say anything for a moment. "Our analysts were aware of an online campaign targeting the firm."

"What kind of campaign?"

"The kind that usually doesn't go beyond the dark corners of the internet."

But this time, it had.

Priest's brow furrowed as he abandoned his coffee and slipped into the bathroom. He had clothes that weren't entirely filthy, and he pressed the phone between his ear and shoulder as he struggled into his jeans. "Oliver's shop hadn't gotten any press recently, right? We can't call that a pattern."

"The targets seem to have some similarities and some noted differences." Jeremiah let out a slow breath. "How fast can you get here?"

"I need five minutes to get dressed and leave a note for Oliver."

"Did you two work things out?"

"More than," Priest said with a smile, satisfaction still humming through his veins.

"Spare me the details and tell me he's not going to take off. We don't have the resources to track him down if he gets a wild hair and tries to go after his friend."

Priest had about a thousand questions, but he'd ask them later. He also ignored Jeremiah's demand. "I'll see you soon. Ping me the address."

He hung up and finished dressing, then dragged wet fingers through his hair to put it in some semblance of order as he rinsed with mouthwash.

He gave himself a quick glance in the mirror and was startled to see what he looked like. His skin was all but glowing, and the dark circles under his eyes had receded to almost nothing. He looked alive. He looked better than he had in years.

And he didn't need a second to understand exactly why that was. He was fairly sure it had nothing to do with the fact that Oliver was part Angel. He'd fed from a full-blooded Angel, and nothing like this had happened. He'd even had a Nephilim lover years and years back, and while he'd felt powerful from it, he didn't feel restored the way he did now. Like his muscles and bones filled out his skin better than they ever had before.

It was something to do with *Oliver*. No, it was *everything* to do with Oliver.

He pinned the thought aside because he didn't have time for it. He would take advantage of the fact that he was feeling more alert and use it to take care of whatever the fuck was going on. He knew Jeremiah likely had a theory, and if Knight had been able to get some downtime and recenter, he probably had ideas as well.

After all, if any of them knew what it was like to escape something like this, it was their Vampire brother.

Heading back into the kitchen, Priest rummaged around his

neglected drawers until he found an old notepad and a pen. The ink in it was half-dry, but he managed to sketch out a quick note telling Oliver that he'd be back, and under no circumstances was he to leave the house. He wished he had better magic abilities so he could ward his wayward little lover inside, but he didn't.

Besides, if Oliver could break his thrall, there was no telling what other bits of Priest's magic he could resist.

Tiptoeing back into his room, Priest stood beside the bed and stared down at his lover. Oliver looked small somehow, nestled in his sheets with the comforter pulled halfway up his chest. He had one arm flung over his head, the other curled in a loose fist at his side, and his lips were gently parted with his breath.

Priest wanted to crawl into the bed and wrap around him and never leave. Instead, he set the note down on the nightstand, brushed a kiss to his temple, taking in a deep breath of his scent, and then he turned and hurried out.

The streets smelled like ash and a little like magic. The same scent that was all over Oliver's bookshop. It had blown into the street, knocking out several windows of nearby shops, and though the police were keeping people back, crowds had gathered.

Priest couldn't help but hear the quiet murmur as he approached. He passed well enough for human, but they still knew.

Demon. Monster. Abomination.

The words slipped past their lips in soft murmurs. They trusted him to save their asses, but none of them would ever shake his hand. His stomach twisted, but he couldn't let himself give a shit about that now. He never had before, and he wasn't about to start in the middle of a job.

Jeremiah was off to the side, speaking to the detective that looked like he was leading the investigation, so Priest slid up to Knight and Slate as they surveyed the scene. He took a deep breath, searching for something besides rubble and the faint lingering hint of magic.

"It's not Fae," Slate said, his voice a low rumble. He would know. Gargoyles were a distant cousin of the Fae, and being that he was once a prince of the oldest bloodline of Gargoyles, he would recognize it anywhere. "I can't pinpoint what it is."

"It's the same as the scene when Jeremiah was almost killed," Knight said.

Priest nodded. It was. Magic manipulated by human hands and wielded by… he didn't know. Not yet.

"I have a gut feeling this is about to get a lot more familiar for me," Knight said quietly. He had his arms wrapped around his middle, his eyes covered by dark glasses, his face paler than usual.

"Was anyone found alive?" Priest asked.

Knight shook his head. "Two people were in the building, DOA when the cops got here."

Priest dragged a hand down his face. "Fuck."

"That's not all." Knight stepped closer to him. "We found a scent trail. One of the firefighters is a Dragon. He said this hasn't been released yet, but a third person has been reported missing."

"Who?" Priest's voice was sharp. He was afraid of the answer.

"One of the senior partners at the firm—his son. He'd been hired recently as an intern. There's no sign of a body."

Senior partner.

"Zimmerson?"

Knight raised a brow. "How'd you know?"

"I want to talk to him," Priest said, ignoring the question.

Jeremiah would fill in the rest of the team as soon as they had a chance to catch their breath.

Slate nodded. "I'm going to sniff around the other alleys and see if I can find anything. Shout if you need me."

He broke away, and Priest moved in close to Knight, who looked like he'd been awake for days. "Tell me you're alright."

Knight grimaced, his fangs showing. "I've been better. You know what this feels like, right?"

Priest did. It wasn't like he was ever going to forget what his brother had been through before he turned. The torment kept him up at night, kept him from being able to be close to anyone. The only thing Priest wanted to do was pull his friend close, but he knew he couldn't. Not now.

"Have you been with your moths?"

Knight paused mid-step and barely held back his smile. "Yes. Four of them cocooned yesterday. They'll be ready for release soon."

Priest grinned, unable to help it. Part of Knight's therapy was finding something he could do—something mindless to take the edge off the pain. Priest had no idea how he got into it, but he'd started breeding Death's head Hawkmoths. Whenever he disappeared, the guys knew exactly where to find him: in his sanctuary beneath his home, sitting in a chair reading with several moths perched on his shoulders.

They spent the next couple of hours examining the scene, talking to witnesses, and conferring with the Bravo Team members who'd come out to help. Any bit of possible evidence was sent back to the analysts at HQ, their search continuing long after the police detectives had headed back to their beds.

There wasn't much to go on, and the frustration from that ate at Priest, enraging his Demon and making his skin itch.

The head of the Bravo Team—Seven—clapped him on the

shoulder just as the city began to rumble with life around them, moving forward despite the devastation happening amidst them. "We're going to head back to HQ, start sifting through everything from this scene and the bookshop. Try and find a connection."

Priest laid a hand over Seven's, feeling a kinship with the Shadow Demon. "Thanks for coming to help. I know you and your team are already covering a lot for us so we can focus on this."

"Don't give it another thought," Seven said, deep voice reverberating through Priest's chest. He gave him a half smile, then dissipated right in front of Priest's eyes, the weight of his hand the last thing to disappear.

Knight wandered over, shoving his phone in his pocket. "Let's find Sunshine and Slate."

They rounded the corner of what was left of the law firm's building, and the two firefighters who were still on scene turned to face them. Priest spotted the Dragon, nodding at him. He broke away from his partner and walked up.

He gave Priest a slow up and down. Dragons didn't often hate the same way others did when they realized he was a Demon, but sometimes, they did. He braced himself, but after a beat, the Dragon's shoulders relaxed.

"Trident, eh?"

"Alpha Team. I'm Pries." He extended his hand.

"Kellan." His palm was warm, as all Dragons were. "I spoke with the head of your team."

"I've been brought up to speed and know about the person who was taken. Can you give us any information on him?"

"He was human," Kellan said, sounding tired. "Young. Barely nineteen. His birthday was a few weeks ago."

There was a sadness in his voice that hit Priest in the sternum.

"Were you two—"

"No," Kellan said with a laugh, and then his face fell. "No, nothing like that. But I've known him a long time. Since he was knee-high. Good kid. Really fucking good kid." His voice cracked. "He doesn't deserve this."

"What's his name?" Priest asked. He had a feeling Jeremiah hadn't gotten details. When he was focused, he missed those small things.

Kellan closed his eyes in a slow blink. "Cody."

Cody. Poe. Gods knew who else. Priest had a feeling this was just the beginning.

"Was he an activist?"

Kellan shrugged. "His parents were—if you want to call it that. He was just a student trying to make some extra cash over the summer. He wanted to buy a convertible before school started." Kellan passed a hand down his face. "He babysat for my Hoard sometimes."

"We're going to do everything we can to get him back."

"Give us your contact information," Knight said, his voice a little stiff. "In case we need more information from you."

"Will you call me if you find him?" Kellan asked.

"Yes," Priest promised him as he took Kellan's information down. "As soon as we know something, I'll send a message."

"Thank you. I'm serious, man. He didn't deserve this."

Knight bowed his head. "We know. None of them do."

They made their way back to Jeremiah, who was leaning against the open door of his SUV. He looked more exhausted than Knight. Glancing up, he relaxed when he saw Priest and Knight, and he pushed away from the door.

"Find anything?"

"Nothing we don't already know. Good kid, name's Cody," Priest said. "Not a vocal activist."

"Neither was Poe, as far as I'm aware. But his family was," Jeremiah said. He was frowning, rubbing at his temples. "And then there's Remi. People didn't love that he was half Siren, but he didn't make a big fuss about it. Neither did his parents. None of this is adding up."

"And the scents are disappearing into thin air," Slate said as he walked up. "I don't like it. I think you need to get Oliver somewhere safe."

"Safer than his town house?" Jeremiah asked.

"Maybe."

Priest raised his brow. "Why?"

"Because so far, we have dead bodies and missing bodies. Oliver's the only one who's survived an attack and is still here. If he was meant to die or be taken as well, whoever did this might come back for him."

Priest's stomach twisted. Fuck, Slate was right. He hadn't sensed any danger around his place, but leaving Oliver alone might have been one giant mistake. Whoever was behind all this shit had to know he'd come running when he heard about another attack. "I need to go."

"What's wrong?" Jeremiah asked.

Priest was already backing away. "I left him there alone."

"Your place is warded," Knight started, then stopped, and his shoulders sagged. "Except that only works if he stays put, and he's a flight risk, isn't he?"

Priest didn't answer. Instead, he turned and fled.

He broke every traffic law getting back to his place, and he flew through the door without ceremony. He could feel his Demon itching to come out. His eyes were black, the heat in the room growing, his claws stretching from his fingertips.

He wanted nothing more than to find his little human in his bed, still sleeping from their night together, but he couldn't feel him.

Knight was right: the wards would have protected him.

But his beloved was a man on a mission, and he would not be stopped.

And now he was gone.

10

OLIVER

*O*liver hadn't known where he was going to go, only that he had to get out now if he didn't want Priest to come home and stop him. The note said he'd be gone a while, that he was free to use anything in the house, and to please not leave.

But Oliver, of course, wasn't going to obey.

Not that order, anyway. He did make himself at home. He showered, he had a cup of tea, he found comfortable clothes that were kind on his body, which was still sore. But he also didn't waste any time. He wasn't trying to openly defy Priest, but he couldn't sit by and do nothing.

It wasn't a lack of patience; it was knowing that the Trident agents didn't fully believe Poe was alive. The more time that passed, the more likely it was Poe wasn't going to survive whatever he was going through. And Oliver did not want to live in a world without his best friend. He couldn't.

He wouldn't survive it.

He didn't bother taking a car. There was a trolley stop a few blocks from the bookshop, and it seemed the most logical place to start. If he was part Angel, it wasn't much, so he

109

couldn't rely on whatever new powers were cropping up. He wouldn't be able to sniff Poe out, but maybe there was something the guys missed.

Something only he would notice. A message Poe left behind or... or... anything that would get him a step closer.

He thought he was prepared to see the damage, but the moment he rounded the corner and saw the rubble, he nearly fell to his knees. The shop was just that: brick and mortar, filled with ink and papers. It was a building full of things.

But they were his things. His and Poe's. It was a lifetime of hard work, of getting to a place Oliver never thought he'd be, considering how he'd grown up. It was blood, sweat, tears, sleepless nights, and endless days reduced to nothing. And whoever had done this had taken one of the only people Oliver considered family.

He hadn't let himself think about what Poe was going through, but it was getting harder and harder to avoid. He stepped past the hole that had once been the shop door and stared at the pieces of twisted metal that had been the frame for his glass counter.

The last time he'd paid attention to that space was when Priest was there. If he closed his eyes long enough, he could picture the moment perfectly—their almost kiss. The almost moment where Oliver thought he'd finally broken him down.

Only he hadn't.

He'd run.

Priest wasn't running now, but was it worth the price to have him if it meant this was his reality? The answer seemed simple enough. Oliver didn't just like him. He didn't just love him. It was more than that. It was something no words could describe. The feeling ran deep, through his soul. When Priest was holding him, kissing him, feeding on him, they were connected in a way Oliver hadn't realized was possible.

Not that he had a lot of experience to go on, but he had enough.

There was something different happening. Something new.

And he was angry he wasn't allowed to dwell on it because every second thinking about Priest was a second lost not finding his best friend.

He swallowed heavily, then flinched when he felt something on the edge of his jaw. His hand flew up to brush it away, and it came back wet. Fuck, he was crying. He realized the tightness in his throat was his body attempting to hold back a sob. This was too much. It was all too much.

His gaze cut to the wall where the stairs were that led to his apartment, but the hole above him told him there was nothing left to find there. Everything was ruined. He ran both hands over his face until his cheeks were dry, and then he squared his shoulders and turned toward the space where the counter used to be.

His eyes moved over everything, but it was all covered in ash from the fire. It smelled like burning rot. Not a single book had survived. Not a single artifact. Not one spell jar. His potions were cooked, leaving smears on the floor.

"Where are you?" Oliver whispered, but there was no one to hear his words.

As he picked his way through the carnage, time passed slowly—like the turn of the Earth was caught in a river of honey. His limbs were still stiff and aching, and after what had to be at least an hour, he had to stop. There was nothing there—and if there was, he wasn't going to find it.

He wasn't a detective. He wasn't a member of the Alpha Team. He might be part Angel, but it wasn't enough to give him the strength he needed to do any of this.

Oliver's gaze cut to Azriel's bar, clearly visible through the gaping holes where his windows used to be. There were no windows at the club, but he had no doubt the Angel was there. He was probably sleeping still… or drinking or fucking. Or some mixture of all three. The last thing he wanted to do was drag Azriel into something he wanted no part of, but he was at a loss. The Alpha Team wasn't prioritizing Poe, so what choice did he have?

He stepped over fallen beams and burnt brick as he made his way back outside. The smoke had long since cleared, but his lungs still felt clogged with ash, and he coughed several times as he made his way into the alley.

That was where they'd picked up a scent. Where they'd found one of Poe's shoes. Maybe there was something left.

He walked from one end to the other, kicking over old takeout containers and soggy cardboard boxes, but if Poe had left anything else behind, Oliver couldn't see it. He wondered if the shoe was even his. If the scent was even his. It wasn't like he could verify for himself.

His stomach ached as he turned back toward the club. He had to get Azriel. He was at the end of the line.

"Poe. Please," he murmured helplessly. Pointlessly.

Why did he have to be this? Why couldn't his new Angel powers come with something useful besides the ability to teleport three feet and be overwhelmed with ridiculous premonitions that never made sense until well after the fact?

"If you're out there—"

Something crawled up his spine. It was so powerful, so intense, he swore it was a physical touch. He spun toward the club, then froze. Nothing was there. No one was with him. Oliver closed his eyes and took a deep breath.

"Poe," he murmured again.

The sensation was back. It was like a second heartbeat beside his own, but it wasn't lodged in his chest. It was moving—tugging him to the right. He took a step, and the feeling increased. Urgency flooded his limbs.

"Poe," he said again, his voice stronger.

The feeling was like a rapid drumbeat. It was Poe. It was the feeling he had before when he knew Poe was alive—it was his heart. He was hurting—he was in danger—but he was alive. He wanted to run, but he needed to think clearly if he was going to have a chance at finding his friend.

"Where are you?"

There was no answer. Then, before he could start to panic that this was one more useless thing now plaguing him, his feet began to move. It was a slow stumble at first, but once he stopped resisting and gave in to his body, he began to run.

It felt like there was a hook lodged in his ribs, pulling him along. He let go to the power, and by the gods, this was what he needed. He started to laugh as the buildings whipped by him. He wasn't moving faster than a human, but it didn't matter. His powers had found Poe.

However they came to be—whatever his horrible family had done and whatever secrets they kept—in this moment, he was grateful. He was going to find him. He was going to bring Poe home and—

Everything stopped.

Powerful arms wrapped around him, gripping him. The creature's heat was white-hot, almost burning Oliver through his shirt. He instantly began to fight. He wasn't going to let himself be taken!

"Let me go! Fuck you, let me g—mpfhhh!" The creature pressed a hand over Oliver's mouth. His claws dug deeply into Oliver's skin, and he began to flail, trying to scream past the warm, sweaty palm pinning his lips together.

"Oliver!"

It took him a moment to recognize the voice and a moment after that for his body to stop fighting.

"Oliver! It's me. It's me."

Priest.

He went still, and the second Priest's arms went lax, he twisted out of his grip and turned to hit him. "What the fuck! What is wrong with you?" he shouted for all of the street to hear. He swung his fist, but Priest caught it midair and stepped into his space.

His eyes were completely black, his claws still pricking at Oliver's skin. "Stop screaming."

"You scared the shit out of me!" Oliver said, refusing to lower his voice.

Priest let out a low growl. "It serves you right. What in the nine hells were you thinking leaving the house on your own?"

"I was thinking that none of you give a shit about Poe!" Oliver shouted. He shoved at Priest hard, but the Demon was an unmovable wall. He was undeterred. "I was thinking that if you're not going to help him, I'm going to do it my gods-damned self, and I don't care if I die in the process!"

Something snapped in Priest. Oliver felt it before he saw it. There was a charge in the air, rippling above Priest's skin. He let out a deep, dangerous growl that shook Oliver to his score. His sharp nails became full claws, his eyes somehow darkened further, sucking him into their endless depths. His face lengthened and sharpened as his pale skin melted into a grayish black, like unpolished hematite, and long, twisted horns rose from his temples.

Priest's Demon, no longer politely hidden beneath his human face.

He towered over Oliver, almost a foot taller than he had been a moment ago, with a broad chest and clawed feet. He was powerful and deadly. His fingers curled against the front of Oliver's throat, his claws pricking his skin. He backed him up so swiftly Oliver's feet left the ground, and he hit the wall with a dull thud.

Priest's anger curled around him as he leaned in close, staring into Oliver's face. There was a faintest flicker of flames in the back of his black eyes, a glimpse of the hell all Demons were born from in one way or another.

"Don't you ever, *ever*, say that again," he snarled through thick fangs, the cute little ones from the day before replaced by teeth that could bite him in half if he wanted to.

Oliver lifted his chin. "I meant it."

Priest's grip tightened, pressing into the sides of his throat, and Oliver felt a warmth rushing through him. Pure lust. Some of it was Priest's, but so much of it was his own. Priest's nostrils flared, his Demon face scrunching in confusion as his tongue flicked out to taste the charge between them.

"Oliver," he growled. "Focus."

He couldn't. He was *drowning*.

He closed his eyes in a slow blink, overwhelmed with need. Carefully, in case Priest didn't like it, he gripped one of those thick horns, squeezing when Priest groaned. He traced his fingers over the hard twists of the black length until he reached the blunt tip, then wrapped his fingers around it once more and gave it a few quick strokes.

Priest's thigh wedged between his, pressing against his aching balls, his other hand landing on Oliver's ass to rock him against the hard muscle.

"Take me home," he gasped, grabbing onto the other horn and rutting against Priest without thought to where they were or who could catch them.

Priest's forked tongue dragged over his lips. Whimpering, he opened to him, letting him taste the inside of his mouth. He tipped his head back against the wall behind him, offering anything to Priest. Offering *everything*.

"Oliver," he said, softer this time. His Demon began to fade back into his skin—not completely, but enough for Oliver to see the face of the man he'd come to know. His horns shrunk down to half their length, so he moved his hands to grip at the back of Priest's neck, pulling him closer. "Don't say it if you don't mean it."

"I mean it. I want you. I need you. *Take me*."

Priest closed his eyes as Oliver's dick throbbed behind his zipper, and he tightened his grip around Oliver's ass and released his hold on his throat.

Much to Oliver's disappointment.

He ached for that possessive recklessness, craving for his Demon to use every filthy trick up his sleeve to bind them together.

"Hold tight, little human. And don't let go."

11

PRIEST

*T*he drive back to his house seemed to take an eternity. But unlike the last time, he followed every traffic law in existence. With Oliver in the car with him, he wouldn't take any chances on being reckless. His Demon was still stirring inside him, agitated at the fact that Oliver had run off after Priest had explicitly asked him not to. And then, when he saw Oliver running away from him—or at least in the opposite direction of where he'd been standing—it had triggered a predator drive inside him. Yes, he wanted to keep Oliver safe, but he also wanted to catch him and claim him.

Remind him where he belonged.

It didn't help that the entire drive, his car was filled with the scent of his little human's lust perfuming the air. Every breath he took, he could taste it on his tongue, in the back of his throat. It made it hard for him to focus, especially when he kept glancing over every few seconds like he was worried Oliver would disappear again.

But his reckless beloved sat in the passenger seat, looking almost relaxed except for his eyes. They had the faintest shimmer to them once more, giving away the stirring of his desires and his Angel blood.

As soon as the car was turned off, he was hustling him inside, tempted to just throw him over his shoulder and carry him through the front door and up to his bedroom.

As soon as the door was shut behind them, Oliver turned to him and wrapped his arms around his neck. "Just because I found you going full Demon uncontrollably attractive doesn't mean I'm going to give up on Poe," Oliver said, his voice wavering as he pushed up onto his toes and rubbed his body all down the front of Priest's.

"I don't want you to forget about your friend," he said, gripping the back of Oliver's thighs and hoisting him up, practically purring when Oliver reflexively wrapped his legs around his waist. "I want you to be safe. I want you to *trust* that me and my team will find him."

Oliver stared down into his face, running his teeth over his bottom lip. "It feels like no one is making Poe the priority. He's my family. I can't just forget about him, even if all I want is to spend every waking moment covered in your come and wrapped in your sheets."

His Demon surged inside him, and he was moving faster than any human could, crossing the house and sprinting up the stairs. Once they were in his bedroom, he kicked the door shut behind him.

"We'll find him together, I promise," Priest said emphatically, holding Oliver's eyes as he slowly lowered him onto the mattress. He followed him right down, bracing his forearms on either side of him. They were so close their breaths mingled, the damp, warm air making his skin tingle. "Do you trust me, little human?"

Oliver stared into his eyes for a moment, and it felt like his answer would be the beginning of something... or the end. They stood on a precipice, and he just hoped Oliver was brave enough to jump off with him.

"Yes, Priest. I trust you," he whispered, lightly caressing his cheek. "We'll do it together."

Relief and happiness and resolution filled his entire being. He dove down and took a long, deep kiss. He moved his lips slowly, trying not to rush despite the fact his Demon was urging him on, demanding they do things he knew Oliver wasn't ready for.

More than that, he was hungry again, starved. Considering he'd woken up that morning feeling more sated than he had in years, it was hard to believe, but fully shifting into his Demonic form always took a lot out of him, sapping his energy when he changed back and bringing his Incubus needs right to the surface.

An ever-present reminder that he could never truly be full. That his Demon was a bottomless well, always looking to be fed again and with more.

He was going to have to work hard to hold back. It wasn't fair to ask Oliver to feed him again, even with whatever Angelic powers he was discovering inside himself. Three times in as many days? That could drain even the most powerful creature. And he wouldn't put him at risk like that.

As if he could hear Priest's thoughts, Oliver broke their kiss and tightened his arms and legs around him. He whispered directly into his ear, "I need you, and I can feel how much you need me. Take it. Take everything you need."

"It's too soon—"

Oliver shook his head, his hair wild and glasses askew. "No, it's not. I felt good this morning. I still do. I can handle it. You don't have to treat me like I'm made of glass."

"Oliver." He shouldn't. He knew that it was dangerous, and yet his Demon whispered in his ear. *He wants it. He craves it. Take. Take. Take.*

"Yes," Oliver moaned. "Take. Do it. *Please.*"

That "please," said so brokenly, so desperately, was more than Priest could handle. He fell forward once more, locking their lips together, pushing his forked tongue into Oliver's mouth and tasting every inch of him, every molecule, from the tea he had for breakfast to the desire burning in his veins.

It took a while to get them undressed. He didn't want to leave that perfect sweet mouth, kept going back in for more kisses. After he kicked off his shoes and then stripped off his shirt, he and Oliver struggled to get Oliver's pants off until Priest finally lost his patience and tore them away.

Oliver stared at him wide-eyed and then laughed. "You're going to have to get me a new pair. Most of my things burned in the explosion."

He said it lightly. But Priest was so in tune with him in that moment he could taste the hints of grief tinging the air around them.

He crawled up onto the bed as Oliver scooted backward and then flipped over, bracing himself on his hands and knees. He peered over his shoulder at Priest and sucked on his lower lip. He was fucking gorgeous like that. All lean muscle and pale white skin.

Priest wanted to taste every single inch of him, and he planned to, but not this time, not when Oliver's lust and his own hunger were driving him forward, edging him toward madness. He didn't have the patience, and neither did his little human, who lowered himself to his elbows and spread his legs wantonly.

"Fuck," Priest snarled, diving forward and burying his face between those perfect cheeks.

Oliver's hair and the skin on his face held a tinge of ash. He knew he had walked through the burned-out shell of the bookshop, and it lingered on him. But here, right here, it was pure Oliver, and the scent was driving him mad.

He ran his tongue from the back of Oliver's balls all the way up over his hole and then kissed the bottom of his spine.

Perfection.

Oliver moaned and spread his legs a little farther, arching his back in offering, an offering that Priest would gladly take.

Gripping a cheek in each hand, he spread him open and used the dexterous tip of his forked tongue to torment him, fluttering it along the sensitive skin of his sac and perineum.

It didn't take long before Oliver was pushing back against him, silently begging for more. And because Priest was a kind and thoughtful Demon, he gave it to him. He finally moved up to Oliver's entrance, licking over the furled muscle over and over until it was nice and wet, and then used the tips of his forked tongue to spear inside of him.

The cry Oliver released riled up his Incubus, his nails sharpening where he clutched at his delicate skin, but he held them back from turning into full-on claws. He didn't stop his torment though, using the strength and more slender makeup of his Demon tongue to breach his little human deeper until he found that perfect spot inside him. That little bundle of nerves that made Oliver dance on the bed when he fluttered his tongue against it.

"Oh gods, oh gods, oh gods," Oliver chanted, pushing back against Priest's face so hard he had to use some of his own strength to hold him still.

He was so focused on giving Oliver pleasure and driving him out of his mind with it that he didn't realize he was feeding on him. Oliver's desire was so thick in the air around them it was making him a little light-headed.

Or at least that's what he thought until he became aware that as he tongue-fucked Oliver into a moaning mess, face pressed into the sheets and the scent of tears on the air, he was taking in all the nourishment he could want, and it didn't seem like Oliver noticed. He had so much inside him Priest taking a little off the top didn't even register for him.

"Priest, please," he cried, reaching back and gripping a handful of Priest's hair. "I'm like two seconds away from coming, but I need you inside me."

He groaned, the sound reverberating straight inside Oliver and making him whimper and thrust back against him. Slowly, he retracted his tongue, massaging the plump globes of Oliver's ass as he went. As soon as he was free, he licked his lips lewdly, meeting Oliver's eyes. "You're fucking delicious, little human," he growled.

He could tell that his eyes were completely black, the heat from Oliver's body like a beacon, drawing him in.

"That tongue of yours should be illegal," Oliver panted, not bothering to move a single muscle, staying exactly where he was with his face pressed against the bed and his ass sticking straight up in the air.

It was a good look on him, and Priest planned on appreciating it as often as he could. He gave his cock a few quick strokes, not that he needed it. The sight and taste and sounds of Oliver were enough to keep him hard for the rest of his life.

He pressed his wide head against Oliver's loosened entrance and started to push in.

"Wait," Oliver said, a hand fluttering in the air.

Priest froze, not moving a muscle.

"Lube. We forgot lube."

He still didn't move, surprised his little bookworm didn't know his saliva was better than any store-bought lube in existence.

Before he could figure out how to tell him that, Oliver rolled his eyes and said, "Oh, wait. Incubus, never mind. Go ahead."

Still a little confused, Priest held his position, one hand on his cock, the other on Oliver's hip. He stared at the side of his flushed face. "Are you sure? I can probably find some somewhere."

He couldn't. He didn't know why he said that. There was no lubricant in his house. He didn't need it.

Oliver shook his head as best he could, stretching his arms out in front of him like a cat. "No, I just forgot. Go ahead. Take me."

Take him was exactly what he wanted to do, that and so

much more. His need for Oliver went beyond anything he'd ever felt before, anything he could ever dream of feeling. Slowly, doing his best to remember that Oliver was mostly human, he sank inside his tight heat, his eyes rolling into the back of his head at how amazing it felt.

He didn't stop until he was all the way inside, his hips pressed flush against Oliver's ass. Taking a deep breath, he squeezed his eyes shut for a minute.

"Oh gods," Oliver moaned, a shudder running through his body.

Eyes snapping back open, Priest ran his hands from Oliver's hips up to his shoulders and back down. "Are you okay? Is it too much?"

He knew that people liked to brag about having sex with a sex Demon, but he also knew that sometimes the size of him could be overwhelming.

"No, it's fucking perfect," Oliver slurred out. "I need you to move."

"Not yet," Priest said, satisfaction filling him. Oliver loved having him inside him. Soon, he'd crave Priest as much as Priest did him.

"Priest, please do *something*."

Smiling, Priest pulled all the way out, the sound of him moving in Oliver's slick passage obscene in the quiet room. His human craned his head around to scowl at him.

"What are you doing?"

Priest smirked and easily flipped him onto his back and then jerked him toward Priest where he knelt on the bed. Oliver went limp beneath him, arms stretched out above him, dazed eyes gazing up at Priest.

"I decided this is how I want to take you, little human. I want to watch your face as I show you where you belong."

Oliver swallowed thickly, watching as Priest lined back up and drove inside faster that time, smacking their skin together in a lewd way. Oliver threw his head back and moaned, long and low.

Priest couldn't resist the temptation of that long, slender column, sliding his hand up Oliver's abs and over his chest until he rested his palm on his throat, curling his fingers around the back of his neck. He held him firmly, not cutting off any air, just holding on possessively.

Oliver tipped his chin back down and met his gaze, his damp lips slack with euphoria.

Priest pulled out and then thrust back in, holding Oliver's eyes. "You're not going to run off like that again, are you?"

Oliver shook his head, but he didn't say anything.

"No. Because if you do, next time, you won't get the pleasure of my cock inside you."

Oliver sucked in a quick breath.

"No, if I have to chase you down again, I will throw you over my shoulder." He thrust hard. "Carry you back home." Another. "And *tie you to this fucking bed*." One more, even harder, driving Oliver an inch up the bed. "Do you understand me?"

"Yes, Priest. I understand," Oliver moaned, still holding Priest's eyes, even though his were heavy-lidded. His long, slender cock lay untouched between them, but it was practically purple, the tip drooling precum obscenely.

"Good. That's good," Priest said through gritted teeth, picking up his pace, beginning to chase his own pleasure as well. Oliver looked like one wrong move and he was flying over the edge, and Priest wanted to be there with him. "You are precious to me, Oliver. I will not be held responsible for what I do if you were to get hurt or be taken from me."

Some of the lust cleared from Oliver's eyes as he blinked a few times. "I'm right here. I'm safe."

But he almost wasn't, was almost lost in an explosion that tore apart his home and store.

And if Priest hadn't come home when he had and found

him gone, would he have been able to find him as fast as he had? Oliver had been sprinting away from the bookshop and club, following something no one else could see. How far would he have gone? Would he have made it? And what would've happened if he did?

Terror began to combat the pleasure growing inside him. Groaning, he fell forward, moving his hand out of the way and pressing his face into the crook of Oliver's neck, shuttling his hips in and out.

He wrapped a hand around Oliver's neglected dick and began to stroke in time with his fast thrusts. Just as they both reached their peak, he murmured against Oliver's skin, "Don't leave me."

He was sure Oliver didn't hear him. How could he over his shouts of ecstasy?

The scent of his come was thick in the air as Priest kept working him, drawing out every drop that he could before finally allowing himself to find his own release, grunting and pushing as deep inside Oliver as he could get, wishing he could crawl inside him. He released his seed into his lax body, sating part of the urge by leaving some of himself behind.

Oliver's eyes were closed, his breaths still ragged, but he peeked up at Priest when he got up from the bed and went into the bathroom to grab a washcloth, bringing it back to clean Oliver up.

When he climbed back in the bed, he didn't bother asking that time, just pulled Oliver into his embrace and held on. His body and his hunger were sated, but his mind couldn't rest. Oliver didn't seem to have the same problem, drifting off to sleep shortly after he curled into Priest.

He lay there with him for a long time, stroking a hand gently down Oliver's bare skin, as much to soothe himself as Oliver. He inhaled their combined scents, taking it deep into his lungs and letting it fill him up, every cell of his being.

He needed to make sure that Oliver stayed safe. Even

though he had said he trusted Priest and that they would find Poe together, he couldn't forget Slate's words from the second bombing site. If Oliver was the only person left from either attack, could someone come after him to try and take him from Priest?

There was no way he could be with him every second of the day if he was working with the team, and if he stayed home with Oliver instead of going to work with the others, Oliver would get pissed off at him, rightfully. They needed all hands on deck to figure out what in the nine hells was going on, but he couldn't be distracted and worried that while he was at the office or out investigating, Oliver was out on his own, playing at detective and trying to use powers he didn't understand yet.

No, things had to change. They had to adapt.

Pressing a quick kiss into Oliver's hair, he carefully extracted himself and grabbed his cell phone from his discarded pants before strolling out of his bedroom naked. He went downstairs and headed straight for the den, pouring himself a large glass of gargoyle whiskey.

He drank down half and then unlocked his phone, pulling up the contact he needed. He didn't let himself stop and think about it too long, worried he'd second-guess or get cold feet. He just hit the number and raised the phone to his ear.

A deep voice answered after two rings. "Hey, Priest. I'm surprised to be hearing from you so soon."

"I need a favor."

12

OLIVER

onsciousness was slow to come to Oliver, like his body was fighting waking up. Though the more he was, the better he felt. There was a faint energy buzzing under his skin. He'd never felt anything like it before. He couldn't be sure if it was from his angelic blood as it continued to wake up and be more aware inside him or if it was from his sexy lust Demon making a whole damn meal out of him.

The longer he was awake, the less he could detect it until it fully faded away, leaving only him and his deliciously sore body behind. He was contemplating falling back asleep, a complete lack of urgency inside him to get up or do anything. Just as he was about to turn onto his side and attempt to drift back off, something thudded on the floor, and then that same lust Demon who'd turned him inside out with the flick of his tongue muttered under his breath, "Oh balls."

Oliver pressed his lips together to hold back a laugh. He peeled his eyes open and glanced over at the clock, surprised to find that it wasn't even dinnertime yet, even though he felt as if he had been asleep for an entire day or maybe longer, rested in a way he'd never really felt before. All of the lingering aches and pains in his body were just... gone. Like the explosion and his near death experience hadn't happened. He had a feeling that was thanks to Priest feeding on him, but he couldn't say why.

He slowly stretched his arms up above his head and his toes down toward the foot of the bed and then propped himself up on his elbows to see what his Demon was up to. He found Priest on the opposite side of the bed, holding what appeared to be a sparkly, purple dildo in one hand and a rather large black butt plug in the other. A duffel bag that was overflowing with clothes sat on the bed in front of him. Oliver could tell from looking at it that it would never zip close. As he watched, Priest, seemingly unaware that Oliver was awake and he now had an audience, tried to push the plug into the side of the bag.

Just as he was about to give the same treatment to the dildo, Oliver asked, "Where are you going?"

Priest jerked his head up and stared at him for a second, eyes wide, and then he held the dildo up, shook it at him, and said in a very calm and firm voice, "This is a kidnapping."

Oliver sat the rest of the way up and raised his brows. "I'm sorry. What was that?"

Waving his arm—and the toy—around in the air, Priest paced down to the end of the bed and back. "Oliver, do not fight me on this. It's too dangerous for us to stay here. Anyone who's had surveillance on you for the last few months will know that there's a good chance you're with me or someone else from Alpha Team. We need to relocate somewhere that's more isolated and secure."

Oliver was shaking his head before he even finished. "I can't just leave. We talked about this earlier. We can work together. I *want* us to work together, but that can't mean we just fuck off to who knows where while the rest of your team maybe gets around to rescuing Poe in a few weeks, if at all."

Priest stopped at the end of the bed and planted his hands

on his hips. Their conversation was so serious, and yet, the sight of him in his tight-as-sin jeans and open button-up shirt showcasing his carved muscles, with that sparkly, purple dildo still clutched in his hand, it was all Oliver could do not to laugh, despite how pissed off he was.

"That's not what's happening. Do you know where I went yesterday when you decided to just take off, even after everything that has happened?"

Oliver glanced away, guilt growing inside him even though he still felt right, and he'd found something when he was at the bookshop. He'd been able to tap into some ability of his, some latent power that had allowed him to track Poe. He was sure of it.

"No, I don't know where you were," he muttered sullenly and then met Priest's gaze again. "You didn't say where you were going in your little note that you left. You were just gone, and I decided that if no one else would find Poe, I would."

"Oliver," Priest said between clenched teeth. "We're all concerned about Poe. You cannot even begin to understand the concern we have about people being kidnapped. But that doesn't mean you can just—"

"Wait," Oliver interrupted, leaning forward slightly. "What do you mean, *people*? Who else is missing?"

Priest went to rub his hands through his hair and nearly poked out his own eye with the dildo. Seeming surprised to find it still in his hand, he tossed it aside and gestured at Oliver emphatically. "That is what I'm trying to tell you. Yesterday, I got a call. There was another attack. This time, on a law firm run by humans that were publicly supportive of supernatural rights."

Oliver's stomach twisted, and he thought he was going to be sick for a second. "They attacked somewhere else?" he said slowly, clarifying despite having heard Priest perfectly fine.

"Yes, little human, they attacked somewhere else. Two

people are dead, and the son of one of the senior partners is missing, presumed taken."

Oliver covered his mouth with both hands. Tears burning his eyes, he shook his head furiously. "Why are they doing this?"

Priest's entire body sagged, and then he threw his hands out to the side. "We don't know. Not for sure. There haven't been any ransom demands. No one's claimed responsibility for the attacks. No manifestos have been printed online or sent to any news outlets. Whoever these people are, they have an agenda, but they don't want us to know what it is yet, and that's even more terrifying than if they were screaming it from the rooftops."

"Why?" Oliver whispered between his fingers.

"Because this is large-scale. This isn't just one or two bad actors pissed off and striking out because they feel like humans who support supernaturals are traitors. This is a well-funded, well-organized group of people with a goal, one that they've probably been working toward for a lot longer than any of us could possibly imagine, and what that goal is might be bigger and more terrifying than any hypotheses we can make right now. There is too much we don't know and very little we do know."

Oliver swallowed and swiped at the damp skin beneath his eyes.

Priest's face softened. "I don't want you to be even more scared, but you need to take this seriously."

He nodded. "I am. I have been since the beginning, but I can't abandon Poe."

"No one is asking you to. We're going to go stay with a Hoard I know. One of the Dragons there, he can help you learn how to harness your abilities."

"Really?" Oliver asked, a little skeptical. "You just happen to know a Hoard of Dragons that's isolated and more secure who's willing to take us in *and* someone there can help me learn about my Angel abilities?"

Priest shrugged and scrubbed at the back of his neck. "I know a lot of people."

It took Oliver a second to realize that his sex Demon was embarrassed at the fact that he had a lot of friends, or at least a lot people he knew well enough he could ask for a favor like this and they'd give it to him immediately based on the fact a day hadn't even passed.

"Okay," Oliver said slowly, running all of the information through his head and trying to see a bigger picture or at least a clearer one, but there were too many holes. "While we're off learning how I can become a better Angel or whatever—" Priest snorted but waved his hand silently, asking him to continue. "—what will the rest of your team be doing? Is there a plan?"

Priest tipped his hand back and forth in the air. "Sort of. At this point, it's all about running down possible leads, finding a connection between you or Poe and the people in the law office, specifically the senior partner or his son, seeing if we can figure out why these two businesses and groups of people were targeted. Were you mentioned in the same article or news story, blog post, social media post? Anything like that."

"Okay. That sounds good." Sounded more than good. Oliver hadn't even considered that aspect of it. Sure, he and Poe weren't overtly vocal in their support of Supernaturals, but they also hadn't kept it a secret, so who knew how they had ended up on the list to get targeted. "Why were we targeted first?"

Priest scratched his jaw, eyes lifted toward the ceiling as he considered the question. "It's hard to say. It might've been convenience. It might've been easier because it was a smaller building, so it was more of a test run before they hit the larger law firm. It could be because there is some sort of personal connection between you and this group or Poe and them, and it could also be that you weren't the first attack. You're just the first one we know about. That'll be something else the team digs into, seeing if there's anything else we've missed over the last few months no matter how minor."

"That's a lot of research," Oliver said quietly.

"It is, and then we'll also probably have some of the other teams working on it. I think Jeremiah is going to assign the Bravo Team to the physical evidence."

Oliver wrinkled his brow. "What physical evidence? There wasn't anything left at the scene."

Priest smiled at him. "There was plenty left. Traces of magic, the explosives that were used, possible footprints. Some of the blood that Knight picked up on could belong to someone other than Poe if he was able to defend himself when he was grabbed. He could have injured one of them. They'll be doing all the lab work, running down where parts could have been purchased from, figuring out what spells could have been used, things like that."

Oliver felt foolish.

He had been so sure he was the only one taking things seriously, that Priest and his team didn't actually really care about one missing human when they had royals and senators and celebrities to protect, and yet, here Priest was, laying out a half dozen next steps he and his people would be taking, and all Oliver had planned on doing was following his instincts.

Not just following them—he'd been *sprinting* toward them, so sure that he would find Poe on the other end of whatever had been pulling him along, but what would he have done then? He had no idea where Poe could be, what kind of building he might be in, how many of these assholes would be with him, or how well armed they might be. And what if he wasn't in the country anymore? They could have taken him outside of the Siren kingdom into any number of more anti-Supe countries, some of them thousands of miles away. Was he going to run that entire distance?

"We don't have to leave," he finally said. "I understand now how much you and your team are doing, and it sounds like you need to be here to help. I promise I won't take off again."

Priest shook his head. "I appreciate you saying that, but even with the warding on the house, I don't want to take a chance of a group coming here with overwhelming force and stronger magic. I can't risk it. I can't risk you."

"But you're needed here," Oliver said again. "Maybe I should go alone to stay with your friends."

"Absolutely not," Priest said emphatically, marching around the side of the bed until he was towering over Oliver. "I can work on doing research just as easily with the Hoard as from the office here. I can call in when there's meetings. And if need be, I could even fly back, but I'm not sending you off to go stay with a bunch of horny Dragons without me."

Oliver couldn't help but chuckle at that. Sure, Hoards were made up of a group of mates—and Dragons were notorious for the number that they took—but they also didn't just invite *anyone* into their family.

He sobered quickly when he remembered how jealous Priest had gotten the day before when he thought Oliver was going to leave and go to Azriel, and then the first chance Oliver got, he left the safety of his warded house to go gallivant around the scene of the crime and play detective. It was no wonder Priest was feeling insecure.

"You're right. I don't know what I was thinking," he said gently and slowly peeled the sheets off his body, pleased when a solid black ring grew around the outside of Priest's irises.

Sure, they weren't his full Demon eyes, but it was still sexy, and it made him feel more attractive than he ever had before in his life. The fact that just the sight of his bare skin was enough to make an Incubus start to lose control of his lust was a heady feeling.

"When do we have to leave?" He said it casually, acting like he wasn't tracing his collarbones with his fingertips before slowly moving down and circling one of his nipples.

Priest's eyes were locked on where he was touching himself, his chest expanding with deeper breaths as he sucked Oliver's desire right out of the air.

When he didn't say anything, Oliver gave his nipple a pinch and then said a little louder, "Priest, when do we have to leave?"

Priest cleared his throat and said in his low, growly Demon voice, "The plane won't be ready for a few hours."

"Once I know how to use my tracking power, we're coming back, and we're finding Poe."

Priest ripped his gaze away from where Oliver was teasing himself and met his eyes. "I promise."

"Thank you," Oliver said softly and then spread his legs, bending his knees and planting his feet flat on the mattress beneath him.

Priest was on him before he could even begin to tempt him with some sexy, come-hither line. He kissed his way up Oliver's stomach and sternum before beelining over for the same nipple that Oliver had been touching. Using his human tongue on it, he licked over the nub several times and then sucked it into his mouth.

Oliver sank his fingers into his hair, keening softly. "You know, you won't always get to boss me around."

Priest grunted, pushing up for a moment and ripping off his shirt and undoing his pants. Oliver licked his lips, taking in the sight of him. He wasn't big and hulky like the Hellhound that led their team, but he was still ripped and gorgeous. His white skin was a soft tan color, like he spent an odd amount of time out in the sun without any clothes on.

Priest grabbed his legs and pushed them up toward his

chest. Oliver bit his lip to hold back a whimper, knowing exactly what was coming and craving it like nothing he'd ever experienced before.

"Okay. *Outside* the bedroom, you won't get to boss me around."

"Yes, dear," Priest muttered, his voice so low and Demonic it shuddered through Oliver, alighting all of the nerve endings in his body, and then he stroked his tongue over Oliver's hole. "Are you too sore?"

He probably should be, considering the size of Priest. He'd known from his research Incubi were generously endowed, but he hadn't really thought about it in regards to Priest until he'd come face-to-face with all ten inches of him. But his desire was already building, bubbling inside him like a freshly uncorked bottle of champagne.

"Never," he said, gasping when Priest licked over his entrance once more. "You can have me whenever you want, however you want, anytime you need."

Priest growled against him. Oliver shuddered and moaned at the sensation, meeting Priest's gaze when he lifted his head to look at him. His eyes were completely black now, his Demon just beneath the surface.

"You shouldn't say things like that to a Demon like me."

Oliver gripped the sides of his face, making sure he had his full attention. "I'm not saying them to a Demon *like* you. I'm saying them *to* you. Because I trust you, and I know you would never take advantage of that."

"I won't," he said, and then he looked back down, his forked tongue appearing as he stared at Oliver's entrance. He glanced up at him once more and said, "You might want to keep hanging on to me."

And then he was devouring Oliver once more, just like he had the night before, using that deliciously dexterous tongue to tease him inside and out, over and over.

All Oliver could do was clutch at Priest's hair and hang

on, moaning and begging for more, even when he thought it was too much. The ecstasy building inside him was almost terrifying in its intensity.

Priest didn't stop like he had the night before though. He just kept going until he found the perfect rhythm of fucking his tongue into his hole, rubbing against his prostate, and then drawing it back out again, fast, driving Oliver out of his mind.

He didn't realize he was crying until after he came, screaming Priest's name and shooting come all over himself. Priest extracted his tongue and reached up, gently wiping the wetness away and bringing his fingers to his mouth to lick clean.

When he started to push inside, Oliver's body couldn't handle it. He was so oversensitive from his orgasm he immediately whimpered and shook his head.

Priest shushed him, stroking his thighs and not moving. "Just this much," he groaned, only the head of his cock breaching Oliver.

He nodded wobbly. "Yeah, just that much."

Priest wrapped a hand around his shaft and jerked himself, staring at where he disappeared inside Oliver's body. Oliver couldn't take his eyes off him. His straining muscles and glistening skin, the barest peek of fangs behind his panting lips.

He was so gorgeous.

When liquid heat splashed against his insides, Oliver moaned, finally letting his legs relax. He mewled pathetically when Priest gripped the back of his thighs and kept them in place, dipping down and using his slender tongue to gently push his come back inside Oliver's aching body. If he had even an ounce of strength left, he was sure he would get hard again just from the feeling.

Once he was satisfied, Priest crawled up to him, plastering himself to Oliver's front, pressing the softest of kisses right over Oliver's thudding heart, and then resting his head on his chest. Oliver caressed his shoulders and neck, scratching at his scalp and just lounging, enjoying the feeling of his fucked-out body and the amazing Demon who had brought him so much pleasure.

He thought maybe Priest had fallen back asleep and was considering taking a short snooze himself before repacking the overflowing duffel bag when Priest said quietly, "I have to protect you. I have to do everything in my power to keep you safe because I don't think I could live in this world without you now that I know how perfect we are together."

Tears burned at the back of his eyes. Oliver stroked his hair, murmuring soft, encouraging words, letting him know he understood.

And he really did. He didn't know how he could feel the same way, that his entire existence was now bound to this sexy and endearingly awkward sex Demon. It should have been terrifying.

But as he lay there, sweat drying on his skin and heart finally slowing, he realized it wasn't scary at all.

It just felt... inevitable.

13

PRIEST

$\mathcal{T}$he flight to the Dragons' lair was mostly silent, just him and Oliver curled up together watching a silly comedy and a few members of Bravo Team stoic in the rear of the plane. He wasn't sure about his sleepy human, but his own subdued nature came down to the fact that he couldn't focus on anything beyond Oliver and their connection.

And that was terrifying.

Especially when he couldn't be sure Oliver wouldn't change his mind again and go off on his own. Rationally, he knew Oliver was smart—brilliant, even—and that he understood the dangers now that he hadn't before. And he'd promised Priest, just as Priest had him, that they were in this together.

But his Demon wanted to lock Oliver in a tower and keep him safe from the whole world, including his own impulsivity. His rampant possessiveness may just be the thing that finally drove him over the edge and into madness despite the fact he felt more levelheaded than he could ever remember and barely had any twinges of hunger after gorging himself on his sweet-but-not-quite-human beloved.

He was grateful when they finally landed at a small,

private airport about thirty minutes from the Dragons' house. The Bellona Mountains loomed around them, dark storm clouds rolling in from the west, teasing them with the occasional drop.

Their ride was already there waiting for them, the bright orange SUV with tinting so dark even he couldn't see through it saved them from the inevitable downpour.

Priest opened the door to the back seat, cringing as the eardrum-rupturing bass hit his sensitive ears. He put an arm in front of Oliver to stop him from climbing in, a wince on his face. Pounding on the driver's window, he threw his hands up in exasperation when Rorick lowered it and just stared at him.

"Turn it down, asshole," Priest snarled, letting his eyes go black. "I'm not going to let you ruin Oliver's hearing because your Hoard lets you get away with being a prick."

Rorick held his gaze as he reached over with one heavily tattooed arm and cranked the volume down to barely audible. "There you go, princess. Now, are you getting in, or do you need to remove the stick that's up your ass before you can comfortably sit?"

Priest stared at the Dragon. He had half a mind to drag Oliver back to the plane and take him to one of their safe houses instead. Rorick didn't move a muscle, his handsome face completely stoic, with just the faintest glimmer of orange in his irises.

Of all the Dragons in the Hoard, he was, by far, Priest's least favorite. His attitude was always grumpy, to say the least, sometimes bordering on hostile. When Priest had spent time with the Hoard while he was babysitting the Siren crown prince's siblings, he'd rarely seen Rorick. The man hadn't been interested in socializing or spending time with him or the young twins, whereas the rest of the Hoard had fawned over them and loved on them like they were little baby Dragons and not half-human, half-siren prince and princess.

Priest knew enough about the Hoard's past to understand *why* Rorick was a giant asshole. But he didn't appreciate the general hostility he was getting from him and wasn't sure he wanted to subject Oliver to it, even for the short drive to the Hoard's house. Sensing his mood shift, Oliver put a hand on his forearm and gave him a light squeeze, stepping in close next to him.

"Thank you for coming to pick us up," Oliver said cheerfully, giving the stoic Dragon a wide smile. "And we truly appreciate you and your mates taking us in temporarily."

Rorick grunted and tipped his chin up slightly, giving Oliver the barest of recognition. Then he turned forward, gazing out of the windshield like he didn't care one way or the other whether they got in the car or not.

Oliver tugged on his arm a little, and Priest relented, giving him a hand up into the back seat and then quickly following him in. The door had barely closed, and Rorick took off, driving faster than Priest was comfortable with, but he knew if he said anything, the Dragon would probably just ignore him. So instead, he hurriedly fastened Oliver's seat belt around him and gave him a tight smile.

Oliver's returning smile was soft and amused. He reached up and caressed Priest's face lightly, holding his gaze for a long moment. Warmth swelled in Priest's chest, affection and something deeper and scarier tickling at the back of his brain.

"For fuck's sake," Rorick growled. "Keep it in your pants until we at least get to the house. Fucking Incubus."

The last part was muttered so softly Oliver definitely didn't catch it, but Priest did, his spine straightening and shoulders going back. It wasn't like he could control his Demon when Oliver was so near to him and offering him such easy affection. His hold on his other side had been tenuous at best long before his little human came into his life. Now, it was all he could do not to mount and feed on him every chance he got.

Clearing his throat, Oliver slipped his hand into Priest's and turned forward. "I've never visited a Dragon Hoard before," he said conversationally. "Though I've read about them extensively. Is there specific etiquette I should be aware of?"

Rorick looked at him in the rearview mirror and then back at the road. Raindrops started coming down harder, the automatic wipers turning on. The music was low but still throbbing in the speakers.

Priest's hackles began to rise at his beloved being ignored, and then Rorick finally spoke.

"No, there's no specific etiquette. We are happy to have you as guests in our home."

The words didn't exactly ring true, and Priest had a feeling Caspian was behind them. No doubt, he had reminded Rorick of that before sending him to fetch them. Priest wished the geneticist could have been the one to pick them up, but it had been too short of notice for him to get out of something for work. He promised he would meet with them as soon as he was finished though, his lab conveniently located in the basement of the Hoard's house.

"And we really do appreciate it," Oliver said hurriedly, ignoring Rorick's tone and general leave-me-the-fuck-alone demeanor.

"We really do," Priest muttered when Oliver elbowed him and gave him a pointed look.

All the Dragon did was grunt at them again.

An amazing conversationalist.

"How many are in your Hoard?" Oliver asked after a few minutes of silence.

Priest winced, giving his hand a quick squeeze and then shaking his head subtly when Oliver glanced at him.

"Oh, I mean…"

Rorick cleared his throat. "There's five of us, but you'll only meet four."

Oliver sent him a confused look, brows scrunched adorably, and Priest tried to convey silently that he would tell him later and to not prod at that particular subject anymore.

Taking the hint, Oliver asked, "Do you enjoy being able to fly over the mountains? It must be a lovely view."

Rorick shrugged. "It's fine."

Priest rolled his eyes, deciding to step in before Rorick strained something. "I know Flint and Tamir like to go out quite often." He'd learned that during his last visit. Flint was an executive chef at a fancy restaurant, but any chance he got, he was in the sky with one or more of his mates. Tamir owned his own garage, mostly restoring classic cars, which gave him a flexible schedule. "Tamir also really likes to hunt in his Dragon form."

Oliver turned to him, looking grateful. "That must be so fun."

"I hope you like venison," Rorick muttered from the front seat.

Oliver looked between the two of them, obviously not sure if that was a joke or not, but just smiled once more. "Yes, of course. I'm not picky."

He and Oliver kept up a light conversation the rest of the way, with Rorick barely participating, though his frostiness seemed to have thawed out a little bit at Oliver's easygoing demeanor and earnest way of asking questions. As they turned around the last bend and the Dragons' home came into view, Priest smiled at Oliver's sharp intake of breath.

Even with how dark the sky had gotten—thanks to the storm now in full force and the rain hindering some of the view—the size and majesty of the Hoard's home couldn't be denied, especially as most of the windows were lit up from the inside, glowing softly like a beacon welcoming them in.

Rorick veered to the left and hit a button on his dash that opened one of the garage doors. He pulled the SUV in, parking between five motorcycles clustered together and a bright yellow sports car that *maybe* would fit three out of four of the Hoard members. There was another SUV parked on the other side of the garage and bicycles mounted on the wall closest to them. As they stepped out, Priest noted the kayaks hanging from the ceiling.

Everything inside the space pointed to a family that enjoyed doing activities together.

Priest grabbed their bags from out of the back, waving Rorick off when he made a half-hearted effort to try and grab one. They followed the Dragon through the garage, a roll of Hoard rumbling around them as the garage door slowly lowered.

They went into the house through a door that brought them into a large mudroom filled with coats and boots and umbrellas. Rorick paused, leaning down to untie his black boots before kicking them off. Oliver glanced at him, and Priest nodded, quickly toeing off his own and using his feet to slide them out of the way.

Dragons were particular about their homes, despite what Rorick had said about not having any particular etiquettes. It was considered rude to wear your shoes while inside, and Priest had learned the hard way the first time he was there with the twins. The shocked and disbelieving looks had made his skin crawl, and he'd been quick to remedy his mistake.

If they would have come in through the front door, they would have walked into the grand entrance. Marble floors, high vaulted ceilings, and two staircases that led up to the second floor. But coming in through the mudroom, you got dumped right into the kitchen. It was grand in its own way and extremely spacious, but it had to be to feed a Hoard of Dragons.

But it was also lived-in and functional, unlike some of the other parts of the house that felt like they were more for display. Dragons could be arrogant about *things*, caring more about material goods than they probably should sometimes.

But they valued nothing more than their mates, their families, so the parts of their homes that were used most often were comfortable and cozy.

Oliver made a startled noise next to him, his gaze glued on the tall, umber-skinned man dicing vegetables at the kitchen island. "Storm?"

Priest laughed, and Flint did as well.

"I get that a lot," the chef said, not slowing down his chopping even as he smiled at Oliver, his knife going a mile a minute. "My brother and I do look an awful lot alike."

Oliver gazed at him with wide eyes, and Priest shrugged. "I told you I knew them."

He slapped at Priest's arm. "You could have mentioned they were family." He grinned at Flint. "It's so nice to meet you. I've only met your brother a handful of times when he was dragging this one out of my..." His voice faltered, his entire demeanor changing in the blink of an eye, his grief so thick Priest could scent it on the air. "Um, m-my shop."

Flint gave him a sympathetic look. "We heard about what happened. I'm so sorry. All that knowledge just lost. It's devastating to the entire supernatural community, but I can't even imagine how you must feel, especially with your friend missing."

Oliver blinked quickly and looked away, swiping beneath one of his eyes and clearing his throat. "At least I still have Poe. We'll find him." He met Priest's eyes, his expression full of fear and longing. "We have to find him."

Priest cupped his face, uncaring what the Dragons thought. "We will."

He and Oliver stared at each other, sharing the moment, breathing each other in and letting the feeling of their skin connecting soothe them both. Rorick groaned behind them, and Flint chuckled.

"Oh, Ro, leave them be. Don't you remember what it was like to be newly mated?"

Oliver started choking on nothing, his face turning beet red, and Priest's heart fell to the floor. Was the idea of being mated to him so horrifying? He thought... Well, he supposed it didn't matter what he'd thought.

He let his hands drop, and he took a step away as Flint hurried to fill a glass and hand it to Oliver. "Sorry, I shouldn't have blurted it out like that."

Oliver waved a hand in the air after taking a long sip. "No, it just caught me by surprise. We haven't..." He glanced at Priest, his smile shy. "We haven't really talked about... you know, everything."

"There's no rush," Flint assured them, clapping Oliver on the shoulder briefly and then rounding the kitchen island once more, gesturing Rorick toward him with a quick flick of his fingers.

Rorick grumbled but complied, not stopping until he was pressed against Flint's front, wrapping his tattooed arms around his mate and taking a deep breath before letting it out noisily.

"Were you polite to our guests?"

Rorick grunted in reply, and Flint chuckled again.

"He was fine, lovely even," Oliver quickly said.

"You don't have to cover for him," Flint said, smiling fondly at the top of Rorick's head.

Rorick ignored them, keeping his face buried in his mate's neck.

"He really is quite sweet once you get to know him though. He can just be a little prickly with new people."

"I'm right here," he grunted.

"Of course you are, dear," Flint said. "Tamir's out back, fiddling with one of the ATVs. Why don't you two go for a quick flight before dinner?"

Rorick was already speed-walking toward the large glass doors that led to the back patio.

"No hunting," he called after him. "Both freezers are already full to capacity."

Rorick waved a hand in the air and then disappeared outside. There was a flash of lightning, followed almost immediately by a rumble of thunder.

Oliver looked at Priest and then Flint. "Is it safe for them to fly in a storm like this?"

Flint laughed, and Priest had to press his lips together to stop from chuckling himself.

"Dragons are pretty hardy," Flint told him, his perfectly white teeth almost blinding from across the room. "Even if they somehow managed to get themselves struck by lightning, it wouldn't penetrate their scales."

"Whoa," Oliver whispered. "That's so cool."

Priest bristled. "Demons are pretty cool too, you know."

Snorting, Flint went back to chopping his vegetables, a huge slab of meat waiting next to the grill top. Priest knew he was being ridiculous, but the words had flown out before he could stop them. He didn't want Oliver admiring any other supernaturals or their abilities.

Oliver leaned against his side and tipped his head back so their faces were only inches apart. "Of course they are. In fact, there's one in particular I'm quite fond of."

He hoped *fond of* meant *wished to be mated to*.

Now that Flint had broken the seal on that word and Priest was finally letting himself acknowledge the possibility, it was all he and his Demon could focus on. He wanted that. He wanted Oliver by his side for the rest of his life, caring for him, and protecting him, and feeding off him.

When he didn't respond, Oliver scrunched his eyebrows at him.

Priest cleared his throat, smiled as best he could, and said to Flint, "Is Caspian still working downstairs?"

Flint nodded. "He'll probably be at least another half an

hour. He had some conference call that he had to hop on, but once that's wrapped up, he'll be done for the day. Dinner won't be ready for an hour or so. If you guys want to head up, we made up the same guest room you were in last time, Priest."

That sounded like a great idea. He needed to chill for a minute before subjecting himself to the entire Hoard. He gave Oliver a more genuine smile. "Let's go get settled in. You can meet Caspian and Tamir at dinner."

Oliver studied his face for a moment, then gave a half shrug and turned to Flint. "Thank you again for letting us stay."

"Of course," Flint said. "Like you said, the Alpha Team is family, even when my brother would prefer us not to be," he added with a wry grin.

Priest led the way out of the kitchen, and as soon as they were out of earshot, Oliver slipped his fingers between Priest and whispered, "What did he mean? Why does Storm sometimes wish you guys weren't considered family by his brother's Hoard?"

He considered what he should say since it wasn't really his story to tell but then decided Storm would understand him sharing with his... future mate. "He has a complicated relationship with his siblings and parents. Flint is the only one he speaks to on a regular basis. His parents won't talk to him at all, and his other siblings only on holidays or when something major happens."

Oliver made a sympathetic noise. "Family can be complicated, that's for sure."

Priest wouldn't know, but he decided not to bring that up. They weren't talking about him and his childhood of growing up on the streets, in and out of foster homes, until he met Jeremiah and the two of them teamed up to keep each other safe. And then, when they were a little older, they found a newly turned Knight, so traumatized from the unspeakable things that had happened to him he was barely functioning.

"You know how Dragons always have multiple mates, right?" Priest said, leading them up one side of the grand staircase.

Oliver's eyes were on the mural on the ceiling, twenty-five feet above them. "Right. Hoards are a minimum of three mates, though usually five to six is more common."

He rattled off the information like he was reciting it from a book, which he probably was. Priest wasn't sure why he found that adorable as fuck, but he did.

"Well, Storm… he's not interested in having more than one mate."

Oliver whipped his head around, nearly stumbling on the next step. "He doesn't want more than one mate?"

"No," Priest said clearly, "and when he told his parents…"

"They disavowed him," Oliver finished for him.

"Essentially. He's not welcome in his parents' home anymore. His mothers and fathers are unwilling to bend in their belief that it's just a phase."

Oliver shook his head, his lip curled up in disgust. "How anyone could think that about their own child…"

"It's more common than you'd think. Humans aren't the only ones who can be intolerant," Priest said, thinking about him and Jeremiah both being cast aside as children. And so many others they encountered in the same circumstances. "Anyway, that's why he sometimes prefers to keep the Alpha Team—his chosen family—away from his brother's Hoard."

"Even though Flint accepts him for who he is?"

"He didn't at first, but eventually, he came around," Priest said, leading him down the hallway in the opposite direction of the Hoard's bedroom on the other side of the house. "They've talked a lot, and I think Flint's mates have also helped him, especially after what happened."

"What do you mean?" Oliver asked.

Priest found the bedroom he'd used the last time he was in the house. The door was cracked open, and a warm light was on inside. He pushed it the rest of the way open and stepped back so Oliver could go in first. He followed right behind and kicked the door shut behind him, dropping their bags at the foot of the enormous bed that was taking up the majority of the large room.

"They had a fifth mate," Priest said, his voice stark. "They don't talk about what happened to him, and Storm has never told us. I don't know if he even knows the details. I don't think they even know if he's dead or alive."

Oliver clapped his hands over his mouth. "Dear gods, they don't know if he's alive?"

"I don't think so. According to Storm, that's why Rorick is as standoffish as he is. He was the closest to their lost mate, and he was never able to get past it. Not that the others have moved on, but they've found a way to cope. Rorick… he's stuck."

"That's so sad," Oliver whispered. "I can't even imagine."

Priest couldn't either. Now that he had found Oliver, he couldn't imagine losing him. Not knowing where he was or what was happening with him, if he was safe or if he was scared and in pain.

The not knowing would be worse than knowing for sure he'd never see him again.

Oliver sniffled and held his arms out. "Will you lay with me for a little while? I just… I need to hold you after hearing that for some reason. I need us to be as close as possible."

Priest's Demon rumbled in his chest. "I need that too, little human."

14

OLIVER

"*Y*ou're part Angel, alright," Caspian said, peering at one of his large monitors through his thick-rimmed glasses. His wavy hair looked a little overgrown, and there was at least two days' worth of stubble on his face, but he still managed to make the look *work*.

"Was that really in doubt?" Priest asked, trying to peer over his shoulder. Oliver wasn't sure why he was bothering. He'd learned over dinner the night before that the Dragon had not one but *two* PhDs and was a geneticist. There was no way either one of them would be able to understand the results of the tests Caspian had run overnight.

"In doubt? No," Caspian said, scrolling through whatever information was on his screen. "But I don't like to deal with assumptions. I like to know all of the facts so I can build the appropriate parameters for the experiment."

"Experiment?" Oliver said loudly, drawing both of their attention to where he was leaning over the continental map spread out on one of Caspian's workstations. He was supposed to be focusing on it to see if he could pinpoint where Poe might be, but he hadn't gotten so much as a tingle in his toes so far.

Caspian glanced over at him, a tiny frown between his brows. He was the palest of his mates, a smattering of freckles on his cheeks the only real color. Both he and Rorick were white, but it was clear Caspian spent *far* less time outside in the sun. Their other mate, Tamir, had a tawny skin tone somewhere between Flint's dark umber and Rorick's taupe.

"'Experiment' might have been the wrong word," Caspian conceded slowly, tugging at the bottom of his sweater vest. "'Testing' would be more accurate in this case. Either way, your angelic friend, Azriel, was right. Somewhere in your recent lineage, a fallen Angel bred a human."

Oliver scrunched up his face. "Bred? Really? That's gross."

Priest spun around, but Oliver still heard his muffled snickering.

"And since then," Caspian continued, not acknowledging either one of them. Oliver had a feeling he was used to interruptions from his mates and was unfazed by them. "From one generation to the next, the angelic blood was there, building in the background. Unlike other supernatural creatures, the more angelic DNA mixes with human, the stronger it becomes."

Eyes feeling like they might fall out of his head, Oliver stared at him. "So, like, I'm stronger than Azriel?"

Caspian shook his head. "Not at this point, but who knows what could happen with concentration and training."

He looked over at Priest. His Demon was staring at him, just as shocked. Oliver knew a lot of supernaturals in passing, thanks to his shop, but it was easy to tell that Azriel was by far the strongest. He *radiated* with power, casting out an aura that could either set you completely at ease or make your skin crawl with agitation, depending on his mood.

"And because of the co-mingling of species," Caspian continued, his attention once more on his computer, "we won't know until your powers fully manifest what they are."

"Well, he can teleport—at least short distances," Priest offered.

Crossing his arms over his chest, Oliver rolled his eyes. "But I didn't do that on purpose. I have no idea how I did it. If you weren't so sure it happened, I'd say you imagined it."

"Oh, it definitely happened," Priest assured him, striding across the lab. "And he has gut feelings that are usually right, including that his friend was still alive before we even realized he'd been taken."

His face began to heat for some reason, like Priest was bragging about him instead of just listing off what they knew so far.

Wrapping an arm around his shoulders, Priest gave him a quick squeeze. "And then Oliver could feel Poe when he was where Poe had been taken, like a hook drawing him to wherever he is."

Caspian was typing quickly and nodding along as Priest recited the facts. "Anything else?"

Priest looked at him expectantly, but Oliver shook his head. "Not that we know of."

"We'll start there, then."

"This isn't working," Oliver said, shoving at the map so that it slid halfway across the table, the top half of the continent hanging precariously over the edge. He squeezed his eyes shut and slammed his fist down twice and then stood there, shoulders hunched, head lowered, palms pressed onto the tabletop.

Whatever abilities he'd tapped into outside of the bookshop must have been a onetime thing because he'd been trying for a week, and nothing had happened. Occasionally he thought he could detect the faintest hum or buzzing, but then it would disappear just as quickly, and he was now convinced he'd been imagining it. He was a fraud. He was the reason they were never gonna find Poe. He was—

Strong arms wrapped around him from behind.

"It's not useless, and you're not powerless. A month ago, you didn't even know about this side of you." Priest's words were low, said right into his ear and calming. Or maybe that was his presence. Just having him near was enough to dial back his ire most days. And the longer they spent holed up with the Dragons, the faster it happened and the easier it seemed to be.

"What if they're hurting him?" he whispered into the quiet of Caspian's lab.

The Dragon had disappeared hours ago, probably off canoodling with one or more of his mates. Oliver was grateful Priest was the only one seeing him lose his cool and finally voicing the concern he'd had ever since he'd known for sure that Poe really was alive.

"What if..." He couldn't say it. He couldn't finish the sentence.

Priest's arms tightened around him. "What if he's not alive anymore?" Priest asked delicately.

Oliver nodded, tears squeezing out behind his lids. Just the idea of a world without his best friend in it felt like a punch to the solar plexus, like he couldn't breathe and his whole body wanted to collapse in on itself.

"Just because he was taken alive doesn't mean he's still... And even if he is, what are the chances they aren't torturing him?"

Priest didn't respond for a moment, and Oliver appreciated that. He didn't want Priest to simply placate him, tell him everything was going to be okay and give him a pat on the head. This was real, and it was dangerous, and he needed to know what Priest actually thought.

"We think he's still alive," Priest said, speaking carefully, and Oliver had to wonder what kind of information he'd been receiving from his regular updates from Jeremiah and Knight. "Taking someone against their will—that's more difficult than you might think. If all they wanted to do was kill him, they wouldn't have bothered to take him."

Oliver choked back a whimper, and Priest's fingers flexed against his abs.

"Same with the lawyer's son; they took him, blew up the building, and left the other two to die."

"And the others?" Oliver prompted. He'd overheard part of a conversation between Priest and the rest of Alpha Team the other night. He knew there had been more attacks.

"Same with the others. One other location had a casualty as well as a missing person. They're being very selective in who they take, which means they have some sort of plan. And they haven't asked for ransom or to negotiate with the families or the royals."

"But they could still be hurting them?" Oliver asked, even as that information eased a little more of the tension in his body.

"They could be," Priest said, not sugarcoating it. "It's very possible, though the purpose of taking multiple people just for the sake of torture doesn't make sense."

"Maybe they're just a bunch of psychos," Oliver muttered.

Priest gave him a squeeze and then stepped back, turning Oliver to face him and cupping the sides of his neck. He pressed his thumbs beneath the edge of Oliver's chin and pushed his face up, forcing him to meet his gaze. "They aren't just a bunch of psychos."

Oliver sighed. "I know."

One side of Priest's mouth went up in a small smile, and he said, not for the first time, "They have a plan. They're professionals. That means they have an endgame. They're not just causing harm to cause harm."

Oliver took a deep breath in through his nose and then let it out noisily through his mouth, trying to shake the last of the anxiety out of his body. "You're right. I know you're right. I'm just so fucking frustrated. I can't seem to control my powers at all, if I even have any."

Priest gave him an unimpressed look. "You have them. Most Supes spend years figuring out how to control themselves and any abilities that they might have, and that's after knowing your whole life you'll grow into the abilities. How long did Caspian say it took him to learn how to fly?"

It was Oliver's turn to roll his eyes. "Three months."

"Three months just to stay off the ground for over a minute," Priest corrected. "It took him two years to be comfortable flying at any altitude or distance that he needed."

Oliver had a feeling Caspian was the exception, that his intellectual brain had possibly hindered him in following his Dragon's instincts, but he'd appreciated what had passed for a pep talk from the scientist.

"Poe doesn't have two years," Oliver said.

"I know, which is why we aren't only depending on you," Priest reminded him, leaning in and pressing his forehead against Oliver's, the soft contact nearly melting the bones in his body. "My team and the Bravo Team are making progress. I know it's not as fast as you want, but we should have answers within the next week or so."

Another week. He wasn't sure he'd be able to handle that. The Dragons were wonderful, fed them well, kept them entertained, had all kinds of activities to try and distract him—everything from board games to SUVs that had been modified to go up the mountain.

But being unable to leave? Not being able to run down the mountain and back into the city, to go back to the bookshop and follow whatever instinct had tried to lead him to Poe, it was killing a little piece of him. No matter how much he loved being able to spend time with Priest, curled up in his arms at night, working on trying to harness his powers during the day, and everything in between.

He couldn't take much more of it.

"Let's take a break," Priest said, like he could read Oliver's mind. "Maybe we should go watch a movie or take the bikes out for a ride, get some fresh air."

Oliver considered those options and then shook his head. "I have a better idea."

He slipped free from Priest's hold but then held out his hand. Priest took it, entwining their fingers, and let Oliver lead him up to the main floor and then up the staircase into the bedroom they'd been given for their stay.

Priest closed the door behind him and leaned back against it, his eyes already beginning to darken. Oliver was pretty sure he was starting to be able to sense when Priest's powers grew, filling the air around them with lust and desire, heightening the feelings he already had.

He held his eyes, slowly stripping out of his clothes and tossing them aside. Climbing up onto the bed, he scooted back until he was in the middle, propped up on his elbows.

"Help me forget for a while," Oliver whispered.

They hadn't turned a light on, but the large, south-facing windows allowed the cheery blue sky to provide plenty of illumination, allowing Oliver to see every detail as Priest followed his lead, holding his gaze as he got rid of his own clothing and then prowled up the bed until he hovered over Oliver's body.

"We'll find him," Priest said, his quiet voice sounding loud in their silent bedroom, but the words sank into Oliver, beneath his skin and muscles, directly into the marrow of his bones.

Priest wasn't just telling him something to make him feel better. He meant it. He *believed* it. He would do everything in his power to make sure it came true.

"I know." Oliver fell back against the mattress, spreading his arms and legs, welcoming his lust Demon easily. "I believe you."

Priest's eyes darkened further, not completely black, but the whites were a dark gray, haunting in their beauty. He knew from his readings that Demons—Incubi especially— had been ostracized for over a century, even within the supernatural community. He knew their black eyes were feared, but all Oliver felt when he saw them was safe.

Well, that and a healthy dose of lust.

Priest closed the distance between them, taking his mouth in a deep, lingering kiss. Neither one of them was in a rush like they usually were when their passions became so heightened they could barely control themselves.

Instead, they spent long minutes tasting each other, Oliver's hands running along Priest's sides as he slowly lowered himself down on top of Oliver's body. In that moment, he knew what it felt like to be consumed.

He also knew he would give everything of himself— including the last spark of his soul—if his Demon asked him for it.

But Priest never would. He would never be so careless or selfish.

The languid kisses went on forever until Priest finally started to move down his body, pausing for achingly drawn-out moments on all his favorite spots. The side of his neck, his collarbones, nipples, and the small protrusion of his belly button.

Oliver was squirming against the mattress by the time Priest ran his forked tongue up the underside of his cock and then wrapped it around him just beneath his weeping head. He threw his head back, crying out in ecstasy as Priest touched him so gently with his fingertips and took him apart with his lips and teeth and tongue.

Gods, his tongue.

One day, Oliver would write a fucking sonnet about it. Just as he reached the edge, his orgasm building to a fever pitch inside him, Priest stopped, shuffling back up the bed and taking his mouth once more, swallowing his groans of frustration. He kissed him deeply as he slowly fingered Oliver open, preparing his body and driving him mad.

When Priest finally sank inside him, filling him in that delicious, over-the-top way he'd never get enough of, Oliver scraped his nails down his back, and then gripped at his firm ass, pulling at him to try and get him deeper.

Priest hushed him, murmuring to him to relax and just enjoy, but relaxing wasn't something he could do anymore, not when Priest had wound him up so tightly. But he did loosen his grip, doing his best to try and touch every inch of Priest's skin, taste the sweat on his neck, see the lust burning in his black eyes.

He was present in the moment, completely and utterly aware of his Demon in a way he never had been with a partner before. It felt like he was opening his soul to him, allowing him inside his body and all the rest of him, every last corner. All the walls inside him crumbled to the ground, every door thrown open. There was nothing barring Priest from accessing every tiny bit of him.

Groaning, Priest dropped his head down into his neck, and Oliver could faintly feel him begin to siphon off some of his desire, feeding off him, allowing Oliver to sustain him in the most primal way.

It drove his desire even higher, pushing him over the edge. When Priest gave one last hard thrust before spilling inside him, ecstasy washed over Oliver in waves, taking him under and filling him up. He could feel when Priest took one more hard draw from him. And as he did, something shifted inside. It was like the strength of Priest's feeding moved Oliver's insides around, reconfiguring him in a new way and locking things into place that had been displaced.

His eyes slowly opened, and he stared at the ceiling, one hand carding through Priest's hair, the other gently stroking his sweat-slicked back. The euphoria from his orgasm began to fade, but he barely even noticed. He could feel it now, that thing inside him that Priest and Caspian had been talking about all week. A well he could dip into and access pure power. It was thrumming inside him now, exploring every inch beneath his skin, making his toes and fingers tingle.

Priest made a soft grunting noise, not lifting his head from Oliver's neck. "What's that?"

Oliver smiled, eyes still on the ceiling, a strip of sunlight lighting up the pale blue color. "I think I'll be able to find him now."

Priest lifted his head, his eyes sleepy and brow scrunched in confusion. "What?"

Oliver laid a hand over his thrumming heart. "I can feel it now. My power. Let's go get Poe."

15

PRIEST

*T*he last thing in the world Priest wanted was to leave the safety of the Dragons' lair, but he knew they were running up against time. Oliver was coming into his power faster than Priest thought he'd be able to, and now they had something. Not a precise location, but at least a geographical area, which was somewhere to start.

Jeremiah sent him the location to one of their safe houses that was closest to the spot Oliver had pointed on the map, and the next thing Priest knew, the plane was touching down, and he could see Knight waiting for him in the dusky glow of the fading sunset.

He pulled Oliver close before they were ready to disembark and tipped his chin up. Their gazes connected, and Priest could feel his Demon close to the surface of his skin. "Kiss me."

Oliver licked his lips, then pushed up onto his toes and did as he asked. Priest felt a surge of power rush through him, like sparks flicking across his tongue. He drank it in, feeling renewed, and he pulled back to see a glowing light in Oliver's eyes.

Was it a trick from the window?

It was gone before he could work it out.

Priest touched the edge of Oliver's jaw. "Ready?"

"I've been ready for weeks." There was a touch of impatience in Oliver's tone, which Priest understood. He would have felt the same way if any of his brothers had been taken. Knight's captivity had been before Priest had known him, but there were moments he saw the pain in his brother's face and wanted to rip apart the veil between the past and present and save him before he went through his torment.

He hated that he'd been one of the people to get in Oliver's way, and the moment they had Poe safe, he planned to make it up to him. Many times. With tongue.

"I can feel that," Oliver breathed, and he rocked forward, letting Priest feel his thick cock before he shoved his hand in the waistband of his pants and adjusted himself so it wasn't visible. "Stop it."

"I can't help it." Priest's voice was a low growl, and he could feel fangs in his mouth. He took a breath, then caught Oliver's hand and kissed his palm. "He wants you all the time."

"Your Demon?"

Priest nodded, but he pushed back gently until it settled under his skin like a low simmer. He linked their fingers, then led Oliver to the door and gave him a gentle push to disembark first. The wind was warmer and a touch more humid now that they were so close to the water again.

Nowhere had really felt like home, but their offices and his place near the palace in Midlona felt more like it than anywhere else he'd been. He hadn't dropped roots, but he had dropped a few seeds, and he wondered if he'd ever be allowed to see them grow. He could picture a calmer, safer future where Oliver had his shop again and the guys lived nearby.

And there was even room for Azriel in that rosy picture because in spite of the small pricks of jealousy he felt from time to time, the Angel was as close to a best friend Priest had outside of the Alphas. And it helped Azriel already adored Oliver.

"The two of you will have plenty of time for that later," Knight grumbled as Priest ushered Oliver toward the car.

Oliver flushed and ducked his head, and Priest shoved his middle finger at his friend. "We weren't doing anything."

"You forget I can feel it," Knight said, grimacing large enough to show his fangs.

"Oh gods," Oliver groaned.

Priest had no defense against that. Supes could sense when nearby Incubi were hungry, and they could also sense when he was feeding if they were close enough. He sighed and opened the door for Oliver, closing it gently behind him before turning to his friend.

"Why are y—"

"Don't," Knight said, an edge to his tone Priest was unused to. "It's bad enough Sunshine and Remi can't keep it in their fucking pants for more than five minutes."

Priest fought back a laugh. "Well, Remi's young and virile."

Knight turned a little green. He was always wary and uncomfortable around people being physical, and while Priest understood why, he also understood how much it made Knight suffer. He was touch starved and unable to seek what he was so desperately craving except in the most desperate moments.

"We promise to keep it in the bedroom," Priest said, giving his friend a break. "Oliver's more focused on Poe anyway."

"And he's sure this is the place?" Knight looked uneasy.

From the information Jeremiah had put together about

Knight's captivity, they were very near where he'd escaped. Knight's memory of the whole thing was foggy, like someone had scooped massive holes out of his brain, but he remembered enough. Priest and Jeremiah had searched the area for years, trying to find a clue or to get lucky and stumble upon the place he'd been held, but they'd always come up empty.

Until now.

"He seems very certain, and his powers are growing. I trust him, and not just because he's…"

"Your mate?"

Priest flushed. "Demon mates are so rare they might as well be nonexistent. You know this."

"We thought the same thing about Hellhounds," he gently reminded him, raising a brow. "And last I checked, Angels could basically find theirs while unconscious."

"But Nephilim—" Priest started, then stopped.

Oliver wasn't a Nephilim. He was something else—something closer to human but still so powerful, and he could feel his lover's strength growing by the day. He was lucky Oliver wasn't one. Because human and Angel pairings were forbidden—a decree from the gods, not some bigoted government official—and Nephilim were cursed at birth to sense their fated mates but never be able to find them. If they did find them, the mate always found some grisly death.

He shuddered at the thought.

Knight hummed, pulling Priest from his thoughts. "There's something we need to talk about at the safe house."

"About mates?" He scrunched his brows in confusion.

"About all of this. Remi got an email from his ex."

The only ex Remi had was a Nephilim he'd dated at Hillsland University. Priest had only met Ozias briefly when he'd come to check on Remi after the team had recovered him from his kidnapping. He was a renowned scholar, and he could hear other people's thoughts. Rumor was he'd been collared with magic by the university, but Priest didn't buy it. He didn't buy that was even *possible*.

"Alright, let's get on the road."

Knight rolled his eyes when Priest climbed in the back with Oliver and pulled him close. He could sense the tension coming off his beloved in waves; there was no way he could leave him to sit and stew on his own.

Oliver was scared for his friend—scared of what they'd find when they got to Poe and scared for what it meant. Something was obviously brewing. Something beyond some fringe group of fanatics who wanted to kill Supes.

Priest just didn't know how deep it went and how the hell they were going to unravel the increasingly complicated ball of string now that they'd started pulling at all the loose threads.

The safe house was tucked into the woods somewhere near a lake. Priest hadn't been to this one before, but the layout was like the others. It was single story, deceptively large inside, and blended well enough into the surroundings that it was almost impossible to pinpoint from an aerial view. The road leading up to it was slightly wider than an average hiking trail, and they used just enough magic to cloak it and stop anyone from accidently stumbling upon it, but not enough to draw attention.

They had a covered garage for their cars with a mossed roof and tunnel that attached to the side door so none of them were exposed walking outside. There were retinal scanners at each end of the tunnel, and he knew there would be another one they could use to escape if the cars were compromised.

Once upon a time, Priest thought Jeremiah had been a little too paranoid.

Now, with Oliver pressed against his side and so achingly vulnerable, he was grateful for it all.

Knight opened the door ahead of them, and Priest immediately got a whiff of rich spices. Slate was obviously there because he cooked when he was stressed, and Priest couldn't help his excitement because he loved Gargoyle cuisine.

"Remind me to stress him out more often," Priest said as the doorway led directly into the kitchen.

"Fuck off," Slate muttered, not turning away from the stove.

Oliver shot Priest a curious look, and Priest kissed the frown off his lips. "He only plays chef when shit's hitting the fan. So, you know, good and bad."

Slate turned and glowered at Priest, then softened his gaze when he locked eyes with Oliver. He was a very quiet, stoic man who kept his cards close to his chest. But nothing enraged him more than those with power using it to ruin the lives of people who had none.

"There's plenty for you if you're hungry."

Oliver blinked. "Oh. Me?"

Slate's mouth twitched, and he gave a single, regal nod. "Mm."

Priest grinned as Oliver stepped forward and stuck out his hand. "Thank you. I'm Oliver, by the way."

"I know. You're pretty famous around here." They shook hands, and Priest fought the urge to yank Oliver away. A little touching was fine, but it was lingering too long.

Slate eventually pulled back and shot Priest a look rich with understanding. "Go put your shit away. Sunshine's waiting to talk to you. Those of us who didn't get a week vacation with a Dragon Hoard have already been briefed."

Priest growled, but he hurried Oliver along through the archway and down a long corridor. His bedroom anywhere they went was always the second to last on the right, and this was no different. He opened the door and found the layout just the way he liked it. A large bed in the center, blinds drawn, a single dresser, a desk, and a doorway that led to an en suite.

He envisioned a long, hot bath with the two of them later. But for now, they didn't have long to explore. He shoved their cases against the far wall, then pressed Oliver next to the door and cradled his face.

"Tell me how you are."

Oliver rolled his eyes and attempted to push Priest back, but he was either weak from travel or not using his newfound strength to move him because Priest didn't budge. "I'm fine."

"Do you still feel him?"

Oliver closed his eyes, breathed, and the heat of his powers reached out, brushing against Priest. He wanted to drag his fingers through the tendrils, but he was afraid to disrupt his lover. "I can feel him. He's closer. He's..." Oliver opened his eyes and licked his lips. "Something's changed."

"How?"

"I don't know. He just... He feels different. Like he's dying, except he's not." Oliver pinched the bridge of his nose and took a breath. "I don't know what this means."

"It means we're on a short timeline," Priest said. "But we're close, and I don't think we're too late."

"Promise me," Oliver said, his voice trembling and his eyes red-rimmed. "Please."

Priest hated himself for lying because he couldn't actually make that promise. He didn't know who had taken Poe and why. He didn't know what the human had been through and what his life would be like after they got him back. If he'd recover from the weeks of captivity.

But he also couldn't stand seeing Oliver so terrified.

"I promise."

Oliver sagged forward, laughing wetly into the front of Priest's shirt. "I know you don't mean that, but thank you."

Priest kissed the side of his neck, then urged him to

straighten. "Come on. The sooner we're debriefed, the sooner—"

"You can eat?" Oliver teased.

Priest growled and darted forward, nipping at his ear. "The sooner we can get started on our rescue mission, little human."

"Not a little human anymore," Oliver murmured.

Priest smudged a kiss over his jaw. "You will always be my little human. I told you that before, and I meant it. I don't care what you actually become. I only care what you are to me."

The mood in the room was somber. Jeremiah insisted they eat first, which Priest appreciated because now that he was being sated by Oliver, his human appetite was growing. They took their meal in the living room, Oliver pressed against Priest's side. He only picked at his food, but Priest didn't pester him about it.

They made quiet conversation about the Dragons, and Jeremiah seemed to know about the missing mate.

"They asked me to look into it a few years ago," he said as he set his empty plate on the table. "We had a few leads, but they dried up pretty early on."

Priest looked over at Storm. "You helped?"

"My brother didn't want me to at the time," he said quietly. "It probably wouldn't have mattered either way."

Oliver wrapped his arms around his middle. "Losing a mate must be…"

"Hell on earth," Storm answered quietly. He took a beat, then pushed to stand. "I need to go make a couple of phone calls. You don't need me for this, right?"

Jeremiah shook his head. "No. I just need Knight to stay."

It wasn't a dismissal, but both Storm and Slate looked

happy to be dismissed. They filed out of the room, and a moment later, Jeremiah gestured to Knight, who rose from his chair. He paced a little in front of the coffee table, and Priest could see how stressed he was. He was more sallow than ever, and his fingers were shaking.

"There's been something oddly familiar about all of this since the attacks began. Not the attack on Remi," he added, glancing at Jeremiah. "But the shop and Poe going missing. Then, the law office. And now the others."

"Do we think they're connected to what happened to the royals?" Priest asked.

"I think that the attack on Remi was a red herring. I think McCornal was a distraction," Jeremiah said. "The more details I uncover, the less sense it all makes."

Priest frowned. "I mean, he's been the spearhead of the anti-supernatural movement for years."

"Yes, but that sentiment isn't new," Jeremiah said. He rubbed his fingers over his mouth. "A bigot gone too far— it's a tale as old as time. But the timing of it all was... convenient. As the sentencing was happening, the shop was blown up and Poe was taken. But the media was fixed on the trial."

Priest had a sinking feeling in his gut, and he turned to Knight. "What aren't you saying?"

Knight fixed his gaze on Oliver, his eyes more red than they normally were when he wasn't feeding. "I'm sure Priest hasn't told you much about what happened to me."

"It's your story to tell," Priest said.

Knight shot him a grateful smile, but he quickly sobered. He shoved his hands into his pockets, and Priest could see him squeezing his fingers into fists. "I was about as young as Poe when I was taken. I don't remember much of it. Fire. Smoke. Screaming. I was in a fog for... I don't know how long. I was in and out of consciousness. I remember a lab and being poked and prodded. They took what felt like gallons of my blood." His breath trembled. "I was injected with things that made my veins feel like ice and then fire."

"I'm sorry," Oliver whispered.

Knight shook his head. "Eventually, I got away, but I was changed into this." He bared his teeth on the right, showing fang.

"How did you escape?"

Knight rubbed a hand down his face. "I don't know. I used to fantasize about it. I had a thousand different plans, all of them as unrealistic as the other. I came to while I was running through the woods, and I've always suspected that maybe I didn't escape at all. Maybe I was let go once I turned."

Priest hadn't heard this before. His heart was pounding in his chest so hard it felt like it was going to break his ribs. "What are you saying?"

"That this is familiar," Knight repeated. "We're near the lab where I was held. I can feel it. I recognized the trees. The paths. The road."

Jeremiah cleared his throat. "Oz sent Remi a detailed message three days ago saying he was cornered in his office a year ago by a couple of people claiming to be students asking questions about Vampires. He didn't think much of it until the media finally started picking up the stories of the kidnappings."

Priest frowned as Oliver sat forward. "What kind of questions did they have?"

"Strange ones. Like if there's a genetic component to the turn. If there could be a trigger. Absurd because everyone knows—"

"Vampires are created through a virus," Knight finished for him. He swallowed heavily. "But apparently, Oz has been working on a theory that there isn't a virus at all. That it's a latent genetic trait that gets triggered."

Priest stared at Knight. "So your family…"

"I don't know if anyone else in my family has ever turned.

They stopped speaking to me the moment I appeared after the change," Knight said. "I was dead to them, and as far as I know, my name has been erased from the family history. It makes sense they'd do the same to anyone else who turned."

Priest stared down at Oliver's hands. He was wringing them in his lap so hard his knuckles were white. "Does Oz have some idea how to tell or anything?"

"We asked," Jeremiah said. "Remi sent a message back, but it's been total radio silence since then. He's worried."

Priest was too. "Then what's the plan?"

"We raid the lab," Knight said. "We have the advantage of surprise."

"Storm and Slate are already working on an attack on the power grid. We cut all electricity, then go in guns blazing, so to speak," Jeremiah said with a grin that told Priest they wouldn't be using guns but fangs and claws instead. Priest's Demon ached to be able to let loose and draw blood. "We rescue whoever they have in the lab and try to take as many of the workers as we can alive."

"High-ranking ones," Knight said. "People who have information."

Priest nodded, then looked over at Oliver, who was pale. "What's wrong?"

Oliver swallowed heavily. "If what you're saying is true— if it's some sort of Vampire lab, does that mean Poe…"

"Maybe," Jeremiah said at the same time as Knight said, "Most likely."

Oliver looked at Priest. "Maybe that's what I've been feeling. The change in him."

Priest didn't want to believe that was right, but what choice did he have? The coincidence was far too strong.

"It's not the end of the world," Jeremiah said softly. "If he is."

"No. It's just the end of anyone ever being kind to him again," Knight answered bitterly. "But I'm sure he's strong."

"There's not a chance in hell I would ever abandon him," Oliver said fiercely.

Priest turned Oliver's face by the chin and met his gaze, holding it. "He'll also be in the best company. You are mine, so my family is yours, and Poe will always be part of that."

Knight took a step closer and said quietly, "Unlike me, he won't have to figure out his new reality or face his future alone."

16

OLIVER

*O*liver didn't quite know how to process everything he was feeling. He was nervous and starting to feel a little hopeful, which might have been dangerous because if they failed, he wasn't sure how he was going to take it. He was also petrified of being wrong.

What if he'd dragged the Alphas all the way out to the middle of nowhere only to find nothing?

But mostly, he couldn't quite process the idea that Poe might be changed. Irrevocably and permanently. Oliver was more than aware of what it was like for Vampires in society. Their suicide rates were high, which was part of the reason there were so few of them. Like Demons and Hellhounds, they weren't allowed to marry, they weren't allowed to procreate, and they rarely—if ever—had fated mates. They also weren't allowed to hold public service jobs or receive government benefits.

There were only two countries that even welcomed them to own property, but the rules there were strict.

What would it mean for Poe if they found him alive and attempted to rebuild the shop? And while Poe's family were activists, would they accept him?

"Beloved."

Oliver turned and saw Priest hovering in the doorway. He said nothing, just watched as his Demon stepped all the way inside and closed the door behind him. The distance between them felt like miles, and Oliver didn't quite know how to reach out.

"You need to feed before we go, don't you?" he asked.

Priest's eyes widened. "You think I'm here for that?"

"You need your strength." And, at the very least, it would be a distraction from everything Oliver was dealing with. He blinked, and between his eyelids closing and opening again, Priest had moved close to him.

Gods, would he ever get used to that? It wasn't teleporting the way he was supposed to be able to do, but it felt the same.

"I wanted to check on you. You're not my own personal power bank," Priest said. His tone was sharp. He was hurt.

Oliver bowed his head. "I'm sorry. I didn't mean it like that. I want you as strong as possible before we go in there. I don't know what I'd do if something happened to you."

"I'm the strongest I've been in years, little human." Priest gently wrapped his arms around Oliver's waist and pulled him close. The heat of him, the smell, the beat of his heart, it was everything Oliver needed right then. "We're going to be okay."

Oliver nodded. "I know. But when we go in there—"

"We?" Priest leaned back and laughed, incredulous.

"When *we* go in there, I don't want to have to worry about you," Oliver said, his jaw tense. "You can't possibly keep me out."

"I can, and I will," Priest said. "You might be getting stronger, but you're not strong enough for this. We have no idea what these people are capable of, and you're far from impervious to harm, and you're not trained."

The words died on the back of Oliver's tongue. He had no real argument, but he couldn't sit back and do nothing. "I won't stay here. I'm sorry, but there's nothing you can do to stop me. If you try and lock me in, I'll use my powers."

Priest held his gaze steadily. "I had a feeling you'd say that."

"So why argue with me?"

As he threw his head back, Priest's laugh boomed around the small room. It lessened into soft chuckles, and instead of answering him, he dipped his head and took Oliver in a long, slow, deep kiss. The heat of it made his toes curl.

"Arguing with you gets my blood pumping, little human. Everything you do gets my blood pumping." He cupped Oliver's cheek and thumbed his lower lip. "I like that you say no to me."

"You like being spoiled," Oliver argued.

"Yes, I do. But it's different with you. I'm used to getting my way simply for being what I am. I like that you're not afraid of me."

Ah. Oliver understood now. He had no idea what it must feel like to be told yes simply because people were terrified of what he might do if they didn't. He didn't think it was that way with the Alphas, but Oliver also wasn't one of them. Not yet.

Maybe not ever. He didn't know how strong he'd get, but he knew he wasn't about to change his entire life just because he learned he was different. He wanted his friend back and his shop back. He wanted his quiet life and his books and spells and trinkets.

He didn't want any of this.

"I know," Priest whispered. "I know."

Had he been speaking aloud? Or could Priest just hear him now? It didn't matter. Oliver swayed into him and let Priest take his weight. "How can I help today?"

"I've called in reinforcements. Azriel."

Oliver's head snapped up, and he looked into Priest's black eyes. "Really?"

"He's one of the most powerful beings we know. And we have no idea what we're getting into."

"I'm just surprised he said yes," Oliver admitted. Azriel had been adamant from the beginning that this was not his fight. He wondered what had changed.

"He didn't give me his reasons. But he's protective of you. Your Guardian Angel." There was a tinge of resentment in Priest's tone.

Oliver rose onto his toes and kissed Priest again. "I will always be grateful to him for saving my life, and he is my friend. He's one of my best friends. But you're the one I trust to keep me safe."

Priest hummed happily, but the expression didn't last. "I won't be able to focus on the mission if I don't have someone protecting you, and I can't be in two places at once. I'll be following Sunshine's orders, so Azriel has agreed to stick by you. Knight thinks the two of you together will be able to, I guess, enhance each other's power. Maybe not by much, but enough to keep you out of harm's way and enough to help us if we need it."

It made sense. Oliver felt different every time Azriel was around. He wished he'd had more time to hone his abilities, but it would have to do. "We're going to find him, right?"

"We are."

"And as much as life might suck for him after…"

"We're not going to let him fall apart," Priest vowed. He lifted Oliver's hand to his lips and pressed a kiss to his palm. Just as he pulled back, he stiffened, and Oliver felt something shift in the air.

The Angel was there, and his power *was* stronger.

"I feel it," he whispered before Priest could announce Azriel's arrival.

Priest nodded, then stepped back, though he kept Oliver's fingers in his tight grasp. "We should go. Storm and Slate have finished their survey of the land. We're moving at moonrise."

Oliver felt a rush of anxiety and fear, mostly about whether or not he would be capable. But this was Poe's life on the line, and he wasn't going to let him down.

He would save him, even if he died trying.

If Oliver wasn't so terrified, the whole thing might have felt like an action movie. He was outfitted in dark earth tones— mossy green pants, boots to match, and a mottled brown, green, and black Lycra shirt that clung to his skin and reached just past his wrists. He was given gloves that were not the best fit and a dark beanie to pull over his hair.

He felt ridiculous, like someone playing pretend, especially as he watched the Alphas get ready. They had weapons on them, though Jeremiah had given strict orders not to use them unless it was absolutely necessary. They looked at home in their gear, not like Oliver, who was just a man playing dress-up.

But then Priest looked at him, and he could feel waves of lust pouring off his Demon.

"Not now," Oliver murmured.

Azriel stood beside him wearing dark pants and a matching shirt without holes in either, more clothes than Oliver had ever seen covering his skin. The Angel laughed and rolled his eyes. "Don't bother. We can all feel it, darling."

Priest was unrepentant. He crossed the room and stood behind Oliver, arms wrapped around his middle as Jeremiah took his place in front of them. The room was full—Dragons, Gargoyles, another Hellhound whose name Oliver hadn't been given. There were Demon species Oliver didn't recognize and two other Vampires.

The Bravo and Charlie Teams, Priest had said when Oliver realized more than just Azriel had been called in for aid.

"Everyone has been briefed," Jeremiah began, pacing a small line in front of everyone. "You all have your orders. This is a rescue mission, but it's also a capture mission. Priority one is the humans, priority two is gathering information. We're also on the lookout for a Nephilim. I don't know for sure he's here, but I know he'll be difficult to sense."

"Not for me," Azriel said. "I'll know the moment we get close enough."

Jeremiah nodded. "This cannot go more than sixty minutes, at most. We've been given raid rights by the Sirens to conduct this mission, but we're under a firm request to keep this from going public. This cannot be a bloodbath."

Everyone nodded along.

Jeremiah rolled his shoulders back, and then he partially shifted, and Oliver sucked in a breath as he was hit with a wave of heat from his Hellfire. He'd never seen a Hellhound in their true form before. "Bravo Team, your job is to secure every human you find. Sound the alarm if there are traps, and make sure every room is thoroughly searched. From the information we have, thanks to Knight, we know that it's likely whoever is running this lab will give the order to abandon ship. It means we'll have seconds to gather information from their computers before they're wiped. It's likely not enough time, but if we can get even one of their people under our control, we can interrogate them."

There were several muttered agreements. It was almost military, minus the "yes, sirs" that Oliver half expected to hear. But he could tell they all respected Jeremiah. They were all ready to follow him into any battle he found worthy.

"Alpha Team Two, roll out. Send the signal when it's time to move," Jeremiah ordered. Storm and Slate turned on their heels and left. "Bravo, Charlie, follow behind them. No more than a thirty-second delay."

Priest released Oliver, and he turned to see his lover almost fully in Demon form. His eyes were black, fangs poking out from behind his lips, horns stretching high. Oliver might have gone hot all over if it weren't for the fact that this could very well be the last time they'd see each other.

"Do we drive?" Oliver asked unsteadily.

Priest shook his head. "No." His voice was now a low, rough, sensual rumble. "You and Azriel will be teleporting. Bravo Team has vans to transport the humans."

"And you?"

Priest rolled his shoulders, and Oliver somehow knew right then that he had wings. Maybe something he should have assumed, but he'd never seen them. "I'll fly. And I will see you there."

His clawed hand took Oliver by the chin, gently pricking him but not drawing blood. His forked tongue teased his lips before Oliver let him in, the kiss drawing power from him.

He could feel the transfer, feel the bond between them growing.

Gods, he needed this to be over so he could properly have Priest again.

"Soon, beloved," Priest rumbled.

Oliver reached up and touched his horns as their foreheads dropped together. "Promise me you'll be safe."

"I promise." Priest pulled away and narrowed his dark gaze on Azriel. "If anything happens to him, I will have your head."

Azriel didn't argue. He just nodded and placed a hand on Oliver's shoulder. "See you soon."

The rest of Alpha Team were gone in a blur, and Oliver felt like the wind had been knocked out of him. He turned helpless eyes on his friend as insecurity took over. "I can't teleport. I barely got control of my tracking ability before we came here."

Azriel took his hand gently. "Then follow my lead. Let your instincts guide you."

Oliver was shaking, but the longer Azriel touched him, the more he could feel it. The pull—not to just anywhere, but to Poe.

"Yes. Search for him. Find him," Azriel murmured.

Something warm rushed through him, then the feeling in his stomach like a massive hook trying to pull him somewhere. Instead of fighting it, instead of trying to study it, Oliver simply gave himself over. There was a rushing sensation and total darkness.

And then, he was there.

Oliver came to in the midst of screaming and gunfire. His ears immediately began to ring, and he felt something small and sharp whizz past him, but Azriel's wings enveloped him like a shield. How had it all gone to shit so fast?

"Do you know where he is?" Azriel said, speaking over the cacophony of noise.

Oliver did everything he could to concentrate. For a moment, his mind wandered to Priest, terrified he wasn't okay, but he had to focus. He closed his eyes and reached out again. For a second, there was nothing. Then...

"Inside. Not too far," Oliver said. His anxiety was turning into hope, and beyond them, the battle began to quiet. He wasn't going to drop his guard, but he had a feeling the tides were turning in their favor.

"Let's go." Azriel took him and moved faster than Oliver was still capable of going. His feet barely touched the ground as he zipped inside a building with metal walls. It was like a giant warehouse, except inside was a maze of corridors.

There were doorways everywhere and people screaming for help.

"The Bravo Team will get them," Azriel reminded him. "Where is Poe?"

Oliver began to run, following the invisible thread leading to his brother. It got stronger as they turned a corner, and then it became burning hot before it fizzled into nothing. The lack of sensation almost sent him to his knees, but Azriel was ahead of him, using his brute strength to rip the door off its hinges.

Inside was a bed, several monitors that were no longer connected to anything... and then there was Poe. He was unconscious but breathing, on top of a white sheet. He was thin and looked like he'd recently been drained of all of his blood.

But he was alive. Oliver could sense it.

He brushed past Azriel and grabbed him, yanking his hands back when they touched his icy skin. "Poe," he whispered. His friend groaned, head lolling to the side, but he didn't wake up. Oliver looked over his shoulder. "Is he dying? Can you tell?"

Azriel's face looked broken, shattered, and Oliver wanted to scream. They could not have come this far only to lose him.

"He's turned," came a voice from just beyond the doorway. Knight appeared, drenched in blood and dragging a struggling man by the front of his throat. "He also needs to feed. There were three other starving Vampires here."

Oliver's stomach twisted as he realized what the man was for. Was his crime worthy of a death sentence?

Knight's gaze challenged him, and Oliver looked back down to Poe. His lips had parted, dry and cracked around the edges, and Oliver could see his fangs. He was clearly starving, and he knew that would eventually kill him.

But would Poe forgive him for letting him feed?

"It's your choice," Knight said, dragging the man closer. He looked Oliver dead in the face. "This one was in charge of the children."

The children.

Oliver turned his head and threw up half his dinner. He didn't have time to stop it. Stumbling to the side, Azriel caught him and wrapped him tightly in his wings as Knight took his place. "Sorry," he gasped, wiping at his mouth. "Sorry I…"

"I know. I know," Azriel said gently. His voice was clearer now that everything was going very quiet. "The most monstrous creatures that live in this world aren't the actual monsters in the end. It's the ones who are given the most and make the choice to do things like this."

Oliver squeezed his eyes shut and buried his face against Azriel's chest. His guardian's arms were warm and comforting. Not the ones he wanted but ones that still protected him. "Is he feeding?"

"He's feeding," Azriel said.

"He's finished," Knight said a moment later. "He won't wake for a while, but Jeremiah asked me to bring him back to the safe house."

Oliver pushed Azriel's wing to the side and peered over. Poe had color now, and his breathing was steadier. "The others?"

Knight shrugged. "There were several unturned humans. The Bravo Team took whoever was alive. No sign of the Nephilim as far as we can tell." His gaze moved to Azriel, who closed his own eyes, then shook his head.

"If he was here, he was gone long enough for his essence to dissipate. That takes about a day."

Poe's heart dropped, but he knew they had to stay focused on what they could do. "So now what?"

"The others are gathering as much information as they can. The computers have been wiped, but the ones running this place are human. They're no match for Sunshine and Priest." Knight turned away and gathered Poe close to his chest. "Meet us at the safe house. There's nothing left here for you."

And then he was gone before Oliver could say a word.

"Well, you heard him," Azriel said, reaching for Oliver's hand again.

Oliver pulled back. "I want to make sure Priest is okay."

Azriel's eyes narrowed. "You'll see him shortly. There's nothing you can do for him now except distract him, and that's the one thing he asked me to make sure didn't happen."

Oliver wanted to be angry. He *was* angry. But he couldn't let himself act on it. That wasn't fair. He wasn't a fighter. All he'd do was get in the way. The compound had gone quiet, but that didn't mean it was over.

Besides, if he went home now, he could be there when Poe woke up, and that was enough to motivate him into taking Azriel's hand. "Alright. Get us there safe."

Azriel nodded. "You have my word."

17

PRIEST

*A*s far as fights went, it was anticlimactic in ways that were almost disappointing. Priest hadn't used his wings in eons. He hadn't been strong enough to draw them out. But feeding on Oliver had given him power he hadn't known he was capable of having, and he beat Jeremiah's Hellhound to the compound.

They were met with immediate gunfire—something he was expecting. Jeremiah was able to shield the three of them as they breached the doors, and it wasn't long before the first guards were taken down. They had just enough time to sound the alarm before Jeremiah was tearing throats, Knight was puncturing carotid arteries, and Priest was sinking teeth and claws into vulnerable flesh.

These were evil humans. He could sense it, taste it on their blood. They were afraid, but only because they had committed hell-worthy sins. Priest could smell fear in that place. He could smell death.

And something else.

Whatever it was, it had taken Knight directly to his knees. He glanced over to find his friend covered in blood, trembling from head to toe. He met Jeremiah's eyes as the Hellhound shifted back and walked over, kneeling beside the Vampire.

"Go and find Poe. Find the others. Let Priest and me handle this."

Knight swallowed heavily, his jaw tense. "It was here. This was the place."

"I know," Jeremiah growled. "And we will burn it to the fucking ground, but first, we need to get as many people out of here as we can." He pressed his finger to his ear, listening to the static on his earpiece. Something in the compound was interfering, but the leader of Charlie Team came through well enough. "Charlie says they're fleeing through underground tunnels."

Knight climbed to his feet, his fight renewed, and then he was gone in the blink of an eye. Priest followed Jeremiah down a maze of tunnels. The Bravo Team was ahead of them, pulling humans from cages, off medical exam tables, and from behind locked doors.

Somewhere in the distance, Priest could hear children crying, and then he heard Knight's roar. Gods have mercy on whatever humans were left behind to guard them. He could feel Knight's rage from where he stood.

"Here," Jeremiah said, leading Priest through a door. It was a massive medical room, and there was a table in the center. The person on the bed was no longer alive and was just starting to smell like decay.

They were emaciated, skin almost translucent, and they were still hooked up to IVs.

"What the fuck?" Priest whispered. Was this what Knight had endured? He glanced over and saw Jeremiah gathering a few leather-bound journals careless humans had left behind before turning his attention back to the body. Something about the man's face looked familiar.

"Zimmerson's son."

The lawyer from the second attack.

Horror washing through him, Priest's knees went weak. "We can't let them find their child like this."

Jeremiah shook his head and tapped the comm in his ear. "We need two members from Charlie for a body extraction. High-profile client. This cannot get out."

Priest swallowed thickly. "Do you think this is what Knight—"

"Yes," Jeremiah said, cutting him off. His voice was tense with emotion. "Yes, I do."

Priest couldn't imagine what his friend had endured. Or why. What was the point of all this? It couldn't be torment for fun, but why would they take ordinary citizens? Children? He didn't want to think that they were doing this all in some sick attempt to turn humans into Vampires, and it seemed so pointless. Vampires were not welcomed in society, so why amass more of them?

After all, the people running the labs were humans. He could sense it, their emotions lingering on the air. What purpose would it serve?

Before he could voice all of that, he heard something—a scuffling sound behind heavy metal. Jeremiah's head whipped to the side, and he jerked his chin at a massive cabinet. Priest rushed over and grabbed the sides, using all of his strength to pull it off the wall. Hinges tore, and there was a passageway behind it.

In the distance, he could hear shoes on concrete.

"Sounds like someone we want to talk to," Jeremiah growled, smoke rising from his shoulders.

They took off like a shot, the gift of their preternatural speed allowing them to catch up in seconds. Two men were just reaching a massive opening—a parking garage with a single car and several oil stains from those who had been coming and going for years, most likely. There was no telling how long they'd been running this lab.

Jeremiah smiled wolfishly at them as Priest tasted their

acrid fear in the air. He half shifted, his skin alighting with Hellfire. "Going somewhere?"

They said nothing.

"We just want a word."

The men glanced at each other, so Priest took a step forward, but before he could do more than that, there was a sound. It was all-encompassing, high-pitched. It was torture. His hands flew to his ears, and he collapsed, barely able to see Jeremiah doing the same in his periphery.

One of the men took something out of his pocket—a strange, orb-like thing Priest swore he'd seen before. He threw it into the air, and then all Priest knew was pain. It felt like every atom in his body was bursting, over and over. His vision whited out, then began to fade to black.

And it was only the sweet relief of unconsciousness that saved him.

Am I dead?

He wasn't sure if he spoke the words aloud, but when Priest tried to open his eyes, everything was white. It was also painful, which might mean he was in one of the hell realms— not that he expected to go anywhere else when he died.

From whence he came and all that.

But then he realized the bed beneath him was soft, and a warm hand was holding his, and a honey-sweet voice was whispering into his ear, "Come on, baby. Open your eyes. You need to feed."

He knew that voice. By the gods, he loved that voice. And the voice was right. He was starved. He groaned, and his vision was dark again, this time with the shadow of a man. He let out a soft hiss, but it was captured by careful lips and a pressing tongue attempting to push past his teeth.

His hunger was overwhelming, his Demon desperate and

exhausted. The temptation of that kiss and all the power he could sense behind it was too much to resist. He opened his mouth to accept the gift he was being given. Power rushed through him, familiar and wonderful.

Oliver, his brain supplied. He was kissing Oliver. He was feeding on Oliver.

He pulled back with a gasp, the memory of the compound rushing back. His limbs felt like they weighed several tons, but he managed to push up and yank his beloved against him. "Are you hurt?" he rasped, squinting around, but everything was too blurry to make out.

Oliver shoved him back and forced him to lie down. "No, jackass. Now, lie still. You're hurt."

"I'll heal," he muttered. And he would. His vision was already beginning to return, and he could finally see Oliver's face. His sweet human was pale, dark circles under his eyes, a smear of something on his cheek. Blood? No, dirt. "How long was I out?"

"An hour at most," came a voice from the other side of the room. He knew that one too. *Azriel.* "I kept my promise. *You* did not."

Priest wheezed a laugh as he reached for Oliver and pressed his dry knuckles to his equally dry lips. "That was a bit out of my hands." He groaned as he sat up again, but his strength was already returning. It was enough to resist Oliver when he tried to push him over again. "I'm okay. I'm okay."

Oliver was shaking. He pressed into Priest's embrace and buried his face against his neck. "You looked dead when Slate dragged you in here." His voice was shaking too. "They didn't know what happened. You and Jeremiah were unconscious."

"Those wily little fuckers had a weapon," Priest growled. He pulled Oliver's head back and nuzzled against his skin, tasting sweat on his neck. He took another pull of his lust, of his love, letting it ease the pain he was still in.

"Jeremiah said the same thing," Azriel replied dryly.

Priest pulled back to look at him. "He's okay?"

"Same condition as you. Healing faster, but it looks like you took the brunt of whatever they threw at you."

Priest swore quietly as he let his head fall back against the wall. "They got away."

"They did. Only one human guard was left alive, but once it was determined he didn't know anything, Knight, ah…" Azriel smiled. "Helped himself."

Knight deserved the hot, fresh meal, and Priest was pretty sure any person willingly working at that lab deserved a painful death. Priest didn't make it a habit to feel sorry for people he didn't know, anyway. He wasn't the most empathetic being and never would be. He'd grown up knowing everything cognizant with a pulse was potential food.

It was only after meeting Jeremiah that he realized there was more than lust—more than power. That he was capable of love. And now, though he was fighting to ignore it, possibly even something more. Something fated.

Turning his face back toward Oliver's neck, he breathed him in. He was starving, and he was going to need more than a small taste to finish healing. Oliver seemed to sense that, but when he turned his head, body tense like he was going to address the room, Priest kissed him quiet.

"Not now," he murmured against Oliver's lips. He felt Oliver's anger, almost as powerful as his lust, and he smiled. "Soon. I need to debrief and figure out what's next. And Poe…"

"Alive," Oliver said. "But…"

It was as they'd suspected.

Priest sat all the way up with a groan. He felt like he'd been hit by a truck, but he'd suffered worse. His gaze fixed on the doorway as a figure appeared. Jeremiah looked almost as bad as he did, though he was walking steadily. He grabbed a chair from against the wall and flipped it around, straddling it.

To an observer, the move would look careless and arrogant, but Priest knew him like he knew himself, and he saw the fatigue and pain running through him. And he could feel Jeremiah's need to leave—to throw himself into Remi's arms and heal.

"Poe will survive. He's past the change," Jeremiah said, his voice raspy. "Knight's helping him through it, but he's going to need protection, somewhere to go, and I can't put any of our people on it right now, so any ideas you have will be helpful."

Priest realized he was addressing Oliver, who shrank back. "Everyone in his family is an ally, but…"

"But we can't be sure they'll accept it in one of their own," Priest finished for him, holding him a little tighter.

Oliver bowed his head. "They're on the side of supernaturals, but Vampires…"

"Demons? Hellhounds?" Jeremiah said with a wry grin. "Trust me, that is a very familiar song and dance. I suppose I can ask the king and queen if they can shelter him, but I hate bringing more danger to their door."

There was a beat of silence, and then Azriel cleared his throat. "He can come with me."

Priest blinked at him in surprise as Jeremiah shook his head. "I don't think a strip club is the best place for a new Vampire."

"I have rooms at the club, but I don't live there," Azriel said, rolling his eyes. "I have an actual home."

Priest felt foolish for being so damn surprised. How had he not known? How had he not even assumed that Azriel had a life outside of the Pearly Gates?

"I'm not going to patronize you and ask if you understand what it will mean to take care of a freshly turned Vampire who is also going to have massive trauma from being kidnapped and tortured," Jeremiah said slowly. "But I need you to acknowledge that I have nowhere to take him if you show up at my door covered in bite marks."

Azriel's lips quirked up into a small smirk. "I know what I'm doing. Trust me."

"I do," Oliver said. He pushed out of Priest's grasp and threw his arms around Azriel. "Thank you. I'm... I don't know what to say."

Azriel's eyes closed, and he held Oliver tightly. Priest should have been feeling jealous. He should want to tear the Angel's throat out, but instead, he was just relieved Oliver hadn't lost his friend and that Poe wouldn't be going through this alone.

"If that's that..." Jeremiah said, moving to stand, but he froze when Priest made a noise of protest.

"That's not that. I'm not done here. I want to know what the fuck took us out at the knees." He dragged a hand through his hair, his muscles screaming with pain. "I want to know what information we got and if we were right."

Jeremiah swallowed thickly. "We were right. At least, as far as Knight and I can tell. We don't know why, and the one person who might actually know something is still missing."

"Ozias," Priest said, sagging backward.

Jeremiah nodded. "Tomorrow, we have to inform Mr. and Mrs. Zimmerson that their son didn't make it. After that, we'll have a meeting of the minds because I have a bad feeling this goes beyond fringe hate groups. There were children in that facility. Two of them were turned."

Priest felt sick. "Where are they now?"

"Rhombus's Hoard took them," Jeremiah said.

Rhombus was a Dragon on the Charlie Team. His Hoard lived on one of the Bellona Mountain peaks, which was probably the best place for children that were, for all intents and purposes, now illegal in every country. Anywhere else, the way they aged so slowly would be noticed easily, outing them. Unless something could be done about society, they would never be welcome.

If Priest had been stronger, he would have put his fist through the wall. "What do we tell their parents?"

"Slate volunteered to talk to them."

Priest couldn't imagine being the one to deliver such devastating news. As much as he wanted to believe the parents would continue to love their children...

He didn't have much hope.

Knight's hadn't. Neither had Jeremiah's.

Priest didn't remember his, his earliest memories of group homes and beatings. He'd been told his mother had abandoned him, and he believed it. No one wanted a child like him, not when the chances of going mad with hunger were basically guaranteed.

"I'm flying back home tonight," Jeremiah said. "Knight's staying here so he can go through the lab after Bravo gets done clearing out the rest of the bodies. Two of the unturned survivors are still here, and he wants to question them."

Priest nodded. "Let him know I'll help."

"You're hurt," Oliver started to protest.

"I am." Priest gave him a knowing smile. "But with a little help, it won't take me long to heal."

As much as Priest would have loved to order everyone out of the room and to take Oliver right there, he couldn't. Poe was calling for him, and Priest wasn't going to stand in his way. Azriel agreed to stay in the safe house for a few more days as Poe gained strength, and it would allow Oliver to help him come to terms with what had happened.

"I don't like this," Priest said to Jeremiah, hobbling with him to the door.

Jeremiah bowed his head. "Neither do I. I thought... Fuck,

when Knight told me what happened to him, I thought it was some random sicko with a Vampire obsession, but he knew that lab. And if they were able to get out so quickly, if they had an escape plan at the ready—"

"Then they've been doing this a long time," Priest finished for him. He rubbed at his temples. "There has to be more than one lab out there."

"I'm terrified to think of how many. But I'm done playing fucking defense." Jeremiah dropped the handle of his suitcase and grabbed Priest, pulling him into a hug. "He's your mate, isn't he?"

Priest swallowed thickly. "I think so. I... I feel this thing inside me, like a thousand impossibly strong threads trying to bind us together. But I don't know how. He's mostly human, and he'd be closer to Nephilim than an Angel. This shouldn't be possible."

Jeremiah rubbed at his chin, and he pulled back. "I have a few theories on that too, but we can talk about it later."

"Do you think whatever this is might be related to finding our mates?"

"I think there's a lot of big, waving flags we've missed over the years," Jeremiah admitted. "But I refuse to believe we're too late to stop whatever the fuck these people are planning." He gave Priest's shoulder a gentle pat. "Go. Feed. Heal. We need you."

Priest nodded, watching as Jeremiah stepped through the door, and then he turned and headed back to his room. It was still empty, and his hunger was gnawing at him, but it was more than that. He didn't just want to feed. He wanted Oliver.

He needed him.

Those invisible threads in his chest began to stretch out. He could feel them reaching, searching. He could feel when they connected to his beloved. Only minutes passed before the bedroom door opened, and Oliver stepped through, locking it behind him.

Priest felt his lingering worry, felt his hunger. His Demon rose to the surface of his skin, ready to take, to feed, to consume the parts of Oliver he was willingly giving. Priest felt pinned to the bed by Oliver's gaze, and he could do nothing except wait for his little human to cross the room.

Oliver's gaze was fixed on him, eyes half-lidded, pupils dilated. He looked like he was in a trance, but then he reached for the hem of his shirt and smiled. "Say please."

Priest's throat went dry. "Please."

Oliver removed the shirt, letting it fall to his feet. He took several more steps. His knees hit the bed. His lithe, perfect, clever fingers touched the button on his jeans. "And this?"

Priest pushed up on his elbows and bared his fangs. "More. All of it. Show me what's mine."

Oliver shuddered as he removed his jeans, letting them pool at his feet along with his thin boxers. His body was unblemished, untouched by the violence of the night, and Priest was grateful for it. The only marks on Oliver's skin should be his own.

He felt his fangs elongate along with his claws as he got his hands around Oliver's hips. With a short grunt, he tugged, and Oliver toppled onto him. The warmth of his skin sent his head into a spin, his hunger taking over.

"Beautiful," Oliver murmured.

For a moment, Priest didn't know what he meant, and then he felt a touch along his horns. The sensation split into two rivers, one flooding his heart, the other his cock. He was torn between lust and love, and he was bewildered that even after showing himself like this, Oliver still wanted him.

His human.

His Angel.

His.

"Kiss me." The words came out jumbled and growled,

tongue thin and forked and flicking out to taste the skin on Oliver's neck. His little human turned and gave him access to his pulse, then leaned in and pressed their lips together, and Priest had to clamp down on his desire to immediately draw power from him.

He was wounded, and his control was thready, but he was going to draw this out. He wanted to feed, but he wanted to love on this man.

"Why are you holding back?"

Priest pulled away and took Oliver's chin carefully in his claws. "I love you."

Oliver shuddered, his eyes closing. "Tell me again."

Priest sank his fangs into Oliver's neck, not enough to break the skin, but nearly. He felt those threads in his chest reaching for Oliver's, twisting together—bright and over-whelming. It was impossible to deny it now. This was his mate. His forever. The soul the universe had chosen to be his and only his.

All he had to do was sink into him and taste him, and they would be bonded forever.

"I love you," he said again. He forced his shift as far back to human as his hunger would allow, and he caught Oliver's gaze. He knew his eyes were still black. His vision was distorted by his Demon, picking up on the heat radiating off Oliver's skin like an aura sunset. He took a breath. "You are mine."

"Yes."

Priest shook his head. "I need you to understand. You... you are mine. My—"

"Your mate," Oliver said. "I know."

How?

Oliver laughed, and Priest realized he had read the question from his mind. "I don't know how. I just do. I feel it. I need you, Claude."

He had never, ever thought he would enjoy hearing his

given name on the lips of anyone until that moment. His eyes went hot, acidic tears threatening to spill down his cheeks.

"I'm not just yours, okay? You're mine too. I want this. I want the bond. I feel like I'm going to die without it."

Priest heard a growl, and it took him a moment to realize it was his own. It was his Demon, ready to possess, to claim, to take what was being given. To offer what he had never thought he'd be allowed to. The fact that he wasn't just wanted but that he belonged to another soul was almost too much for him.

But his Demon wouldn't let him spiral. It was taking over. His fangs dropped again, his face shifting, his horns stretching high above his head. He flipped Oliver onto the mattress and pressed his hands on either side of his head.

"Tell me now if—"

"I want it. I want you. Take me," Oliver begged, cutting him off.

And that was all Priest needed to hear before his Demon took over and descended to make Oliver his.

18

OLIVER

*H*e should have been petrified, but he wasn't. The sight of Priest's entirely changed form would have sent even the strongest human running. But for him, all he saw was the primal, gorgeous, powerful being Priest was. He no longer thought of them as separate.

This was Priest. His beloved. His Demon.

His horns were shiny onyx, twisting up from his temples. Oliver stroked them, and Priest purred loudly before shoving his face in Oliver's neck. His fangs touched him again, not biting yet, and Oliver wanted to scream. He needed it. His end of the bond was frayed and bleeding, aching to be complete.

Instead, Priest pulled back, and his forked tongue flicked over Oliver's nipples. He dipped lower, to his belly button, over his hips, tasting every inch of his skin. The palm of Priest's hand was rough as it took Oliver's cock in a firm grip, and the tip of his tongue dipped into his slit, sending tendrils of ecstasy rushing through him.

"Please," he begged in a shattered whisper.

Priest growled and pressed his free hand to Oliver's throat, silencing him. The pressure was overwhelming in the best way. Oliver's entire body went limp, and Priest let out another happy purr as he shoved Oliver's leg up toward his chest and then began to devour him.

A forked tongue inside him was still one of the best sensations Oliver had ever experienced. He was floating on waves of pleasure, body trembling with need, unfulfilled and suddenly afraid Priest would spend the rest of their lives tormenting him with the promise of being filled, the promise of being allowed to come and never letting him have it.

Priest's low, dangerous chuckle penetrated his thoughts, and Oliver blinked heavily, looking down to find Priest watching him. "Beg me."

Oliver's throat went tight. "I…"

"Beg me for what you want."

"Your cock," Oliver rasped. He tried to move, but Priest kept him pinned. "I want your cock inside me."

"You want it?"

"I need it." Oliver started to feel more frantic. He suddenly felt like prey, like breaking free and running.

Priest's eyes darkened, and the grip on Oliver's throat tightened. "Soon, little human. Soon, you'll be free to run while I hunt you. Tonight, though, I'm going to claim you."

Oliver's cock throbbed, dripping a river of precome over Priest's fist as he squeezed his cock. "Make me yours. I can't live without you. I love you."

Priest groaned, and then suddenly, his hands moved, bracing himself on either side of Oliver's head. The tip of his cock pressed against Oliver's hole—hot, thick, wet. He fucked his hips forward, and his cock caught on the rim of Oliver's hole, hesitating before his body relaxed, and then Priest slipped inside him an inch.

The familiar feeling of Priest's thrall began to wrap around him. Oliver knew he would never lose himself to it like the others, but he could still feel it. Like a gentle buzz of Siren Water, it made him feel good. Soft. Eager.

"So eager," Priest agreed, dragging the tip of his claw over Oliver's lips. "Tell me you want this."

Oliver knew what he meant. Not just sex. Not just to be together. This was it. The moment he gave himself to Priest, there was no turning back. But he wasn't afraid. He turned his head, baring his neck, and he spread his legs as far as he could manage. Priest's cock throbbed inside him, but he didn't move.

"I want this," Oliver said. "It's you. Only you. And always will be."

His eyes had just enough time to close before Priest thrust all the way inside and sank his fangs into Oliver's neck. He felt them pierce his skin, felt the first rush of blood, felt the thin tongue lap against the flow. But there was no pain. There was a bright spark and a thousand threads coming together.

There was the beat of his own heart and the beat of Priest's. There was ecstasy, eternal and overwhelming, rushing through his veins. Nothing had ever felt so good. Nothing ever would. He was moving, his body writhing on instinct, taking every push, every pull, as though he was made for it.

He felt Priest feeding, felt him drawing strength from Oliver and giving him strength in return. His Angel blood inside him sang, reaching for Priest's Demon, sealing them together.

"My love, my love," Priest gasped. He kissed Oliver, sharing the metal tang of blood. And then Priest was shoving Oliver's face into his own neck. "Now you. Seal us. Make me yours."

Oliver had no fangs, but he did as Priest said, biting down and feeling something give beneath his teeth. There was no blood, but there was something else. A white-hot rush of lust that was better than any orgasm he'd ever experienced.

For a moment, he thought he might die from it. He thought it might last forever, and somehow, it would be both heaven and hell. His vision went completely white and then black. He felt himself coming in hot, thick ropes, Priest fucking deep inside him, filling him.

And then he felt the moment the bond was in place. It settled in his chest like a second heartbeat, a gentle thrum of his beloved that would never be silent. He would never be alone. Not really.

He was complete.

Oliver didn't realize he was crying until Priest's rough tongue was swiping tears from his cheeks, and he blinked his eyes open, surprised to see Priest's human face and black eyes looking down at him.

"Regrets?"

"Never." Oliver's voice was barely a whisper, incapable of going louder. But it didn't matter. He knew Priest could now feel the honesty of his words. He would always know when he was telling the truth. And he would always know when he lied.

Priest cupped his face, hands still clawed but so gentle. He was stronger again. Healed.

Thanks to you, little human.

He smiled gently and then kissed the corner of Oliver's lips. "We need rest."

"We need to clean up," Oliver countered.

Priest rumbled a protest and nuzzled against the tender bite on Oliver's neck. "Let me have you like this. Let me wake up and smell us on your skin. Just this once."

Oliver sighed. How could he say no?

"Is it weird that I can smell it?"

Oliver looked up from his phone. It was the first thing Poe had said to him since greeting him when he came in. Oliver had rambled a little—the way he always did when he was nervous. He half expected to be more confident or... more charming, maybe, now that he shared a bond with an Incubus.

But he was simply himself with the press of Priest's love behind his ribs.

"Please tell me you're not talking about my blood," Oliver said.

Poe grimaced. He was very pale and still trembled whenever he tried to move too fast. Knight said that was normal—at least, it was normal for Vampires who had been turned under that sort of trauma. He'd been keeping his distance from Poe other than to help him feed, and Oliver understood why. But he knew Poe was terrified of his new reality, and he hated that there was nothing he could do to take it away.

"I meant the bond," Poe said. He stretched his arms above his head and then shuffled to sit up a little more. He pulled one leg close to his chest, and for the first time since he'd woken, he looked more like himself. "Is it... how is it? What does it feel like?"

Oliver bit his lip as he stretched his legs out, and he closed his eyes, poking at the sensation. "It's... I don't know how to describe it. It's like, I know where he is at all times—and he knows where I am. But it's not intrusive."

"It sounds..."

"Awful?" He knew Poe would have hated it. Poe was always fiercely protective of his privacy.

"Interesting. Comforting." When Oliver lifted a brow at him, Poe ducked his head. "Maybe that's just the trauma talking. I never thought I was going to see anyone I loved ever again."

Oliver ached to reach for him, but Poe was hesitant about being touched. He could hear blood flowing when he got too close, and he was still working on his control. He was also jumpy, and Oliver knew it was from whatever the humans had done to him. He still wouldn't talk about it, but he was going to know soon enough. Priest was speaking with the other survivors, and they were willing to share their experiences.

"I guess I was right," Poe said after a beat, laughing. "About you two."

Oliver groaned, throwing his hands over his face. "I didn't think it was going to be this deep. I mean, don't get me wrong, I love him."

I love you too.

Oliver tried to hide his smile. "I don't think I'd trade it for the world, but it was a complete mindfuck, dealing with that and trying to find you."

Poe stared at him, and Oliver almost jumped out of his skin when Poe's cool hand met his own. He did nothing, letting Poe take the lead. Holding hands felt different now. Not better, not worse. Just changed.

Poe bowed his head. "Will I ever stop being angry, do you think?"

"Knight hasn't."

"Yeah." Poe glanced out the window, where they could both see Knight sitting outside under a tree. He never went far from the house, but he seemed to prefer being outdoors. "He was with them a lot longer than I was though."

"Did he tell you that?"

Poe nodded. He bit his lip again, and this time, Oliver could see his fangs. "He really doesn't like talking about it. Any of it." Poe swallowed heavily, and Oliver could see the heartbreak on his face, which killed him. "I understand why. I... I hate what I remember. I *hate* it."

Oliver wanted to hold him as his voice cracked, but he wasn't sure what Poe needed. He extended his other hand, and Poe stared at it for a moment, then let out a watery laugh as he linked their fingers together.

"I hate that you're afraid to touch me. I hate that you're afraid of me."

"Is that—oh gods, Poe," Oliver said. He shifted closer and cupped Poe's cheek. His skin was so cold now. "I'm not afraid of you. I just didn't want to make it worse. Knight hates being touched. Priest said that's one way to send him into a frenzy, and I didn't want to do that to you."

Poe let go of Oliver's hand and wrapped his arms around his middle. "I want to be touched. I want… I want to know that I'm not some *thing*. Some monster. But everyone seems to—"

Oliver cut him off. He couldn't stop himself. He wrapped his arms around Poe and pulled him until he was spooning him, holding on as tightly as he dared.

"Every touch hurt when I was with them," Poe said in a small voice. "Every single person came with some kind of agony at their hands, and… and I need to remember not everyone will be like that."

Oliver pressed his forehead to the back of Poe's neck. "It'll never hurt here. Not with me, not with the Alphas, and not with Azriel."

Poe took in a deep breath, and it trembled on his exhale. "He said he's taking me to his place. I didn't think an Angel would want to deal with a messy newborn Vampire."

Oliver couldn't help a laugh. "Messy newborn Vampire sounds like his dream job. Come on, you've met him."

Poe snorted and snuggled backward. "That's fair. And, uh… thank you. Thank you for not giving up on me."

Oliver tightened his arms, and he felt a small pang of grief when Poe didn't grunt from the force of it. Because of course he didn't. He wasn't human anymore.

"I will never give up on you, okay? You're more than a friend. You're more than family to me. Priest might be my mate and my bonded, but you've been my other half for as long as I can remember. You saved me. Even if they'd brought me a lifeless corpse, I would have forced Priest or Jeremiah to show me to the gates of the afterlife, and I would have come for you."

Poe laughed, but it sounded close to a sob, and he twisted in Oliver's arms. "I feel the same way about you. I think that's why they couldn't break me. Not completely. I knew you'd find me eventually."

Oliver stared into his eyes, irises almost fully red now, and he knew once Poe had fed enough, they'd be completely scarlet when he fed or lost control of his emotions. "They did enough to make you turn."

Poe nodded and bit his lip so hard his fangs broke skin. He swiped at the drops with his tongue, then shuddered. "To be honest, I don't know how it happened. It's not what they tell people though. They didn't infect me with a virus. I never got sick. It was like... It was like they were using pain to invoke some kind of reaction or something. Like they were trying to wake something up inside me."

Just like Jeremiah had suspected. Like their missing Nephilim friend had been studying.

He ducked his head and caught Poe's gaze. "Was there a Nephilim at the lab?"

"The Hellhound guy already asked me that when I woke up, and if there was one, I don't remember," Poe told him, looking sorry. "I remember the sound of kids. I... I think that made me angrier than anything else. I asked the Hellhound how many of them died, but he wouldn't tell me."

"I don't think he has numbers on how many were there before the raid," Oliver told him. "But I know there were a handful of kids that were alive and two that were turned."

"Oh gods," Poe groaned, flopping his head back. "I had these ridiculous plans about how I was going to escape and save them, but I failed."

"You didn't. You called to me—you kept calling to me, and I heard you. I found you."

Poe studied him for a beat. "So it's true. You're—"

"Part Angel, I guess. Some sort of family secret shame," he said bitterly. "Part of me wants to go confront my parents, but I also never want to see their faces again."

"Does it make you a Nephilim?"

Oliver laughed and shrugged. "I don't think so, but no one seems to know what it makes me. Priest still calls me his little human, though because of my powers, I can feed him without getting hurt. Azriel thinks that the more I use my abilities—like, the more I learn about them and hone them—the more powerful I'll get."

You'll always be my little human, beloved.

I know.

"So we're both freaks?"

"Yup. You and me until the end," Oliver said with a grin.

Poe started to laugh, but it turned into a yawn, and he glanced away with embarrassment. "Sorry. I think I'm still tired."

"After what you went through?" Oliver shifted his arms back and pulled the blanket up to Poe's chest. "It'll be time for you to eat soon, right?"

Poe swallowed heavily. "Would you mind if—if you didn't watch that part?"

Oliver wanted to tell him he'd seen enough bloodshed and death that watching Poe feed wouldn't faze him at all. But he also knew Poe was still struggling with needing to keep himself alive on the blood of others. "Just call me when you need me, okay? Priest and I are staying here with you and Azriel until you're ready to leave."

"Thank you," Poe said sleepily.

By the time Oliver extracted himself from the bed, Poe was already asleep. He let himself out and almost collided with Knight, who jumped back to avoid being touched. Oliver offered him a sheepish grin.

"Sorry. Sorry. I was just, uh…"

"Visiting your friend?"

"Right. That." He rubbed the back of his neck, then blurted, "Can your friends touch you?"

Knight blinked at him.

"Gods, that's such a rude question, but I just... Poe needed to be touched. He felt like the way everyone was avoiding him was because they were scared of him being a monster. And I know it's hard for you, but does it... does it help?"

Knight was quiet for so long Oliver was pretty sure he'd crossed about a dozen lines. Then he took a breath and said, "It helps sometimes. But my experience was different from Poe's. I think I was one of the first experiments. I was there for a long, long time. Being touched by someone I trust is everything, but even then, sometimes it's too much."

"What helped?"

"Time," Knight said with a shrug. "Surrounding myself with people who understood what it was like to be considered a monster and learning that I wasn't one. Destigmatizing the shame that comes with what I am. And my moths."

Oliver smiled. He knew a little bit about his moths. "You'll help him, right? You and Azriel. I can't lose him."

Knight's jaw ticked. "You won't lose him. He'll find his way. I promise."

Priest was gone through dinner, so Oliver made up a small plate and brought it back to their room. He trudged in an hour and a half later, looking dead on his feet, though he perked up at the sight of Oliver lounging on the bed with a book. Oliver's heart kicked up a notch when Priest's did.

"Oh. That's different." Oliver pressed a hand to his sternum. "I feel that."

"How much I want you?"

"How much you want to hold me. It's more than lust."

Priest shed his outer layer of clothes, then slipped into sweats from his suitcase before climbing beside Oliver, bare-chested and so warm. "That's a new feeling for me too. Feelings were always separated into lust and friendship. It's how I determined who was food and who wasn't. But with you, I've always wanted more. That's why I was such a complete fucking jackass every time I came into your shop."

It still hurt to talk about the shop, but Oliver smiled in spite of the pain. The memories were tinged with bitterness of a thing they could no longer have. Life would never be easy. He and Poe would never be human again. There would never again be a day where things were monotonous and safe.

"I don't believe that," Priest said, picking up on his thoughts. He brushed his fingers through Oliver's hair as he pulled him close. "There will be simple days again. It might take a while, but we'll get there."

"You have a lot more faith than me," Oliver said.

Priest pinched his chin and took his lips in a slow, posses-sive kiss. "I can have as much faith as I need to until you feel ready for your own. That's one of the perks of being bonded."

One among many.

Oliver rolled his eyes, so Priest bit him over his mating mark, and he burst into laughter. "You're so fucking annoying."

"You love it."

Oliver pulled back and met his gaze. "Yes. I do."

He kissed him again until they were both a little breath-less, but Priest was well-fed, and they were both too tired to do much more than that. Priest cradled his cheeks and eased him onto his back before snuggling close.

"How was the... What do you call it? Debriefing?"

"It was long and painful," Priest admitted. "The survivors —the ones that weren't turned—they're going to need a lot of help that they can't get right now because they need to be kept hidden. We have no idea how deep this goes, and with the journals Jeremiah found, he's pretty sure several governments are involved."

Shock rushed through him. "Governments? Like, not just humans?"

"High-ranking members," Priest said. "Jeremiah thinks that most people are largely unaware and that several ruling families and heads of democracy are out of the loop. But enough people in power are in on this."

"That's… a lot."

"I think it's more than Jeremiah bargained for," Priest admitted. "But we have somewhere to start now." He yawned so wide his jaw cracked, and then he nestled close. "Knight wants to check out the lab tomorrow. See if we missed anything."

"Do you think that's safe? Won't they be watching it?"

Priest laughed. "They might be, but they already know who raided them. Trust me, little human, we are never subtle. We're not afraid to let them all know they're our next target."

Oliver was suddenly overwhelmed with fear that something could happen to Priest. He clung tightly. "Weren't you just a bodyguard, like, six months ago?"

Priest pushed up and brushed a lock of hair off Oliver's forehead. "And you were just a human. But things change. Taking contracts the way we did was part of our job. The other part is to deal with injustice. All of us deal with it. We're pariahs in almost every corner of the continent just because we have the misfortune of being an unacceptable form of supernatural. Pushed to the edges of society, doomed to mateless existences. Creatures like me condemned to an eventual life of insanity and hunger from never being completely sated."

Oliver frowned. "But you have a mate. You can feed on me and be sated. Like, actually sated."

"I…" Priest froze, cocking his head. "I am sated. Fully. Completely."

"So will that still be your fate?"

"I don't know." Priest closed his eyes. "I don't know if there's ever been a mated Incubus before."

"That's ridiculous," Oliver said, and Priest opened his eyes, raising a brow at him. "I'm just saying, you can't possibly be the first. I mean, if you were somehow mated to a fallen Angel or something, I could see that maybe it had never happened before in history, but you're not. I'm mostly human. Whatever this bond was, it didn't come directly from me. I didn't create it in you."

Priest shook his head, looking confused. "Incubi... I've never heard of one of us bonding. It's incredibly rare for a Demon to have a fated mate, but Incubi... we simply succumb to the hunger."

"But do you know that? Or is that what you've always been taught to believe?"

Priest stared.

"I don't mean to be a dick or—or a know-it-all. I just mean there's so much we all thought about Vampires. Things we were so sure were fact. Even Knight believed he was infected, but the more we uncover, the more he seems to be remembering differently. So how much of what you know about yourself is real? It's not like you had family to teach you, right?"

Priest's face paled. "Fuck."

"I'm sorry," Oliver said in a rush. He could feel that it was too much—that after everything, Priest didn't need another revelation about himself. He cupped his face and kissed him fiercely. "I'm sorry. I didn't mean to make it worse."

"You couldn't possibly," Priest said roughly. "But I... Gods, I think you might be onto something. I need to speak with Jeremiah the second we get back to the city."

"We're going home?"

Priest nodded. "Once Poe's ready to be moved to Azriel's, we'll meet the Alphas."

"You mean you."

Priest shook his head, meeting Oliver's gaze intensely. "We. You're clever, beloved, and it's becoming more and more obvious that we need you. That you see things we don't. And that's not your Angel powers. That's just you."

Oliver opened his mouth to protest, but Priest kissed him until the words died on the back of his tongue, and all he knew was the taste of his bonded and the warmth that surrounded him made up entirely of how much the Demon adored him.

Wanted him.

Needed him.

Loved him.

19

PRIEST

$\mathcal{H}$e didn't sleep.

He was comforted by the fact that Oliver was in his arms. That he was safe and for the moment, it was all over. Poe was alive, and apart from him and Jeremiah, they'd walked away unscathed. He and Oliver were fully bonded, they loved each other, and Oliver accepted every facet of him just as Priest did him.

But...

Oliver's words about mates wouldn't leave him.

Do you know that? Or is that what you've always been taught to believe?

Before Remi, they hadn't thought Hellhounds could have mates either. Priest was pretty sure that was part of why Jeremiah had resisted so hard—he'd been so sure it wasn't possible, so he hadn't even let himself think about it.

And it had been the same for Priest.

How many months had he been drawn to the bookshop but then forced himself away, doubting the innate connection that had sparked to life the first time he'd seen Oliver through the shop's front window?

Even after Jeremiah mated with the prince, Priest had

convinced himself it was mostly because Remi was half Siren —and a royal on top of that. That had to be some extra-strong genes.

But that didn't explain him and Oliver. The amount of Angel blood in his human made it unlikely, if not impossible, for their bond to start with Oliver. Maybe if he'd been aware and developing his abilities before they'd met, Priest could convince himself.

Which meant it came from him.

An Incubus.

A Demon breed so feared and reviled he wasn't welcome in several countries.

And their bond was as strong as the one Jeremiah had with Remi. Oliver was like a second heartbeat in his chest now—always with him, always aware of him.

He fed him in ways that Priest had never been fed before. He was starting to forget what it felt like to be truly hungry. He was capable of being sated, which meant his fate of insanity from starvation might not be his fate at all anymore.

So what else about themselves had they been lied to about? Where had the misinformation come from, and why did Supes just accept it?

Priest was brought up knowing down to his very bones that he was not ever meant to be. That his purpose was to live, serve, and die in pain and anguish. Just like Jeremiah knew his purpose was to live, serve, and die completely alone. Never loved. Never mated.

But look at them now.

When he was certain Oliver was fast asleep, Priest crept from the bed, grabbing a T-shirt on the way out, and made his way through the house until he heard voices. He stopped near the corner of the kitchen, and he could hear Azriel speaking to someone.

"… a lot of pain, but it'll pass. This is early days. But the more you fight it, the harder it'll be."

"How do you know? You're an Angel? I'm... I'm this."

"This is no less worthy. I don't give a shit what some bigots on conservative TV say."

"I literally have to eat people to survive."

Azriel snorted. "No, you don't. Knight survives on blood donations delivered in bags, and he's not weak for that. No one has to die. But even if you choose to feed on people, that doesn't mean you can't find a balance."

"Kill evil ones?"

"Maybe. Though I suppose evil is a bit subjective. But there are plenty of willing donors. They don't have to be human, you know. There are strong beings out there who will happily and willingly donate."

"There has to be a price for that." Poe's voice was soft, almost broken, and Priest hated that for him.

Azriel laughed softly. "Yes, my darling. There's always a price. But there's a price for food you eat too, right? And for what you drink. For where you lay your head at night. You might have changed, but the world hasn't. You just need to take a breath and let yourself adjust."

Priest didn't want to interrupt. The moment was soft, a little tender, and a lot painful. It wasn't his place.

Moving past the kitchen, he found his way to the side door that led to the garden. It was safer at night with the cover of trees, and he didn't have to go far to find his friend. Knight was sitting against a wide trunk of a tall oak, his head tipped back, eyes closed. He tensed a little when Priest sat down, but it was obvious the Vampire had sensed him.

"Do you think we're doing the right thing?" Knight asked after a beat.

"Taking down this organization?"

Knight opened his eyes but didn't turn to face Priest. "With Poe. I want these labs burned to the ground. Not just for me but for everyone they hurt. Everyone they killed. The children—" His voice cracked, and he cleared his throat. "But I know what it's like to live as this. And I hate it."

Priest offered his hand, and after a long beat, Knight took it. Sometimes, he wanted more touch than this, but Priest knew this wasn't one of those moments. The careful brush of palm against palm was more than he was expecting.

"We found Poe in weeks. You were there for…"

Years. Neither of them were brave enough to say it. Knight didn't know how long he'd been under the lab's control, only that he was very young when they took him, and he'd already started to age when he escaped. Most of his torment had been when he was human… but not all of it.

"Poe will heal. He has a support system here that took you years to find," Priest told him. He stroked his thumb over Knight's wrist. "The point of helping people the way we do is so they don't have to suffer like us."

Knight bowed his head, nodding as he stared at their joined hands. "Oliver asked me if it always hurt to touch people. I told him no, but it was a lie. I dream about it— about, about being able to just hold someone. It feels so fucking good. And then I wake up, and every time I try, it makes me want to tear my own skin off."

Priest tried to pull away, but Knight clung to him. "I don't want to hurt you."

"You're not. I need this. I need to stop running from the things that scare me. I'm never going to get past this if I don't." He swallowed heavily. "I want to be able to have what you and Sunshine do."

"A mate?"

Knight shrugged. "Just a lover would be enough for me. The ability to touch and be touched without thinking about them. The ability to sink my fangs into someone who wanted to feed me the way Oliver feeds you. Tiny sips of life from their veins, knowing they want to be there in my arms. I mean, I'm a Vampire, so I know that finding someone capable of making me their mate is next to impossible, but—"

Priest squeezed his fingers. "About that. Ah. Well." He bit his lip. He didn't want to give Knight false hope, but he also knew this was a thread worth pulling because the tapestry that would unweave from this meant giving the gift of mates and life and purpose to so many beings who didn't believe they were allowed to have those things.

"What?" Knight pressed.

Priest blew out a puff of air. "Oliver pointed something out to me. We have a bond, he and I, like Jeremiah and Remy. But it didn't come from him."

Knight stared at him, and Priest hunched his shoulders.

"It didn't come entirely from him," he clarified. "I felt something when I first saw him, I just didn't understand what it was. But if we were entirely wrong about how Vampires were made, what if we're wrong about a lot of things?"

"Like what?"

"Like the fact that Incubi will eventually go mad and starve to death. Oliver satiates me. Completely. The hunger is entirely gone after I feed on him."

Knight looked unsure. He pulled his hand back. "And you think that'll be forever?"

"I don't know. All I know is that it's different with him. Even in my younger days, when feeding would allow me to be full, it was never like this. There was always a little pang of hunger left behind—a want for more. And that's gone."

Knight pulled one leg toward his chest and wrapped his arms around it. "That doesn't mean someone like me is destined for a mate. I'm... barely a Supe. I was born human and made into this."

"Except..." Priest sighed. "Oz's theory seems to be right. Sunshine finished going through the journals, and it documented some of the experiments they did to trigger the change. It's genetic, brother. This was always in you."

Knight looked away. "That doesn't make me feel any better."

"Okay, fine. But it means we have to question everything now. Everything we know about beings like us says we're unnatural. That we're abominations that weren't ever supposed to exist. But what if that's all bullshit?"

"What would be the point?" Knight stressed.

Priest didn't know, but he also couldn't deny he was onto something. Maybe he was just getting his hopes up, but from the moment he'd fed on Oliver, things had been different. Oliver hadn't been drained, and Priest felt almost like he'd been reborn into something else. And he refused to believe all of these things weren't tied together.

"Once we get back, we can talk to Sunshine about it. But I think I want to go back to the lab and see if there's anything left behind," Priest said.

Knight nodded, his jaw tense but his eyes determined. "I'll go with you."

"Knight—"

"No. Like I said, I'm tired of running from everything that scares me. It's time to face this head-on. Sunshine thinks Remi's ex—that Nephilim—might have some of the answers we're looking for. About more than just how Vampires come into existence. I spoke to him tonight, and he said our number one priority after we get Poe somewhere safe is to find Oz."

"Then we should start at the lab and work our way out from there. But I don't want you to push yourself beyond what you can come back from," Priest stressed.

Knight smiled at him—a small, sad thing. But it still reached his eyes. "I know. And you'll never know how much you and the others mean to me for how you've protected me. But it's time to take my power back from them."

Priest grinned and offered his hand again, and he felt something unfurl in his chest when his friend took it. Without hesitation.

"Did you sleep at all?"

Priest looked up from where he was feasting on Oliver's collarbones and smiled at him, shrugging. "Not really, no. But I don't need sleep the same way you do. This is enough for me." He licked a stripe up Oliver's neck, making his back arch.

It was both alien and beautiful the way he could feel Oliver's lust rushing through him. Before, he could scent it, could taste it in the air between them, but now, it was like it was his own. They hadn't fucked since they'd bonded, both of them emotionally and physically spent, but he had a feeling it would be different than it had been before.

"Kiss me," Oliver whispered, turning his body toward Priest.

Their lips met, lazy and sloppy and no less fantastic than when Oliver was frantic and desperate for him. Priest felt his eyes darken, his tongue lengthen, as he tasted his beloved's mouth. "Love you."

Oliver pulled out of the kiss and smiled. "You like saying that, don't you?"

"I wasn't sure I'd ever get the chance. Not with someone like you." Priest raked his claws through Oliver's hair before forcing himself to shift back fully. They didn't have much time for this. Knight wanted to visit the lab early before whoever had been running it sent people to clear up what was left behind. They needed every bit of evidence they could gather.

Oliver hummed contently as he arched his back, then sat up and looked down at Priest. "Do you know you purr?"

Priest laughed. "Yeah." He dragged the tips of his fingers up the inside of Oliver's naked thigh. "I think somewhere in the long ago, Incubi came from some sort of cat shifter."

"The purr?"

Priest nodded, then sat up and shifted enough for his eyes to change. It took extreme effort to do what he was about to do, and it usually only happened when his instincts were to protect his face. But when he heard Oliver gasp, he knew he was successful.

"You have inner eyelids?"

Priest grinned, showing a little fang. "Claws, fangs, a purr, and my eyelids are pretty solid proof."

"Also proof that maybe I'm right about the whole societal mythos bullshit about your species," Oliver said. "Gods, I wish my shop wasn't blown to pieces. We had a whole library of books I hadn't gotten to yet, and some of them were ancient history texts."

Priest frowned. He thought blowing up the shop was a random act of violence to distract from the people who wanted to steal Poe, but maybe there was more to it. Which also meant there might be something more to blowing up the law office than suspecting the poor bastard they'd taken and killed was a vampire.

"What's that frown?" Oliver brushed his fingers between Priest's eyebrows.

"Nothing. Just more food for thought." He swung his legs off the bed, then yanked Oliver to his feet and buried his face in his mate's neck. He could feel heat radiating off the mating bite, and he licked it, feeling a surge of lust rushing into him, giving him the boost he needed.

"If you don't stop that, we're never going to get going," Oliver murmured.

Priest forced himself to pull away, turning so he could grab his jeans and shirt from the top of his suitcase. He threw his clothes on, then raked fingers through his hair before turning back to Oliver, who was delicately picking through his things.

"I'll get some coffee going and see if Knight's ready. Meet you in the kitchen?"

Oliver waved him off, and to stop himself from pouncing and taking what he wanted, Priest made himself walk out the door. He could hear voices, slightly raised and agitated, as he made his way to the kitchen, and he found Poe standing against the counter with his arms crossed.

Knight and Azriel were across from him, both looking determined.

"We need a vote," Poe said as soon as he locked eyes on Priest. He was definitely angry. His fangs had drawn pinpricks of blood over his lower lip. "He wants to leave me with Azriel while you all go to the lab."

Priest raised a brow and looked at Knight and Azriel, who both nodded. "This is a bad idea, why? Because I can see you're still healing from here."

"I want to see where they were keeping me. I was drugged and tortured while they had me, and I was half fucking dead when your friend pulled me out," Poe snapped. "And I'm not made of glass. I'm hurting, but I'm not going to fall apart."

Priest turned to his friends. "He's got a point."

Azriel looked mildly surprised, but Knight looked outraged. "You cannot be serious."

Priest shrugged. "What would you do in his shoes?"

"I was in his shoes," Knight hissed. "And I most certainly didn't look for a way back."

"That's because the lab was still operational when you escaped," Priest pointed out. "And you've never been in his shoes. What happened to you was different."

"I—" But then Knight deflated. He turned to Poe. "I think this could be a mistake, but it's on your head."

He stormed out, and Priest held back a sigh.

Poe looked torn, but Azriel closed the distance between them and set his hands on Poe's shoulders. "Don't take it personally. He's like that with the people he cares about."

Poe laughed bitterly. "He doesn't even know me."

"He knows you better than you think," Priest said, slipping past them to grab coffee. For a moment, he swore he could taste tendrils of lust in the air, but before he could flick his tongue out to verify, it was gone. "You need to be patient with him. This is harder for him than he wants to let on."

Poe let out a short breath. "I don't want to hold you up or anything, but I really need to do this."

"We're not going to stop you," Azriel said. "So long as you promise you'll say something if it becomes too much."

"I promise," Poe said quietly.

There it was again. Priest flicked his tongue out, and Azriel smacked him. "Stop that. I know what you're doing, and I will rip your tongue out if I have to."

Priest raised a brow at him. "I'm not hungry. I was just curious."

Poe looked confused, but Priest wasn't about to fill him in.

After a beat, Poe sighed. "I'm going to go check on Oliver."

The moment he was out of the room, Priest rounded on his friend. "A baby Vampire?"

"It's not coming from me. He's dealing with a lot of confusing feelings and emotions. Everything is heightened, and he feels a little... grateful to the people who rescued him," Azriel explained. "Trust me, it'll pass. And for the record, I would never prey on someone in his position. Do I think he's attractive? I mean, look at him."

Priest snorted. Objectively, he supposed Poe was good-looking, but now that he and Oliver had bonded, he struggled to see beauty in anyone else.

"He's adorable in that weird, humanly awkward way. Like a baby giraffe. But I don't want to fuck baby giraffes," Azriel said.

"Protest much?"

"Fuck you."

Between one blink and the next, Azriel was gone, leaving

Priest to the coffee. He didn't think there was actually something going on, and he did understand what Azriel was trying to say. But he also couldn't deny that now Poe had turned, his life was going to be different.

Not only that, but if they were right about the mates thing, his prospects about any happily ever after he might have would be drastically and completely changed.

OLIVER

*O*liver wasn't entirely on board with Poe coming to the compound, but he understood why his friend needed to do it. He could also see how frustrated Poe was by how careful the others were being with him. Priest was mostly hands-off, and so was Knight for obvious reasons. But he hovered a little too close, and Azriel didn't let Poe get more than a few feet away from him without putting a hand on his shoulder or his back.

Poe looked like he wanted to pounce on the Angel and drain him, and Oliver wondered if Az would let him if he did. Poe had clearly been feeding, though Oliver couldn't bring himself to ask on what—or who. But he could tell Poe was still hungry.

He wished he knew more about Vampires. He never thought they deserved the sort of treatment they got, but he'd never put much study into them either. For so many years, he believed they were caused by a viral infection in humans. Now, realizing it was a genetic mutation or something, it changed everything.

He could only hope the lab had something left behind

because he wanted to help figure it out. Not just for Poe's sake but for everyone who had been turned against their will.

The drive to the compound wasn't terribly long, but Oliver considered asking if they could just use their powers to close the distance. Knight seemed happy behind the wheel though, and Azriel looked at ease. Priest seemed to sense his discomfort because he picked up Oliver's hand and gently played with his fingers.

It was distracting enough to pass the time, and before long, they were there. It was difficult to see at first with the thick brush, but eventually, the road opened up into a clearing with a path that led to an underground garage. The tire tracks were fresh and dug deeply into the dirt from the hasty escape the humans had made that night.

It was odd to see the place in the middle of the day. It looked so unassuming and yet oddly sinister in the same way. It was massive—way bigger than Oliver had assumed. It stretched far into the trees, blending almost as seamlessly as the safe house.

It was no real wonder how it had operated undetected for so many years. It just broke Oliver's heart that it had taken Poe's capture to bring it down. His best friend did not deserve that kind of fate. If he was to become a Vampire, it should have been on his own terms. And Knight sure as hell deserved justice far sooner than he was getting now.

The tension in the SUV ramped up as they pulled to a stop, and Priest quickly clambered out, taking Oliver with him. Azriel followed suit, and the two Vampires remained inside.

"They need a moment," Azriel said.

Oliver knew. He could feel it. He took Priest's hand in his and tugged him toward the door, which had been blasted off the hinges by what he assumed had been either the Bravo or Charlie Teams. "Do you think there's anything we should be worried about right now?"

Priest shook his head, lifting Oliver's hand to his lips and kissing his knuckles. "No. There's no chance in hell they don't know who raided the place, and they won't be foolish enough to come back. They might have government officials on their side—at least, we think they do—but they don't have the law on their side. Not yet. Now's the best time to collect as much evidence as we can."

Oliver didn't have much hope that anything had been left behind, but he followed Priest inside and stuck close as they began to explore the first set of rooms.

It took the better part of three hours to get through the whole compound, but by the time they were done, they found little more than a few handwritten journals and one single computer terminal that hadn't been wiped. Unfortunately, the only thing on there was security footage of the guards coming and going.

Priest hooked a tablet up to it, downloaded everything onto a zip file, and immediately sent it to HQ for the analysts to go through, but he wasn't confident they were going to find anything there. So far, Priest hadn't recognized anyone, and facial recognition would take forever since each country or kingdom had its own database that would have to be searched.

"I doubt they send anyone high-ranking to these facilities," Knight said. He'd been quiet as he perused the rooms. Everyone had left him to his thoughts, and while he seemed tense, he wasn't shaking the way he had been the night of the raid. "They're not too clever to get away with this forever, but they're clever enough to cover their tracks."

Azriel rubbed at his chin, glancing over at Poe, who was leaning against the far wall with his arms wrapped around his middle. "Were you able to piece anything together?"

Knight shrugged. "Odd, broken memories. Kind of like dreams." He massaged his temples. "I'm starting to wonder if they fucked with my mind."

"It's entirely possible. They have access to every drug on the market and many that aren't. There are plenty of spells too," Priest said. "It wouldn't take much to affect the memory of a newly turned Vampire."

Knight lifted his chin, looking furious. "Then I need to find someone to unlock this shit."

"Are you sure that's a good idea? You know that could—"

"I godsdamned know exactly what it could do to me," Knight interrupted, glowering at Priest. "But do you really think the better alternative is to let me live in this fog?"

Priest sighed heavily, and Oliver moved closer, taking his hand. Priest shot him a grateful smile before turning back to Knight, his eyes glowing crimson. "You're right. I'm sorry. I just don't want you to have to suffer more."

Knight let out a bitter laugh. "My entire life has been a nightmare since they took me. Starting the agency saved my life, but that doesn't mean it erased the torment. But I can't move past something I don't remember."

"He's right," Poe cut in. He pushed away from the wall and walked toward them. "A lot of what I went through is a foggy mess, and I know it would have been so much worse if I'd been here as long as him. Being here is awful, but it helps. Being able to see it with sober eyes and totally free?" He glanced away. "I'm ready to leave now, but I'm glad I came."

Azriel looked at Poe, then Priest, then Knight. Finally, his gaze settled on Oliver. "Are you ready to say goodbye for a while?"

He wasn't. Shit. His chest was tight like he had a boulder lodged behind his sternum, and he swallowed thickly. He knew he had to let his best friend go. At least for a little while. Poe needed time to adapt and to heal. He needed time to accept that whatever had been done was forever.

And Oliver knew he'd just be in the way. He'd want to shield Poe from feeling anything bad, and that wouldn't help him in the moment. No, he needed someone like Azriel who would let him suffer because it wouldn't be forever.

But it sucked.

"Are you ready?" Oliver asked.

Poe looked at him, his gaze shuttered. It was the first time since meeting Poe that Oliver couldn't read his expression. He felt like he was being gutted. "I'm ready."

When Oliver tried to take a step forward, Poe took a step back and shook his head.

"Okay." The word came out a tattered whisper, and Priest quickly pulled him close.

"I'm sorry," Poe said. "But I just... I can't. Not right now. Not here." He turned on his heel and hurried out of the room, his footsteps echoing off the metal walls like gunshots.

Knight turned to Oliver and met his gaze. "It won't be forever. I promise. Just give him a little time."

"You'll come by soon, right?" Azriel asked.

Knight offered a wry grin. "If I can find the place."

Oliver had no idea what that meant, but he watched as Azriel leaned in and whispered something into Knight's ear. The Vampire nodded, then shoved his hands into his pockets and backed away like the closeness was becoming too much.

"I'll call you soon," Azriel said to Oliver. "When he's ready for a visit."

All Oliver could do was nod and let the Angel pull him into a firm embrace. He felt the pulse of Priest's jealousy, just a gentle simmer, really, so he indulged in the hug until Azriel let him go. "Thank you."

Azriel cradled his face gently. "Don't thank me, little brother. We're family. This is what we do." He pressed a kiss to Oliver's forehead, ignoring Priest's clear growl, then pulled away and turned. In the blink of an eye, he was gone, and just like he'd felt it when Poe was gone before, he felt the same thing now.

Only there was no fear. No pain. No desperation. There was just the absence of him and the knowledge that as soon as he was ready, Oliver would see him again.

Back at the safe house, Priest and Oliver were alone. Knight packed quickly after finishing up with the compound, and then he took one of the two remaining cars and said he'd see them back at HQ. He and Priest spoke quietly for a few minutes in the driveway, and Oliver watched from the window as he got in and eventually disappeared down the narrow road.

The door opened again, and Priest gathered Oliver close. "And then there were two."

Oliver was profoundly aware this was the first time they'd been alone together after bonding. It felt important, and yet it also felt so natural, like it was part of who they were. He turned his face up, and Priest took him in a firm, lingering kiss.

"Take me to bed," Oliver murmured.

Priest didn't obey immediately. He pushed Oliver against the wall, kissing him harder, then lifted him until Oliver was wrapping his legs around Priest's waist. He was hard, needy, aching for more, and Priest let out a soft growl as he scraped his teeth along the tendon in Oliver's neck.

"Want you," Priest said.

Oliver knocked their foreheads together. "You have me. I'm yours."

Priest began to purr again, more vibration than sound, rushing under Oliver's skin. He shuddered with a mix of pleasure and contentment, rocking himself against Priest.

"Bed. Now."

Oliver laughed. "That's what I've been *saying*."

Priest ran faster than Oliver could process, and in a single breath, they were behind their closed bedroom door. Priest laid Oliver out on the bed, and then he lifted a clawed hand and tore the shirt from his body.

"I liked that! I don't have many things to my name right now!"

Priest smirked as he went after his slacks the same way. "I'll buy you more. I'll buy you an entire department store of adorable, nerdy librarian clothes the moment we get back."

Oliver shuddered. The moment was tender yet oddly feral. It was a glimpse of what was to come—of everything he was still waiting to learn about Priest. He could see himself naked in the forest, running, Priest in full Demon form going after him.

A moment like they'd shared in the alley, but instead of racing home to feed, Priest would take him there, surrounded by nature, observed by the moon and stars. He groaned as Priest dropped to his knees and lifted his cock, taking the head between his lips. He suckled, dipping his forked tongue into his slit, and Oliver's eyes rolled back in his head.

"Gods. Gods," he gasped.

"Demon, but close," Priest said, sinking his teeth into Oliver's thigh. He broke the skin, then licked away droplets of blood before kissing his way up Oliver's chest. "I want to be inside you, my little human."

"Yes," Oliver said. He watched as Priest spat in his hand and slicked his cock, and then he wrapped his legs around Priest's waist, moaning when that thickness dragged over his hole. Priest sucked his fingers into his mouth, then reached between them and pushed inside, lubing and stretching him.

Oliver groaned at the sudden fullness, at the heat of it, at how perfect it all was.

This was fate. It had to be. There was no other explanation.

"Yes. Fate decided you are mine, so I took you," Priest rasped, fucking his fingers in and out. He added a third, then a fourth.

Oliver had never been stretched so wide before, but gods, he wanted more.

Priest groaned as he lifted higher, shoving Oliver farther onto the bed, and then he pushed and slipped inside with a single thrust. Oliver's eyes went wide and sightless as he took all of his mate. It was different. He felt his own pleasure wrapped in Priest's, ricocheting back and forth.

It was almost too much.

"I didn't realize it would be like this," Priest gasped, his hips moving fast, thrusts shallow and rapid like he was chasing both their orgasms. He was trembling, clinging to Oliver like he needed him to stay weighted to Earth. "Fuck. Fuck. I feel you taking me. I feel it."

Oliver understood. He could feel himself being fucked, but he could feel the ecstasy coursing off his mate. Their bond threads were twisting together, bright gold, pulsing with the beats of their hearts. His balls went tight as Priest lifted his leg and changed angles, hitting his prostate with every thrust.

"More," Oliver gasped. "Harder."

"Yes. Yes. Take it. Gods, look at you take it."

Oliver opened his eyes to see Priest staring down at where they were joined. He grabbed him by the back of his hair and yanked him in for a kiss. The moment the forked tongue wrapped around his own, he was lost. His orgasm crashed over him like a tsunami, whiting out his vision, consuming his limbs, tearing him from the mortal plane.

And Priest went with him. There was a single, still moment, and then he was spilling deep inside Oliver. He clung hard, claws drawing blood, fangs sinking into their mating bite. There were no words in any language to describe the way Oliver felt.

Only that it was right. It was theirs.

No one else would ever—could ever—feel this way. It was them. Together.

For as long as the universe allowed them to live.

21

PRIEST

*T*he flight back home was strange.

Everything was changed, and yet it was exactly the same. Oliver kept close to him, and Priest stayed curled around him as long as it was physically possible to do so. They stopped for dinner on the way to his house, holding hands in the drive-thru, kissing when they were at traffic lights.

It was easy, and nothing in Priest's life had ever been easy before. It should have terrified him, but a lot of it was Oliver's calm that kept Priest from sinking into the what-ifs. They had a few days of peace before he was supposed to head to HQ to meet with Jeremiah and the others, which meant a few days of giving in to his desire to touch Oliver. To make him beg, and sob, and come.

It was satisfying in ways Priest didn't think he could be.

Once upon a time, the idea of relationships had sent his skin crawling. The idea of monogamy was so foreign to him it was like an unknown, undeciphered language. But now, the thought of looking at someone else—at feeding on anyone else—made him feel sick. He was happy. He was content.

And that's what terrified him the most because they could

lose this battle. They could fight this war Jeremiah wanted to bring down on these people, and they could lose. Oliver could die, and if that happened, Priest knew he'd go with him.

If he didn't perish right away, the madness would take him because nothing would ever sate his hunger again.

Part of him wanted to pick Oliver up and squirrel him away back with the Dragons until the people fighting consumed each other. He could live in a wasteland so long as Oliver was by his side. But he also knew he owed it to Knight to do better. To do something to bring him the justice he deserved.

They all had earned that. And he wasn't done searching for the answers to all the new questions that had arisen.

Who was he? What was he, really? A Demon, yes. An Incubus, yes. But what defined those two things now? It was strange enough coming to the realization that he could live his life fully and completely without the threat of madness and starvation hanging over his head.

So could that be the same fate for others out there like himself? And gods, but would things have been different—would his mother have kept him—if she'd known?

"Baby?"

Priest blinked in surprise when he realized Oliver was talking to him. No one in his life had ever thought to call him something sweet. His heart felt thick in his chest as he opened his arms and let Oliver crawl into them.

They were lounging on the couch, stomachs full, sleepy and lazy. It was the perfect evening, especially now with Oliver resting against him.

"You were thinking really hard. I could almost hear it in my head," Oliver told him when he was settled.

Priest dragged fingers through Oliver's hair. "There's been a lot on my mind since, well, everything."

"Because of me?"

"Yes, but not because I have you. It's because of what you said about our bond and how it wasn't just you." Priest's fingers trailed down the side of Oliver's face as he stared into his eyes. They were blacker now, almost matching his pupil. He wondered if Oliver had noticed yet, if he'd hate the change that came from their bond.

"You mean the starvation thing, right?"

Priest bit his lip, then said, "I have no idea how many Incubi are out there. We've spent eons trying not to breed because the last thing any of us wanted to do was condemn another soul to this torment. And those of us who do abandon our young."

"Have you abandoned—"

"No," Priest interrupted in a rush. The idea of children horrified him, but if it had happened, he could have never left his child. Not after what he'd suffered. "No. But my mother left me at a group home for Supes like me. It was... lonely. Terrifying some nights. Painful. We were educated on what we were and what we were meant to become. They told me if I wanted to survive, I should go into the service of a royal household."

Oliver sat up a little. "You mean..."

"Yes," Priest said softly. "That kind of service. They said there would be no stopping the madness—that I would eventually succumb—but being employed in the service of someone wealthy meant I might delay it for longer than an Incubus who had to find food on their own."

"So they'd get sex and what? Power? I mean, you're capable of doing a lot of damage," Oliver said. "You're strong."

Priest wasn't sure where he was going with that, but he could feel in the bond that Oliver had a point. "Yes. Like Hellhounds, Incubi can be trained as a sort of attack dog... with perks. And I'd have the ability to feed more often than finding a willing being, and it would keep me from going over the edge too young."

"Convenient," Oliver spat.

Priest rubbed a hand down his face. "It's not complete bullshit, my love. I felt it. I felt the gnawing hunger. I felt the madness. And the time I could go between feeds was growing less and less."

"Yeah, but..." Oliver's brow furrowed. "Did you ever try to find someone? Not like a one-off, but someone you cared about?"

Priest snorted. "I'm a Demon, little human. Most people—supernatural or not—aren't like you."

"I feel like that's kind of my point. You believed it, and everyone else around you believed it. But you and I just proved it's bullshit. Jeremiah and Remi proved it's bullshit. And Knight—"

They didn't know if it was bullshit for Knight, but Priest was terrified that no matter what his friend wanted, he might not ever be in a place he could accept it.

"We know the virus is bullshit, so what's to say that the reason Incubi have all gone mad is because they've spent centuries believing a lie and have turned away from their true nature."

"This *is* my true nature," Priest said, starting to feel defensive.

Oliver twisted, pushing up onto his knees, and he cradled Priest's face between both hands. "This is your nature, Claude. This. With me. The rest is bullshit. I refuse to believe that any creature was created only to die in agony. That there are beings out there who are meant to be alone and unloved. That's just... it's not possible."

"You're optimistic."

"I'm following a trail of evidence. I'm a nerd and a historian. It's what I do." Oliver leaned in and kissed him. "Believe me. Please."

The truth was, Priest did believe him, but it scared him. If it was true—if it was *all* true—it meant thousands before him had lived and died because of a lie. It meant he was abandoned by his family because of a lie. It meant that their numbers were almost nonexistent now because of a lie.

But why? What was the point?

"We need to talk to Jeremiah," Oliver said, settling back into his arms. "I think he'll see my point."

"I think you're right," Priest murmured. He dipped his head low and took Oliver in a sweet, lingering kiss.

Maybe he was right. Maybe he was wrong.

But the only thing that really mattered was right there, in that moment. Whatever the truth was for others, Oliver was right. Loving his little human was his true nature now.

Priest watched as Oliver paced the room, his hands moving as he spoke. It was like an intricate dance, and he fought the urge to grab him and pin him to the chair so he could kiss the breath out of him. He didn't because Jeremiah would have mauled him, though he had a feeling Remi might enjoy the show.

But Oliver had an audience now, and he'd been working on the smaller details of his theory the whole trip to the Trident Headquarters.

It helped that Jeremiah was riveted. It didn't show in his face, but it showed in the way one hand was clenching into a fist and relaxing, revealing a hint of claw. And in the way he kept his thumb running over Remi's wrist like he needed the physical touch since everything Oliver was saying was overwhelming.

"It makes sense," Remi said after a long beat.

Jeremiah turned and quirked a brow at him. "Does it?"

"I mean, it's just as likely you'd be capable of creating a bond as I would. I'm half human, and you're full Hellhound."

"Your parents—" Jeremiah began.

"What if my dad isn't actually all human? I mean, if Oliver never noticed he was part Angel, what's to say there's not some sort of supernatural line in my dad's family? It's not like they took DNA tests."

Jeremiah sat back in his chair with a slight thud. His face looked the way Priest's must have when he realized Oliver had a point. There was something happening. Something was wrong about everything they thought they understood.

"The journals I took are beyond my education," Jeremiah admitted. "But I have Caspian looking over them and trying to transcribe the information in more layman's terms. What I could understand is that they've come up with a way to trigger what they call the Genetic Awakening. Vampires are like Nephilim—they only come from human lines."

"And?" Priest asked.

"Maybe we need to—" Remi started, then blushed when Priest looked at him. "Sorry, I was going over the journals too."

"Don't be sorry. Obviously, we need all the help we can get," Priest told him.

Remi nodded, then looked torn. "It would help if we could find Oz. He used to talk about this stuff all the time when we were dating." Jeremiah growled, and Remi rolled his eyes but otherwise ignored him. "I didn't always understand it, but I absorbed some of it. He thinks that there was a... divergence in history, when the continent was being divided. A war that didn't involve humans, and a lot of the records were lost. There's some in stories. But everyone assumed they were myths."

Priest leaned forward. "Like what?"

"A war between Gargoyles and Sirens in the Oceanus Tales," Remi said.

Priest had no idea what that was, but Oliver nodded along.

"They made an alliance to fight an army full of Hellhounds who were eventually defeated and enslaved. But so far, there's been no actual evidence of that happening."

"So what does that have to do with this?" Jeremiah asked.

Remi bit his thumbnail for a moment. "Well, in the Oceanus Tales, the Sirens subjugated the Hellhounds and basically sterilized them to keep them from breeding. They decided the most humane thing to do was to let them die off without mass killing them all."

"Charming," Jeremiah growled.

Remi cast his eyes down. "Yeah, it doesn't make my people look great."

"I just don't see what that has to do with anything," Priest cut in. "I mean, I get it. Sterilize them and let them die off, but that clearly didn't happen."

"Well," Oliver said softly, "the thing is, you can't really mass sterilize an entire population. The army, sure, but what about the others? The average citizen? The children? How do you subjugate them all?"

Priest lifted a brow, waiting for the answer.

"Create a massive lie. A myth rooted in some truth. Tell the world that Hellhounds are different—that they're not like us because they don't have mates. They live and die alone. They're weaker and mostly infertile. Work laws into the system that prevent them from being welcome on most continents. Slowly, over time, that becomes public knowledge."

Priest felt like he'd been punched in the gut. "We have no evidence that's true."

"No, not really." He glanced at his mate. "Except you. And the notes saying that everything everyone has believed about Vampires is a lie. And if they're lying about that—and if both of you can have a mate bond, then it's possible that's a lie too. It's possible that other Hellhounds and other Demons who have found their mates have kept it quiet for fear of what might happen to them if they told anyone."

Priest swallowed heavily. "What would be the point?"

"It's hard to say," Remi answered. "Maybe something to do with the war. Maybe it's about power."

"It's usually about power," Oliver says, a haunted look on his face.

"And if we can find your friend, he might know more, right?" Priest said.

Remi hugged his middle, and Jeremiah pulled him close, smudging a kiss over his temple. "Yeah. I think he would. He's dedicated almost all of his life to ancient history, long before he decided to attend Hillsland. And if this is true—if we're getting close to something—it's probably why he was taken."

"You're so sure he was?" Oliver asked.

At that, Jeremiah looked up, and his expression was far from happy. "We found something in that security footage."

Pulling out his phone, he tapped on it a few times, then handed it over to Priest. Oliver hovered over him to watch, and together, they saw a grainy, black-and-white image of a tall man with dark hair in tattered clothes and glasses with bent rims dragged past a doorway.

"That sort of looks like him," Priest says, handing the phone back.

Remi nodded miserably. "I'm a thousand percent sure it's him. But I don't understand how. He should be able to crush them."

"Yeah, but they had something that brought me and Priest to our knees," Jeremiah said, running his nose along Remi's hairline. "So it's safe to say they might have had a weapon that could work against him too."

Priest sat forward and smiled grimly as Oliver began to rub his lower back. "So we know they have him. Now we just have to figure out where he is and get him back. Any ideas?"

Oliver tapped him gently. "Azriel and I are both Angels. Well... I'm part Angel. I managed to find Poe, and he's stronger than me, and he could feel the power in me. So maybe if we have somewhere to start, he and I can work together to get some kind of location."

"It's as good a plan as any," Jeremiah said. "Will Azriel be willing?"

"All we can do is ask. He promised to call me soon," Oliver said. "As soon as Poe is ready to see other people."

Priest hated the plan. He hated it because it put Oliver front and center, but he also knew that his beloved little human wouldn't have it any other way. Besides, this was all of their fight now. "I can send him a text, but right now, I think all we can do is wait and see if—"

"This is him," Oliver said, cutting Priest off. He was holding his phone. "He must have sensed I needed him."

Jeremiah looked at Priest, who nodded. "Take it. Make the plan to see him. At this point, I don't think we have any other choice."

EPILOGUE

OLIVER

"*H*oney, I'm home."

Oliver toed off his shoes and hung up his jacket, more tired than he'd even been after nearly getting blown all to hell. Working his new Angelic abilities for hours alongside Azriel was draining for him in a way he wasn't used to, but they were making progress.

He hoped.

It was hard to tell most days, but Azriel seemed satisfied with what they were accomplishing.

He knew the rest of the Agency was trying to hunt down other leads on where Oz could be or the location of any other lab compounds. Each day, he went to Azriel's, and Priest went to HQ or out to run down a possible lead with Knight, Slate, or Storm.

Priest had texted him an hour ago to say he was home for the day and making dinner. Oliver smiled to himself, warmth filling him. Things were still chaotic and scary, but in their home—because Priest had insisted it was both of theirs now that they were mated—away from the bigotry and hatred and threats, it was peaceful. Domestic.

He padded through the house, smiling when he entered

the kitchen and found his sweet Demon stirring a large pot of something that smelled divine, wearing an apron that said *Tongue-fuck the cook.*

Which he planned on doing, after he ate.

"Hey," Priest said, smiling as he set his spoon aside and stepped around the kitchen island. "You look a little tired, love."

"I'm a lot tired, so I'll take that as a compliment."

Priest frowned, not appreciating his joke.

"I'm okay." He stepped up into his mate's space and tipped his face up, silently asking for a kiss. He got one, of course.

Priest devoured his mouth, acting like he hadn't seen Oliver for weeks instead of hours. Not that he minded. Sighing, he wrapped his arms around his Demon's shoulders and held on to his hair, opening for Priest's flickering tongue.

After several molasses-thick minutes, Priest raised his head, running his thumb along Oliver's lower lip. His eyes were black as sin, a match to Oliver's new irises.

"Did you see him today?"

Oliver's heart twisted in his chest as he shook his head. "Not today."

He'd been going to Azriel's every day for two weeks, working on focusing their powers on the lost Nephilim, and he hadn't seen or spoken to Poe once. He knew he was there —he could sense him as soon as he was within the wards that hid Azriel's place—and Az reassured him he was doing okay. But Poe wasn't ready to see him or be seen. Not yet.

As much as Oliver understood, it still hurt to be so close to him and be kept at arm's length. He knew that Poe had been hoping for peace and quiet, and Oliver showing up not long after he and Azriel had retreated there wasn't helping. Oliver had offered his and Priest's place to work, but Azriel hadn't wanted to be away from Poe for hours every day.

"I'm sure he'll be ready soon," Priest reassured him, just like he did each evening.

"Me too." He nuzzled against Priest's face. Soon was subjective, after all. Now that Poe was a Vampire and Oliver was part Angel and mated to a Demon—who knew how many decades or centuries they'd have on Earth together.

"Hungry? Dinner is ready."

He brushed Priest's hair back from his forehead. "Always."

"Unf, yes," Oliver moaned, arching his back to try and take Priest deeper. He sank onto his forearms and pressed his forehead against the mattress. "Just like that, baby."

He felt a surge of happiness from his mate at the endearment, just like always, but it was quickly swallowed up by the raw lust enveloping them. Priest's clawed hands were holding his hips as he rammed into him fast and hard, pricking at his skin and sending sparks of pleasure shooting through him.

He loved when they came together slowly and tenderly, making love for hours until they were both sated and dehydrated. But he also loved this, when it was borderline aggressive as Priest *took* him with his huge Incubus cock.

Priest shuttled in and out of his body, his growly purr filling the air around them as he siphoned off some of Oliver's power to top himself off. The tug on his essence sent him higher, filling him up in a different way instead of stealing from him like everyone said it would.

Warmth settled on his back, Priest's voice rasping in his ear. "You weren't lying; you are hungry."

Oliver smiled against their soft sheets. "Starved. Give me more. Harder."

"Hold on, little human," Priest ordered, voice barely more than a rumble.

He wrapped his fingers in the bedding, grunting with each slam of Priest's cock in his ass. His whole body jolted forward and then was jerked back by Priest's bruising grip. It was overwhelming. The wet sounds, Priest's rumbling purr, the rough friction on his knees and forearms. It all combined with the mounting pleasure inside him, driven higher every time Priest sank fully inside him, stretching him to the max.

He wanted the feelings to go on forever, but he knew it couldn't. He was already so close, and Priest's orgasm was barreling down on him as well. Just as he was reaching the pinnacle, his throbbing cock untouched where it swung with each of Priest's thrusts, his Demon's warm body covered his once more.

Instead of words though, sharp teeth bit into his neck, causing an explosion of euphoria to explode beneath his skin. "Oh gods!"

Priest growled, fangs still inside him, and his hips jerked a few more times before pressing as deep as possible and holding. Warmth filled Oliver—in his wrecked hole and spreading from his refreshened mate bite. It would never even heal all the way if Priest didn't sneakily use his powers on Oliver. It was such a small wound it didn't take much strength from him, but Oliver didn't like the idea of his Demon going out searching for the evil people who'd terrorized their friends without a full tank.

It was a while before Priest pulled his softened cock out and then gave them a bare-minimum cleanup before flopping onto the bed, half on Oliver's back and pressing his face against his neck.

"Mm. We should go eat dinner," Oliver said sleepily, his limbs feeling like they weighed a thousand pounds.

"It'll keep." Priest didn't move a muscle. "How was the rest of your day?"

"Slow," he mumbled, turning his head to try and peer down at his mate, but all he could see was the top of his disheveled head. "Az swears we're making progress, but I can't feel it. What about you?"

Priest grunted and squirmed up on the bed until they were face-to-face. He was practically glowing, so full from constantly feeding off Oliver. It filled him with immeasurable pride, knowing he kept his sweet Incubus completely sated.

"We might have a lead."

That woke Oliver up a bit more. "Really?"

Priest nodded, the tips of their noses brushing. "One of the analysts ID'd one of the guys in the video with Oz. Turns out, he's the son of some obscure prince from the Pravaria Kingdom in the south that borders the Griffin's empire."

"Wow." Oliver turned that new information over in his head. "He's a long way from home. Do you think they have Oz stashed in Pravaria?"

"Maybe," Priest conceded. "But it seems more likely to keep everything here, where whoever is in charge can keep a tight grip on the ranks."

"How does IDing this guy help then?"

"The royal family owns estates in pretty much every country on the continent."

Oliver's eyes widened. "You think he has access to all of them and they have Oz hidden away right under our noses."

"That's exactly what we think."

He chewed on his lip until Priest stopped him with a gentle touch.

"What's wrong? I thought you'd be happy now that you and Azriel will have somewhere more specific to focus your searches."

"That'll be really helpful. It's just... Keeping someone as powerful as a Nephilim locked down—even with magic— would be extremely difficult and dangerous. It would take someone, or a group of someones, with incredible strength to do it." He met Priest's understanding eyes. "Getting him free will be a lot more difficult than Poe and the others from the compound. And you and Jeremiah got really hurt already."

Priest cupped the side of his face. "My sweet, worried little human. We have tricks up our sleeves we haven't come close to losing. We'll get him back."

But at what cost?

He did his best to shield the thought, not wanting Priest to think he doubted him and his Demon even for a second. But he hated knowing he'd have to watch Priest walk into danger over and over again. That was who he was, who the whole Trident Agency was. They stepped in when no one else would or could.

It pleased him to no end that his mate was such an amazing person.

But it also terrified him.

He couldn't lose him.

"Shh." Priest brushed his thumb over Oliver's cheekbone. "You won't. I love you, and I'm not going anywhere. I'll always come home to you. If nothing else, trust in that."

He nodded, eyes burning with tears, and buried himself in Priest's chest, holding him tightly. They lay like that for a long time, stroking each other, dropping random kisses on whatever body part they could reach, and soaking in each other's warmth and love.

When his stomach started growling, Priest dragged him out of bed and downstairs to the kitchen, neither of them bothering to get dressed. Priest dished up an incredibly aromatic beef stew, and they sat together, eating quietly and holding hands.

He was almost finished with his second bowl when Priest's phone went off where he'd left it earlier on the kitchen counter. Sighing, Priest went to check it, his back muscles freezing as he gazed down at the screen.

"What's wrong?"

"It's from Knight," Priest said slowly, spinning to face Oliver. His jaw was tense, and he fisted his hair with his free hand. "He says he found where Oz is being kept, and he's going to try and break in tonight."

"On his own?" Oliver asked, voice pitching up as he scrambled to his feet.

"Fucking martyr." Priest typed something into his phone and then tossed it back onto the counter. He strode over and clasped Oliver's face between his hands. "Sweetheart, I might have to go back into the office for a little while. Unexpected late-night meeting."

Oliver rolled his eyes at his odd sense of humor. "Yes, dear. But I'm coming with you. Time for a sit-down and firm talk with that troubled coworker of yours."

Priest gazed into his eyes as his emotions swirled, bombarding Oliver. Fear was most prevalent, but acceptance was right behind it. "Have you been working on your teleporting with Azriel?"

Nodding, Oliver slowly took a breath and let it out, then used his powers to move his body to the other side of the kitchen and back. He didn't land *exactly* where he'd been before—one of Priest's fingers ended up in his mouth—but it was still pretty damn impressive if he did say so himself.

"Together," Oliver said softly.

Priest clasped the back of his neck and pulled him close, pressing a sweet kiss to his lips. "Together."

Always.

Thank you for reading Priest and Oliver's story! We hope you enjoyed it and will join the Trident Agency again when Knight's book arrives in 2025!

ALSO BY EM LINDSEY

<u>Kindle Unlimited Books:</u>

<u>Broken Chains</u>

<u>The Carnal Tower</u>

<u>Hit and Run</u>

<u>Irons and Works</u>

<u>The Sin Bin: West Coast</u>

<u>Malicious Compliance</u>

<u>Collaborations with Other Authors</u>

<u>Foreign Translations</u>

<u>AudioBooks</u>

ALSO BY KIKI CLARK

Kincaid Pack

Leather & Chrome

Blue Collar Hearts

Forever Family Trilogy

Audiobooks

ABOUT EM LINDSEY

E.M. Lindsey is a non-binary, MM Romance author who lives on the East Coast of the United States. When they're not working, EM is spending time on the beach, kayaking, swimming, and playing with their dogs.

Ream Stories
Website
Free Short Stories
Amazon
Instagram
BookBub

ABOUT KIKI CLARK

A small-town Michigan girl, Kiki has enjoyed reading since she first picked up a YA fantasy as a child. After that, she devoured everything she could get her hands on and dreamed of one time writing her own books that touched people's hearts.

In 2020, she proudly joined the ranks of authors releasing character-driven, emotionally satisfying books showcasing that everyone deserves to find love.

To keep up-to-date with Kiki, sign up for her newsletter: http://www.kikiclark.com/newsletter.

Keep in touch by following her on any of these platforms:

facebook.com/kikiclarkauthor
instagram.com/kikiclark2017
amazon.com/author/kikiclark
bookbub.com/authors/kiki-clark
goodreads.com/kikiclark